SAMURAI & SNIPERS

A World War II Thriller

DAVID HEALEY

INTRACOASTAL

SAMURAI & SNIPERS

A World War II Thriller

By David Healey

Intracoastal Media digital edition published 2025. Print edition ISBN 979-8-9872808-4-3

BISAC Subject Headings:

FIC014000 FICTION/Historical

FIC032000 FICTION/War & Military

"My country kept the faith. Your capital city, cruelly punished though it be, has regained its rightful place —citadel of democracy in the East."

—General Douglas MacArthur

PART ONE

CHAPTER ONE

DEACON COLE KEPT a wary eye on the trees, looking for any sign of the enemy. The Japanese troops that had escaped the fall of Ormoc and then Palompon had retreated into the Filipino forest, using the jungle shadows for cover as they picked off the Americans traveling the roads. It never ceased to amaze him how one enemy soldier with a rifle could harass an entire company of infantry. No wonder the enemy was proving so hard to beat.

"You see anything?" Philly whispered beside him.

"Just keep your eyes open," Deke replied. "They're in those trees, all right, sure as a hound has fleas."

He felt an itching between his shoulder blades as if a target had been pinned there. The unrelenting combat was finally getting to him, the constant tension wearing on him like a millstone grinding corn, leaving him feeling thin. He pushed back the brim of the bush hat that he'd gotten from a wounded Australian back on Guam and wiped sweat off his forehead before it dripped into his eyes. A few rivulets of sweat ran like rivers through the rough landscape of scars etching one side of his face and neck.

Deke and Philly were part of Patrol Easy, scouts and snipers whose job it was to escort this convoy and do what they could to discourage Japanese snipers—and not get themselves killed in the process. Patrol Easy was made up of a motley group who never would have come together anywhere but the army, Deke thought.

Though Deke was the best shot of the bunch, they all had their own skills and talents that united their unlikely crew. Philly was a damn good spotter who always had Deke's back. Rodeo hauled the radio for Lieutenant Steele, who might've been the oldest lieutenant in the Pacific. Their Filipino guide was a tough jungle fighter named Danilo. Yoshio was their Nisei interpreter and the most erudite of the bunch, always with his nose in a paperback novel. From time to time, they were joined by Private Egan and his war dog, Thor.

Patrol Easy had been fighting together since Guam and had made the landing at Red Beach, near Palo, in a hailstorm of enemy fire that greeted the American arrival in the Philippines. From there they had been grinding their way across the island of Leyte.

Over the last few weeks, one by one the Americans had cleaned out the enemy's pillboxes and concrete batteries on Leyte. Most of these fortifications had been built using Filipino slave labor. These fortifications and their defenders gradually had been eliminated—blown up, burned out, or shot to pieces. More than a few GIs and Filipino fighters had died in the process. They had paid dearly for each fortification destroyed.

But it hadn't been enough. It turned out that for the enemy, the green jungle was the only fortress needed. Now their convoy was making its way through this deadly jungle, the soldiers escorting supply trucks making their way from the coast to the inland towns that the GIs had wrested from the Japanese.

Under different circumstances, the forested hills and sunny open fields would have been a pleasant place to explore. But now, the country that they passed through was littered with signs of war, the worst being the bodies of innocent Filipino civilians who had been murdered by the Japanese. The bodies were mostly those of women or older men, bayoneted or shot at close range.

There was no apparent reason for the killings other than a thirst for violence. These civilians weren't guerrilla fighters, and they certainly had nothing worth stealing. No, the murders were simply another sign of the enemy's penchant for cruelty and revenge against the civilian population. If the average GI had been hanging on to some thread of compassion toward his enemy, the sight of those torn and bloody civilian victims had broken it. Any Japanese they captured tended to have a short life expectancy. In contrast, the Americans did everything they could to avoid harming civilians.

For now, the enemy still held the upper hand, firing from cover at the convoy. The GIs fired back, but the enemy remained frustratingly elusive.

It had been like this all morning. As the sun rose, the air grew muggy. The convoy moving from Palompon to the American outpost near Valencia crept at a snail's pace along the winding road that ran beside a narrow, rain-swollen jungle river no more than twenty-five feet wide. If the river had a name, Deke couldn't remember it and didn't much care. The river cut through the countryside for many miles before eventually flowing into the sea near Palompon, which until recently had been a Japanese supply port. The port was now in American hands, and supplies were being brought inland.

Normally the river was more like a stream, rocky and shallow enough that soldiers could easily wade across. Deke had seen it in this stage, and it reminded him of the upper reaches of the Clinch River, which he was familiar with back home.

But recent rains had transformed the river into a raging torrent in places. They had even seen the drowned carcass of a cow float past in the swift brown water. The terrain on both sides of the river was rugged and hilly, covered in dense forest. The meandering road was the only practical way to cross this territory. The enemy knew this all too well.

They had lost at least a half dozen men so far to enemy snipers. The frustrated GIs had started hosing down the jungle with the machine gun mounted on one of two M8 armored cars spaced between the trucks like chunks of meat between the vegetables on a shish kebab skewer. The M4 Sherman tank at the head of the convoy used its own .30 caliber Browning machine gun to discourage the Japanese. But the bursts of machine-gun fire did little more than eat up ammo without having much effect on the enemy. The Japanese just kept their heads down, then picked off another target once the suppressing fire stopped.

Even Lieutenant Steele was started to show signs that the random Japanese attacks were getting to him. Just a minute ago, he had turned and fired several rounds from his 12-gauge combat shotgun into the underbrush, pumping out the hulls that went spinning away into the mud. The military hulls were made of brass because the typical waxed paper shotgun shells that were familiar to hunters swelled in the humidity and jammed the gun.

"What are you shooting at, Honcho?" Philly asked.

"Thought I saw something in those bushes," the lieutenant muttered. He shoved fresh shells into his shotgun.

He preferred to be called Honcho by his men because being addressed by his rank or as "sir" was a surefire way to be targeted by the enemy. Considering that the word came from a Japanese term for a squad leader, the joke was on the enemy.

The tall, taciturn lieutenant had lost an eye on Guadalcanal and now wore an eye patch that Deke had crafted for him out of scrap leather. Honcho's hair was touched with gray and his men figured that he had pulled some strings not only to avoid being sent home after losing an eye but also to remain a mere first lieutenant. Being a captain meant more headaches. He was more than content to command their squad of scouts and snipers.

Shotgun at the ready, Honcho moved off to check on the rest of the convoy.

"Dammit, we're sitting ducks out here," Philly grumbled. He walked a few paces behind Deke, his own rifle at the ready. They both knew that Deke was the better shot, but that didn't stop Philly from needling him about his marksmanship from time to time. Because Philly was Philly, and Deke's closest buddy in the army, maybe even in the world, Deke put up with it. "How can we fight the bastards if we can't even see 'em, huh? This is a suicide mission."

"I've got news for you, city boy. Life is a suicide mission," Deke said. "Keep your head down and your eyes open."

They were maintaining their "dime"—keeping a distance about ten feet apart to lessen the chances that a burst of fire from the jungle would take them both out. Deke heard the crack of a rifle. Another GI sprawled unmoving in the mud at the side of the road.

"Sniper!" someone shouted, and once again the GIs scrambled off the road like ants, taking shelter in ditches or under the trucks. They weren't quick enough. Another shot rang out, and another man went down, wounded. A medic crawled over to help him.

Deke hid behind a truck tire and swung his rifle in the direction from where his keen hearing told him the shots had originated, but all he saw through the sniper scope was a wall of green, so dense that it looked as if a bullet wouldn't pierce the veil. He couldn't see anything to shoot at.

He felt a shiver along his spine, wondering again if he was in the enemy's sights at this very moment. That imaginary target itched on his back. *Dammit.* He much preferred being the hunter to being the hunted.

"Did you see where that shot came from?" Philly wanted to know. "I swear, this convoy is nothing but target practice for the Japanese."

"These snipers are crafty," said Yoshio as he studied the brush that hid the enemy. "We need to outsmart them."

"When you figure out how to do that, Yoshio, let me know," Deke said.

Yoshio could move as silently as any of them when he needed to. The sight of the Japanese American in his GI uniform still brought stares of suspicion, like he might be an infiltrator rather than a soldier in the United States Army. But Deke and the rest of Patrol Easy had come to trust Yoshio with their lives because he had proved his bravery more than once.

Yoshio had been born in Washington State, which made him just as American as anybody else, even if he had grown up speaking Japanese. Although his parents and grandparents had also been born in America, their Japanese heritage meant that they were now sitting in an internment camp, behind barbed wire and under guard, designated as potential enemies of the United States. Yoshio had never expressed any bitterness about that situation, but he had opted to prove his loyalty by enlisting to fight for a country that treated his family with suspicion.

"I guess the best we can do is keep our heads down and pray," Philly said.

"When your number is up, it's up," Rodeo offered.

The only member of the patrol who hadn't spoken up was

Danilo, their Filipino guide. It was always a mystery as to how much English the tough guerrilla knew.

Deke had his rifle to his shoulder, his eye to the scope, and his finger on the trigger. Now and then he spotted a trembling leaf in the breeze or a bird flitting through the branches, but nothing that looked like a Japanese sniper. He had no doubt that the Japanese were watching *them*.

"I can't see these fools," Deke muttered. Behind him, the agonized cries of a wounded GI faded as morphine began to course through his system. "It's a regular cattywampus, I can tell you that much."

"A catty-what?" Philly asked.

"He means it's a hot mess," Yoshio explained. "Lucky for you, I speak a little hillbilly."

"You must have picked it up from all those Westerns you read," Philly muttered.

No more shots came from the green curtain. The wounded man was loaded into the back of a truck; the dead man went into another. Once again, the convoy began to roll.

Bad as things were, the slow-moving column's luck was about to go from bad to worse, because the Japanese had cleverly prepared a trap for them. The convoy reached a bend in the road between two bridges, one just in front of the column and one behind. The captain in charge checked the bridges and gave the all clear. But as they were to find out, the Japanese had managed to hide the surprise that they had in store for the Americans. The front half of the convoy, led by the Sherman tank, had just crossed the first bridge when the structure erupted in flames and roiling smoke. The Japanese had set off a charge to destroy the bridge, leaving the convoy suddenly cut in half.

From the rear of the convoy, there came the sound of another explosion as the Japanese destroyed the bridge that the column had just crossed. The second half of the convoy that included Patrol Easy was now stranded on the road, with the bridges gone in front of it and behind it, the river on one side and a steep bank hemming them in on the other side.

Not good, Deke thought.

Debris was still raining down when the Japanese opened fire, hitting the trapped portion of the convoy with two machine guns that strafed up and down the line of vehicles. Men dove for shelter wherever they could, crawling under the trucks or behind the thick tires. A few enemy grenades arced down from the steep banks above.

The convoy's front half had the Sherman tank and one of the M8s to defend it, while the stranded portion of the column had the other M8. Up front, the captain was trying to organize a defense from the other side of the ruined first bridge, but he was cut down and killed by a burst of fire. Technically, that left Lieutenant Steele in charge as the highest-ranking officer still breathing.

"Damn it all to hell, but at least we can see the bastards for a change," Steele said, nodding toward the muzzle flashes and tracer fire.

Snipers were able to hide in the greenery, but the machine guns were easy enough to spot, and they were within buckshot range. Exposing himself to the hail of lead, Steele walked out from behind a truck and began firing shotgun blasts at the machine-gun team. That gun fell silent, and two quick shots from Deke and Philly silenced the other machine gunners. The M8 accompanying their marooned portion of the convoy added its firepower.

However, the Japanese were far from done. Rifle fire continued to pepper the pinned-down convoy. The vegetation hid the enemy snipers so well that picking them off was next to impossible.

Deke decided that he'd had enough. He could shoot back all

day and never hit any of the enemy who lay hidden in the jungle-covered riverbank.

"C'mon, fellas," he said. "Follow me."

Using the trucks for cover, Deke ran toward the rear of the column, with Philly and Danilo following him. The small bridge back here had been shattered by the blast, but the debris had fallen in such a way that a single beam remained stretched across the narrow waterway. Brown floodwater tugged and pulled at the beam, making it bob more like a bit of straw than a heavy wood stringer. It was dicey, but it was the only way across.

Here goes nothin', Deke thought, then raced across the beam without waiting for the others. He was moving too fast to lose his balance, carried across by sheer momentum. His boots got wet where the current washed over the beam, but he managed to dash across and reach the far bank. He dove for cover as first Philly, then Danilo, followed him. Lucky for them, the Japanese were so intent on picking apart the convoy that they scarcely paid any attention to the three men, other than sending a few random shots in their direction.

"What the hell are you up to?" Philly asked, once he lay panting in the jungle underbrush.

"I'm making it up as I go along," Deke said. "C'mon."

The three men pushed their way up the steep riverbank. The mud and dense undergrowth made it tough going. They had no choice but to bull their way through the thick weeds and tangled branches. Something slithered past Deke's boot and he thought, *Snake*. He ignored it. At the moment he had bigger worries.

At the top of the bank, they were rewarded with the discovery of a narrow dirt track that ran parallel to the river. The trail was likely used by animals, but someone else had been through here—the telltale prints left by Japanese boots were visible in the mud. The Japanese were using this trail to move parallel to the convoy and harass the Americans on the other side of the river.

Deke motioned for the others to follow him. Up ahead, it was clear from the sound of firing that the enemy was tearing up the column. There wasn't a moment to waste.

He broke into a run, sprinting down the narrow trail. Palm fronds and pendulous tree branches sodden from the previous night's rain tore at him from the edges of the trail, thorns and sharp leaf edges cutting deep enough to scratch out blood, but he ignored the sting. There was no point in being quiet anymore. As Deke charged, a visceral sound came from deep within him, a keening wail that was Deke's bloodcurdling version of a rebel yell. Deke leaped a tree limb and found himself face-to-face with the enemy.

His rebel yell startled the first Japanese soldier that Deke encountered. The man turned to him, wide-eyed, and Deke threw the rifle to his shoulder and shot him down.

He kept going. Philly was shouting now, and even Danilo let loose with something that could only be described as a jungle roar.

Screaming their battle cries at the top of their lungs, they rolled up the Japanese positioned along the trail. Deke couldn't fire the rifle fast enough, so he switched to his pistol. Behind him, Danilo used his wicked bolo knife to finish off any Japanese who still had any fight left.

It was all over in a few seconds. Their madcap attack had worked. It was hard to say how many Japanese had been part of the ambush, because the ones that they didn't kill had scattered into the forest. The only fire now came from the American side of the river. Bullets tore through the greenery, the so-called friendly fire too close for comfort as Deke, Philly, and Danilo hugged the dirt.

"Stop shooting, dammit!" Philly shouted. "Honcho, tell them

to stop!"

On the other side of the river, they heard Lieutenant Steele give the order. Once the shooting stopped, they retraced their steps along the trail to the bridge and crossed over again.

The lieutenant was waiting for them. "You crazy bastards," he said. But he was grinning with pride. "You three saved this whole damn column—or what's left of it, anyhow."

Slowly, they picked up the pieces left by the Japanese ambush. Several of the trucks had been shot to pieces. Two men had been killed and a half dozen were wounded. It was likely that the damage would have been far worse if Deke, Philly, and Danilo hadn't been able to cross the river and blunt the attack. Oddly enough, the front half of the convoy that had made it across the first bridge had mostly been spared.

But the destruction of the bridges had left the divided convoy in a quandary. The bridges could be repaired—to a point. "There's no way we're getting these trucks and that M8 across," Steele said. "We'll have to take what we can carry, plus the wounded. We'll have to leave the vehicles, including that armored car. Hopefully, we can get some engineers back here to make those bridges operational. We'll have to—this is the main road between Valencia and Palompon."

"Those Japanese knew exactly what they were doing," Deke agreed. "They hit us right where it hurts."

Working in the heat and humidity, a crew of GIs was able to rig a crossing using the bridge to their front. It wasn't much—just a couple of closely spaced beams that had been wrestled into place. There would be no hope of getting any vehicles across, but it would support the weight of a few soldiers at a time. One of the beams bounced and swayed as soon as any weight was placed on it, threatening to spill the soldiers into the brown water, but they didn't have much choice. Later, a team of engineers might be able to return and properly repair the bridge so that the road could reopen and the vehicles, with their precious supplies, could be delivered.

Having to abandon the vehicles and the supplies they carried, Patrol Easy and the rest of the soldiers from the stranded group in the convoy made their way across the mangled remains of the bridge to join the front half of the convoy. Reluctantly, the four-man crew of the M8 abandoned their vehicle, hoping that they would get it back soon enough.

The hardest part of the operation was carrying the wounded across the rickety bridge, each step threatening to send the stretchers and the stretcher-bearers into the swollen river. The task was made even more nerve-racking when a rifle cracked from the opposite bank, reminding them that the Japanese were still present. Fortunately, the enemy's potshots didn't cause any harm.

"Let's move out!" Honcho shouted, once the last of the wounded had been carried across. What was left of the convoy got rolling again.

They were hardly out of sight of the smashed bridges when they began to see black smoke roiling into the sky behind them. Evidently, the Japanese had returned to the ambush site and set the abandoned vehicles on fire. So much for the plan to return and salvage the supply vehicles and the armored car.

Meanwhile, the heat increased as the sun came out again, encouraging flocks of insects that pestered the sweating troops and tortured the wounded. The heat grew until it triggered a sudden thunderstorm, bringing fresh torrents of rain that drenched the men. They slogged on through the mud and downpour.

"Just another day in paradise," Philly muttered.

CHAPTER TWO

THE CONVOY REACHED the division's supply base near Valencia without further incident, other than a few potshots from Japanese snipers. Patrol Easy dealt with them, giving as good as they got. The town itself was comprised of neat single-story houses set close to the road, with mountains visible in the distance.

When they finally came to a halt, Deke dropped into the shade offered by a truck, glad to get out of the sun. The truck itself was shot to pieces and covered in scorch marks. Now that the truck had stopped, the steam from under the hood and its leaking fluids indicated that the truck wasn't likely to move again. Lieutenant Steele had told Deke to stick close because he was going to want him around when he addressed what was left of the convoy, but for now Deke just wanted to get off his feet. Meanwhile, rumors were spreading that a Christmas dinner awaited them, even at this remote base. *I'll believe it when I see it,* Deke thought.

Between the warmth and the jungle surroundings, it was strange to think that it was the Christmas season. This was one of the cooler months in the Philippines, but there wasn't any hope of a white Christmas, considering that it hadn't snowed on Leyte since maybe the Ice Age, if then. Back home, the folks who could afford it would be roasting a turkey or a ham in the oven. His nose seemed to fill with the delicious smells. The thought of home cooking made Deke's mouth water. There had been plenty of lean times growing up, but his mother had always managed to make holiday meals special, right down to an apple pie.

As the remembered smells of Deke's pleasant reverie dissipated, the smells that replaced them were the humid jungle, the fetid mud, and the faint odor of a Jap corpse in a ditch.

A shadow loomed over him. "Don't think you can keep all that shade for yourself," Philly declared.

"I'm only renting it," Deke said.

"That's good to know," Philly said, then sat down so close to Deke that he was forced to move over until he was partially in the sun again.

Deke grumbled. "Now who's keeping the shade all to himself?"

"Quit your griping, hillbilly. Skinny as you're getting, you could sit under a blade of grass and not get sunburned."

There was some truth to that for all of them, Deke thought. How long had it been since they had eaten a decent meal? Anyhow, the shade was a welcome relief, although both men tried to ignore the stink of burned rubber and leaking gasoline that clung to the wreckage providing the shade. The division's hardworking mechanics did what they could to get damaged trucks back into action, but this one wasn't going anywhere—it had been shot full of holes, its lifeblood of oil and fluids leaking into the soil.

The wrecked vehicle was a reminder that the fighting had become a war of attrition. The loss of each ship, each plane, each tank, each truck, each soldier, was felt keenly as the American forces slowly wore down the Japanese. It wasn't easy, given a supply line that stretched clear across the Pacific, but the Americans could eventually replace what was lost, while the Japanese could not.

Even so, the enemy didn't have the good sense to surrender, so there was no choice but to keep fighting.

The combat on Leyte had certainly taken its toll on Patrol Easy. It turned out that Patrol Easy wasn't going to stay undermanned for long. They'd been assigned a dozen new men, some of them combat veterans who had been separated from their units for one reason or another, and others support staff who'd made the mistake of saying they wanted to get into the fight. Given the losses in the Philippines so far, division command was happy to oblige them.

Now those men were gathered around Lieutenant Steele in the shade of an immense balete tree that grew beside the road. Impatiently, Steele motioned for Deke and Philly to join them. While the Americans sat on the ground, Danilo squatted on his haunches in true Filipino fashion.

Danilo's dark, watchful eyes studied the branches of the balete tree with trepidation, but it wasn't enemy snipers he was looking for. Balete trees grew to be even more massive than this one, with some centuries old. There were more than a few local legends of these balete trees being inhabited by the spirits of the dead. When the breeze stirred the leaves, making them dance as if with a mind of their own, it was easy to understand why some believed the trees to be haunted.

Before speaking, Steele took a moment to look around at the men, his gaze settling briefly on each man as if taking his measure before moving on. By the time he finally spoke, he had their full attention.

"A lot of you are probably wondering what's next," Steele

began. "Well, our strategy is straightforward, boys. When you see the enemy, shoot him."

That comment brought a murmur of approval and even some laughter. However, the lieutenant's face didn't show any traces of humor.

"It's kind of like getting rid of rats," Philly said. "Except these rats can shoot back."

"The more of them we kill, the fewer there are to shoot back," Steele pointed out. "It's that simple, boys. We go where they send us, and we shoot Japs."

"C'mon, Lieutenant, haven't we done enough?" Philly wanted to know. "We haven't even had our Christmas dinner yet—unless rumors are the only thing being served up."

"Keep talking, Philly, and the only thing you're gonna get is some cold C rations and no can opener except your bayonet."

That response made some of the new men snicker. Patrol Easy made up the core of the undersized platoon Steele had been put in charge of since before the ambush on the convoy. Officers were in short supply. The others clammed up when Deke glared at them. Some of them met his eyes, then quickly looked away. With his gray eyes and the deep scars on one side of his face, Deke had that effect on people.

Philly muttered something under his breath, then fell silent. With another officer, Philly would likely have earned himself a chewing-out with his smart-aleck comments, but Steele put up with him. The lieutenant was used to it, and he knew that when push came to shove, Philly was a good soldier, so he gave him some leeway.

Steele went on to confirm what the gathered men already suspected, which was that Japanese forces had scattered into the hills, but they had not given up. In some places, entire regiments were still holding out, remaining a thorn in the side of the U.S Army's advance. However, most of the enemy had been reduced to smaller units or even handfuls of determined men. That was old news to Deke.

As long as there's one enemy soldier out there with a sharp stick, he'll be fighting us, Deke thought. He knew from experience that most of the Japanese were armed with far more than sharp sticks.

"One more thing," Steele said. "I want to introduce our acting sergeant, Deacon Cole. Some of you new guys don't know him, but he's the hillbilly over there with the pretty face. What he says is as good as what I say."

Deke looked up in surprise.

Philly nudged him with an elbow and muttered. "There you go, Deke. Merry freakin' Christmas, *Sergeant.*"

Steele wrapped up, although Deke's head was spinning so that he barely heard the rest. They'd be moving out again in the morning.

One of the new men approach him. "Deacon, huh? You're not some kind of religious fella, are you?"

Philly answered for him. "He's especially good at funerals. He'll be glad to say a few words when we bury you, buddy."

That shut the new guy up, and he suddenly took an intense interest in his boot laces.

Meanwhile, Steele had another surprise in addition to Deke's promotion. It turned out that they really were having a Christmas dinner, even if it was a day late.

The decision to serve a traditional Christmas dinner on December 26, rather than on the holiday itself, had been made quite deliberately by General Bruce, commander of the 77th Infantry Division. Throughout the Pacific, similar decisions had been made to align with the time difference. Their dinner would coincide with what was actually Christmas Day in the continental United States. Across the thousands of miles of ocean, the troops would be celebrating Christmas at the same time as folks back home. It was an important real-time connection that had nothing to do with dates on a calendar.

A makeshift mess hall had been erected, and cooks were at work preparing the meal. There were no tables—each man had to sit on the ground to eat—and everyone kept his rifle within reach. That was OK, considering the wonderful smells that greeted them.

Steele explained that the supplies for their holiday meal had come from an air drop. Again, it was a testimonial to the miracle of the American supply line juggernaut that the troops on Leyte were soon eating roasted turkey, glazed ham, real mashed potatoes, stuffing, and canned string beans. Each man got a slice of apple pie made with canned apples. The boys had even been allotted one beer each to wash it all down, or all the fresh coffee they wanted. The nondrinkers did quite well trading their beer for extra pie.

"Can you believe this, fellas?" Philly asked in wonder, balancing a heavily laden plate on his knees as he settled onto the ground. "It sure as hell beats canned lima beans and ham."

Philly was referring to the least favorite "flavor" of C ration. More than one man would return from the Pacific vowing to never allow a lima bean anywhere near his plate.

"It's sure somethin'," Deke agreed. His belly growled at the sight, but staring down at the plate, he felt overwhelmed. The mess crew had loaded his plate with more food than he could eat. Their stomachs had all shrunk after weeks and months of living on so little. Philly hadn't been far wrong when he had kidded Deke about being able to find shade under a blade of grass. Deke was now as lean as a bayonet, and just as sharp and hard.

He took a mouthful of mashed potatoes swimming in butter, closing his eyes as the taste took him back home to better times, before they had lost his family's mountain home to greedy bankers, when they had still been a family. His father had died in an accident at the sawmill where he'd been working in an attempt to keep the family farm from going under. His mother had died not long after that, most likely of a broken heart and broken dreams. Now it was just he and his sister, Sadie, who was a female police officer in Washington, DC.

He raised a forkful of mashed potatoes in a silent toast. *Merry Christmas, Sadie.* He hoped that his sister was enjoying her own Christmas dinner, and hopefully not eating it alone. Then again, Sadie was a loner, just like him.

He forced himself to eat another bite because it was so delicious, but he was already getting full. He ended up just looking down at his plate, feasting with his eyes, thinking, *Ain't it a wonder?*

His thoughts wandered. When other men recalled the holidays, they spoke of things like presents under the Christmas tree or sled riding. He just recalled it only ever being the four of them, the sole present being an orange, its color almost glowing unnaturally in the winter drabness of the Cole family's modest home. At other times there might not be enough to eat, but not on Christmas. Ma had cooked buckwheat pancakes and bacon on their flat-topped potbelly stove, the pancakes drizzled with molasses, and Deke had thought himself a prince.

Looking around, he could see that Philly was eating like it was his job, pausing just long enough to shoo the flies away. Nobody dwelled on the thought that these same flies might have been crawling on the Japanese dead just beyond the tree line.

The feast also drew the newspaper reporters and photographers who had been embedded with the troops, covering the war.

One of those reporters caused a stir. He was an older man—much older than the soldiers, at least—with a narrow, hangdog face and a sad smile as he listened to the GIs tell their stories.

He was skinny to the point of looking unhealthy. A cigarette hung from the corner of his mouth.

"I'll be damned, it's Ernie Pyle!" Philly declared. "Hey, Ernie, put me in your story!"

Pyle was famous among the GIs and well loved for telling their side of things with his folksy, everyman style of writing. He had done just that in Europe and was now covering the Pacific, although he was something of a latecomer to the war in this part of the world.

Part of his appeal was that he was old enough to be their father, and there was something fatherly in his attitude toward the soldiers. It might be his job to write about them, but it was clear that Pyle gave a damn while he was doing it—and then some.

The reporter made his way over to where Patrol Easy sat, and they made room for him on the bench.

"Where you from, soldier?" Pyle asked, his pencil poised over his notebook.

"Philadelphia," Philly said, clearly delighted by the thought of getting his name in the newspaper.

Carefully, Pyle wrote down their names and hometowns.

"Mr. Pyle, you want some of this?" Deke asked. "I reckon my stomach is so shrunk up that I can't eat it all."

Pyle noticed the scars on Deke's face but didn't look away. Even the journalist in him was too polite to ask where Deke had gotten them. He seemed touched by Deke's offer to share his meal. He thanked him but shook his head. "You just do the best you can."

One of the new guys surprised them by producing a bag of pecans. "Now you can say you've had everything from soup to nuts with this dinner," the GI said with a grin. Nobody bothered to point out that there hadn't been any soup. He shook the bag, then shared it around. "It's hard to believe I was on the farm pruning these trees two years ago."

"If you're lucky, you'll be back on that farm two years from now—maybe," Philly said.

Later, Pyle would describe that moment for his readers and add a few insights: "That's the way conversation at the front goes all the time. The minutes hardly ever go by without some nostalgic reference to home, how long you've been away, how long before you get back, what you'll do first when you hit the States, what your chances are for returning before the war is over."

Finally, the famous reporter straightened up. "Merry Christmas, boys," he said. "Do me a favor and keep your heads down."

CHAPTER THREE

For the most part, the town had been cleared of the enemy and Patrol Easy got some decent sleep for once. Their full bellies helped. By the next day, they had new orders. Lieutenant Steele explained that he would be leading a squad to hunt the enemy in the jungles and hills surrounding the base. He seemed glad to have shed his duties as a platoon leader to focus on leading these scouts and snipers. The veterans of Patrol Easy didn't bother to learn the names of the new guys. There would be time for that if the new guys made it through the first couple of days.

"The plan is to bring the fight to the enemy before they get organized enough to hit the base," Steele explained. "You might say an ounce of prevention is worth a pound of cure."

"More like an ounce of lead," Philly muttered.

By now the veterans of Patrol Easy knew all too well what bringing the fight to the enemy meant. It involved creeping down the jungle trails and across the low hills, stalking the enemy. Deke and Danilo took point, leading the way into the forest. Philly trailed behind them.

For this patrol, they would be heading deep into the hilly

terrain. The trees thickened, and the ground grew steeper. Soon they were all panting and sweating with the effort of climbing the hill. Clouds of gnats appeared, sticking to their skin and flying into their eyes.

"Do you think this hill has got a name?" Philly wondered.

"To hell if I know," Deke replied. "I could think of a couple ideas."

"How about this? We'll name the hill after the first guy that gets killed."

"That's a hell of a way to be remembered," Deke replied. "Believe me, I'm in no hurry to have a hill named after me, if that's what it takes."

Philly's suggestion came from the fact that it was common practice to name geographic locations after the men who had died fighting on them. Across the Pacific there were places that soldiers had given names to, such as Anton's Gulch, Sergeant Darby Hill, or Lefty's Mountain. These unofficial names couldn't be found on a map, but they were written in the hearts of the soldiers. Whether it was the 25th Infantry Division or the 77th, they all had similar landmarks named for men who had lost their lives in these places.

Deke decided it wasn't all that different from back home, where the mountains and gaps—a low crossing point in the hills—usually took the name of some man or event that would have otherwise been forgotten, such as Dead Indian Creek or Frenchman's Gap. Attached to those names was usually some legend that had been passed down through the years. Those names had staying power, but he wasn't sure that would be the case once the US Army packed up and left this part of the world.

They continued climbing, coming to a dirt road that led to higher ground. The road was so steep and slick with mud that a group of soldiers struggled to get vehicles up the hill. This was a problem for the supply trucks and jeeps being used to carry away the wounded. Deke could hear mortars and small-arms fire in the distance, indicating that there were still plenty of Japanese soldiers around. Each footstep carried them closer to the fighting.

They saw that the soldiers had rigged a system to get the vehicles up the hill by lashing a gasoline-powered winch to a thick tree near the top. A heavy rope was tied to the bumper of whatever vehicle was trying to ascend the road. The winch kicked in, snorting and belching smoke as soldiers strained at the corners of the vehicle, adding their muscle power to get the vehicle up the incline.

The winch was a large, hulking machine, its metal body caked with mud and grease. It must have been a bear to get it into place at the top of the steep incline. As it kicked in, its gears turned and smoke poured from its exhaust pipes, adding to the already thick air of the jungle.

Meanwhile, soldiers tugged on the ropes, their muscles bulging and sweat dripping down their faces as they strained to guide a heavy truck up the steep incline. Foot by foot, tires spinning, the vehicle climbed the hill.

"Should we help?" one of the new members of Patrol Easy asked.

"Nope. Looks to me like they got it just fine on their own," Philly said.

After all, a smart soldier knew better than to volunteer for any form of physical work that he could avoid.

They kept going up the hill, passing the crew struggling with the vehicle, and found that the road ended. Soon after that, it was clear the Japanese had been there before them. Instead of a dirt trail leading higher, there were steps cut into the sides of the hill and lined with logs to keep the dirt from washing away. The steps were rough and shot through with roots and rocks, but it made the going a lot easier.

"And one thing's for sure, we're going to get plenty of exercise this morning," Philly said.

They kept climbing as the sound of the winch behind them faded and the sounds of fighting grew more intense.

"We are not joining in that fight," Steele clarified. "Our job is to go around the edges and catch any Japs trying to sneak in behind us. So keep your eyes open."

"In other words, shoot first and ask questions later," Philly said.

Deke ignored Philly's banter. To say that Philly shared his thoughts half baked was an understatement. Most of the time, Philly's thoughts didn't even make it into the oven.

All Deke's attention was now focused on the surrounding forest. The Japanese could be anywhere. The trees pressed in close, creating a dense green wall of vegetation. There could be an entire company of Japanese not more than fifty feet away in all that greenery, and they would never see them until the enemy opened fire and it was too late. It had happened to more than one patrol, and the division's losses were mounting.

Deke used every sense he had to try to detect the enemy. His ears strained to hear anything that wasn't a bird or a droning insect. Some rustle of leaves or crack of branches would give the enemy away. His eyes searched for any flicker of movement, which was the best way of determining whether there was anyone in these woods.

He even pressed his nose into service, sniffing the humid air. The Japanese smelled different, just as he was sure *they* could smell the Americans. Some said the Japanese had a kind of fishy scent because of their diet, but Deke wasn't so sure about that. He would've been at a loss for words to describe the smell, other than to say it was *different*.

A sniper rifle wasn't much use here in this dense forest, with its limited sight lines. Instead, they would've been better off with a submachine gun. That was all right. He would get off at least one shot with the Springfield before unloading the .45 that hung in a holster on his utility belt. It was also reassuring that Lieutenant Steele was behind him with his 12-gauge shotgun at the ready.

Deke had seen that one-eyed bastard do a lot of damage with that shotgun.

"I don't like this one bit," Philly muttered, watching their surroundings nervously.

"Shut up, Philly," the lieutenant said quietly. "Less talking and more looking. Keep your eyes open."

All of Deke's senses vibrated on high alert, expecting at any moment for the enemy to come swarming at them out of the brush. Bugs buzzed in his ears, but he scarcely noticed. He was a lot more worried about the buzzing of bullets that might come at any moment.

They came to a small clearing, and Deke went into a tense crouch, weapon at the ready. When he saw two forms lying prone in the middle of the clearing behind a log, half hidden by the dappled shade, he automatically raised the rifle to his shoulder, getting ready to fire.

But as the target sprang closer through the telescopic sight, he could see that something wasn't right. The two figures were tangled together like lovers. When he looked closer, he saw the staring eyes and bloated skin of corpses that had been dead for at least a day.

These were Japanese, all right, probably killed in the shelling that had been done to soften up the area. Their comrades had either left them behind or the two men had simply been forgotten. Flies covered the dead like they always did, giving the soldiers the unsettling appearance that they were moving. Deke just hoped to hell that if he got killed, somebody would bury him before he got covered in flies like that. The ants, too, had gone to work on the bodies. Nature was relentless here, offering the dead no dignity. The dead simply provided a feast for all the creepy-crawlies of these hilly jungles.

"What is it?" Honcho asked, coming up beside him.

"I damn near shot them just for good measure. Just dead Japs," Deke said.

Honcho touched his shoulder reassuringly. "All right, let's keep going," he said.

Deke skirted the clearing, keeping an eye out for any trip wires or booby traps. One of the new guys approached the bodies as if to look them over for souvenirs, which was always a popular pastime.

"Don't even think about it," the lieutenant warned. "For all we know, those dead Nips are lying on top of a couple of grenades."

The GI had gotten close enough to disturb the flies, which swarmed up around the Americans.

"Damn it," Philly said, wiping at his face. "These flies were just licking dead Japs a second ago. Now they're licking me. I hope to hell they don't think I taste better." He picked up the pace to follow Deke away from the clearing and back into the forest trail. The smell of death subsided behind them. "Do you think somebody already counted these dead guys?"

All the men knew that emphasis had been placed on counting the number of dead. HQ constantly demanded updates.

"Yeah, we'll add them to the total. You know how the brass is about these reports," Deke replied.

Toward the top of the hill, the crest was honeycombed with trenches and small caves. Lucky for them, the ground had been plowed by the artillery bombardment, clearing out the enemy. A few more dead Japanese sprawled in the trenches. One of them had been impaled on the shattered trunk of a sapling, his limbs now hanging stiffly down. It was a gruesome sight, but at least it seemed to indicate that the area was cleared of Japanese.

Suddenly a shot rang out, and one of the new guys dropped as if he'd been felled by an ax. He was dead as soon as he hit the ground. Everybody else dove for cover in the bottoms of the muddy trenches.

"Sniper!" one of the new guys yelled.

The warning was understandable but unnecessary. The problem was that every damn Japanese was a sniper, and every damn GI was a target. Another shot whipped overhead, and then another.

"Where the hell are they?" Philly shouted.

"Who's got eyes on these damn Nips?" Deke said.

He had eased his rifle over the lip of the trench, resting it on a log. Movement caught his eye, and he saw the outline of a Japanese helmet. When he looked closer, he could also see that the Japanese soldier held a rifle. Deke lined up his sights on the enemy soldier and squeezed the trigger. The firing fell silent.

"Nice shot, hillbilly. That's one down," Philly said.

When there were no other shots, the soldiers slowly emerged from the trenches. Philly looked down at the dead guy. "Anybody know his name?"

"I think that was Carlson," Yoshio offered.

"Anybody know his first name?"

Nobody did.

"Doesn't matter," Philly said. "Now it's Carlson's Ridge."

The thought didn't cheer anyone up. Then came another flurry of shots. This wasn't a lone sniper this time, but a squad of Japanese who had come into sight, retreating down a long ditch that had been cut into the hillside. Every soldier in Patrol Easy brought his weapon into play, firing at the enemy. Several Japanese dropped immediately, but the reminder were still shooting at Patrol Easy as they ran.

Honcho surprised them by jumping out of the ditch and running straight at the Japanese, screaming like a madman and firing his shotgun as he went. The Japanese scattered before his onslaught like leaves before a windstorm. A couple of men stood their ground and were promptly cut down by shotgun blasts. Deke fired and took out a third soldier.

While the lieutenant was busy reloading the shotgun, the rest of Patrol Easy followed, shouting as they ran.

They kept running, firing wildly as they followed Honcho's lead, racing after the fleeing Japanese. Not all the Japanese were intent on escaping. Some turned to fire at the Americans. Behind him, Deke heard another man cry out as he was hit, but there was no time to stop. The men shouted with a mad rage, amplified by the knowledge that the Japanese had drawn blood.

Deke dropped to one knee and fired at a Japanese soldier who had turned to make a stand. The man promptly fell, and Deke raced ahead. Somehow Honcho was already far in front, leaping across a trench and firing down at a Japanese soldier cowering at the bottom.

The rest of the men caught up, and now it was just a turkey shoot. Deke thought they were all like hounds chasing rabbits as they raced down the trench, firing as they went. Finally, whatever Japanese remained were either killed or had hidden themselves in the small caves that dotted the hilltop.

Deke caught up to Honcho, both men panting for breath.

"Damn," Deke muttered.

"Yeah," the lieutenant said, racking another shell into his shotgun, then nodded at the dead enemy soldiers. "Count 'em up."

"Twenty-seven," Philly announced with a smack of satisfaction. "If you count the dead ones we found. Somebody has to get credit for them. Not so bad for a day's work, right?"

"Day's not over yet," Honcho corrected. The men had

reached the point where the dead were just numbers, not husbands, fathers, sons, or brothers who would never return home. The faces of the newly dead looked almost peaceful, at least the ones not contorted in pain from their dying throes.

Deke didn't dwell on such thoughts for long. He reloaded his rifle and pistol.

"All right, let's keep going," Honcho said. "We're here to hunt the enemy, not sit around."

"Yeah," Philly added. "Besides, it's starting to stink around here."

In the heat and humidity under the trees, flies were already buzzing around the faces of the dead and the blood-drenched soil of the trench.

"Stay sharp," Honcho warned. "No telling if these Nips had any friends around. Deke, you take point."

Deke moved past the others to lead the way. There was a kind of trail through the forest that the Japanese had clearly been using for moving troops and supplies. Soon the trees began to thin out, and they reached the top of a ridge. The ridge was ringed with forest but covered with tall grass, almost like the tonsure of an old-fashioned monk. The grasslands were covered in knobs, and Deke worried that many Japanese could be hiding in the waving grass. A man could easily remain unseen until you were right on top of him.

"Watch your spacing," Philly muttered, reminding the newcomers to keep alert and stay spread out to be more difficult targets if a Nambu machine gun suddenly opened fire.

Deke's fears about hidden enemy troops proved true when a single rifle shot split the air, and another man was hit by a Japanese sniper.

Another new guy started running toward the man. There was another shot, and the soldier went down.

"Son of a bitch! Somebody get that sniper!"

The other soldiers had all gone into a crouch, using the grass for cover. The problem was that the sniper was up on one of the grassy knobs, giving him a view of the soldiers below. He fired again, and a bullet whistled past them.

By now Deke had a good idea of the sniper's location, but he would only be firing blindly. He took a grenade off his belt, pulled the pin, and threw it with everything he had toward the grassy knoll. The shattering blast fell short, but it was enough to rattle the sniper, who jumped up and started running away. He was crouched over, barely visible above the swaying tops of the taller clumps of grass.

That was the only target Deke needed. He swung the rifle to a point just ahead of the fleeing sniper and squeezed the trigger. The man ran directly into the bullet and fell headlong.

"He won't be bothering us anymore," Deke said.

"All right, nice work," Honcho said. "Everybody, keep your eyes peeled. I've got a bad feeling about this. This place is too damn quiet and too damn wide open."

They kept going, crossing more of the rolling grassland, on the lookout for more hidden Japanese. They waited for the crack of a sniper rifle. The very thought made every man itchy between the shoulder blades. Deke kept his eyes high.

Out of nowhere, they heard the roar of an approaching engine. It was not a plane. The sound came from the landscape ahead rather than from the sky. To their surprise, they saw an expensive Lincoln sedan racing through the grass, bouncing its way over the rugged spots.

"What in the world?" Philly said. "Get a load of this guy. What the hell does he think he's doing?"

"One thing for sure, he's not out for a Sunday drive," Deke said.

"Who the hell is driving that thing?"

Although it was an American car, the fact that someone

began shooting at them out the window settled the question about whether it was friend or foe at the wheel. The Philippines had once been filled with American cars before the war, and it was clear that the Japanese had commandeered this one.

It was time for another grenade. This one was thrown by Rodeo, who probably had the best arm in the unit.

It was a great throw. The grenade went right through the open window and exploded. The car kept going until the gas tank ignited. Even then it kept rolling, setting the dry grass on fire as it went, but the shooting had stopped. The car was no longer a threat, but there were still plenty of Japanese to deal with.

They climbed a bit farther and reached an observation post in a house that was elevated on stilts with a thatched roof.

"I don't like the looks of that place," Philly warned.

Sure enough, they heard the crack of a rifle, and they all ducked as the noise echoed and rolled across the knobby peaks. But it wasn't just a rifle that was situated in that hut, because moments later there was the dreaded sound of a machine gun opening fire with the steady tap, tap, tap, tap of the deadly Nambu machine gun.

"Everybody down!" Honcho shouted. Although the warning wasn't necessary, because the men were already hugging the ground, as the bullets flashed and flared overhead, the tracers visible even in the daylight.

"Deke!" somebody shouted.

He already had the rifle lined up on the muzzle flash in the shack. He fired, worked the bolt, and fired again. For his trouble, a bullet snapped past his head. Deke had damn near forgotten about the sniper in there too. Off to his left, a rifle fired, and the sniper in the shack fell silent.

"That's one for me," Philly said with a grin.

CHAPTER FOUR

UNDERSTANDING the situation in the Philippines required going all the way back to December 8, 1941. Within hours of the attack on Pearl Harbor, Japanese forces had begun their invasion of the US territory. The enemy had quickly overwhelmed the defenders, ending with the capture of more than seventy-five thousand troops and the cruel Bataan Death March that had resulted in so many deaths.

The commander of the defeated forces, General Douglas MacArthur, had left only on the direct orders of the president, vowing that "I shall return."

Nearly three years later, on October 17, 1944, with the landing on Leyte, MacArthur had made good on his promise. Since then, the fighting had continued unabated.

The fierce fighting was a result of the Japanese decision to make a stand in the Philippines. The Japanese poured more men and supplies into the fight for Leyte, intent on hurling the Americans back into the sea.

However, the situation did not go as planned for General Tomoyuki Yamashita, hailed as the "Tiger of Malaya" for his defeat of British forces early in the war. The Americans and Australian forces had proved to be a tough nut to crack. As it turned out, it was the Japanese themselves who were cracking. For the men fighting on the beaches and hills and forests, that wasn't happening fast enough.

The Philippines and Okinawa weren't the only military operations taking place. As Patrol Easy made their way through the jungle, the US Navy and Marines were steaming toward Iwo Jima. There, the Japanese had turned the entire island into a fortress. More than twenty thousand Japanese troops were waiting for the Americans to arrive. Nobody expected it to be an easy fight.

All that anyone had to do was look at a map to be reminded of the vast arena that was the Pacific theater, spreading across more than 20 percent of the earth's surface. To be able to fight a war in two spheres of the world, and supply men and materials to remote islands across thousands of miles of ocean, demonstrated the growing power of the United States.

In the Pacific, everything now seemed to be happening quickly and on a grand scale, even if each day passed much too slowly for the average soldier, sailor, marine, nurse, WAC, or WAVE. Those last two were the acronyms for Women's Army Corps and Women Accepted for Volunteer Emergency Service. For these men and women, home seemed far away and long ago.

Even after months of fighting, there was still plenty of mopping up to do on Leyte, which was just what Patrol Easy and the rest of the 77th Infantry Division were finding out. After all, an enemy ambush had just made mincemeat out of one of their supply convoys. The back of the Japanese defense had been broken, but the arms and legs and fingers and toes were still engaged in fighting. It didn't help that the rugged terrain favored defensive fighting.

Once Leyte and its airfields were taken from the Japanese,

the US plan of attack was to move on to Luzon, the largest island in the Philippines and the location of the capital city of Manila. General MacArthur wanted this crown jewel of the Philippines, and the Japanese were not eager to give it up.

By early 1945 the Japanese had more than one hundred thousand troops on Luzon, nearly a thousand artillery units, plus aircraft and ships at sea—although the Japanese Navy had taken a beating and was no longer the power that it had been. Even so, the combined Japanese forces seemed to be more than enough to meet the invasion.

Or so they thought.

* * *

ABOARD THE LIGHT cruiser USS *Boise*, General Douglas MacArthur managed the whole operation. There was still so much fighting going on that he had not transferred his base of operations to shore since landing and making his famous "I have returned" statement. The formidable "light" cruiser, named for the capital city of Idaho, was six hundred feet in length and carried an armament of fifteen six-inch guns that could spit a shell more than a dozen miles, along with antiaircraft guns and machine guns that could make short work of anything from a Zero to a Betty bomber. No ship was immune to a kamikaze attack, but so far USS *Boise* had not been targeted.

In addition to the security provided by the light cruiser, coordination with land forces and the US Navy was much easier from the ship. The living conditions weren't so bad, either—at least compared to living on land. For starters, there were the three squares a day served up by the navy cooks—also plenty of hot coffee. There weren't any mosquitoes to deal with at sea like there were on land. They *did* have to contend with flies that swarmed in through the portholes that had been opened to capture the ocean breezes and provide fresh air. Then again, this was no luxury cruise. No part of the ship was air-conditioned and not even the general had a fan.

MacArthur's heart ached as he pondered the potential devastation that would befall the Philippines in the midst of war. His love for the islands and its people ran deep, rooted in their rich history that intertwined the culture of the Filipino people with that of the Europeans who had settled there. From the Spanish arrival in the sixteenth century to the American influence since 1898, Manila had become a charming blend of old-world charm and modern flair.

But now, the forces of Imperial Japan sought to leave destruction in their wake. MacArthur feared for the future of Manila and all its beauty. The city's lovely avenues and historic buildings could soon be reduced to rubble and ruin by the cruel hands of war.

As much as he longed for victory, MacArthur knew that there was always a price to pay in times of conflict. Lives would be lost, farmland burned, towns and villages left in ruins, perhaps Manila itself would be destroyed. It was a harsh reality that the general never forgot, even in his moments of hope for a better tomorrow.

* * *

Captain Jim Oatmire had gotten a taste of conditions on shore, and he wasn't eager to return. As one of General MacArthur's junior staff members, he was more than happy to remain on the ship, with its regular hot meals and relative comforts compared to sleeping in a foxhole.

He had moved with the general's staff to the new ship from USS *Nashville*, which had been hit by a kamikaze attack in December that had killed nearly two hundred sailors. All too well, Oatmire remembered that terrifying attack. Despite the *Nashville*'s many guns, it was hard to bring down a single Japanese Zero flying hundreds of miles per hour, with no other intent than to crash into the ship.

There had been no real warning. One moment was quiet, and the next moment the gun crews had been banging away. Two planes had been targeting the ship and the antiaircraft fire brought one of them down. However, the second plane had somehow run the gauntlet of flack and machine-gun fire. In the blink of an eye, the diving plane had struck the ship, erupting in a fireball.

Oatmire recalled how a tremendous shudder had run through the ship after the plane impacted on a five-inch gun battery, the explosion killing every sailor in the vicinity. Fire had quickly spread from the blast and the burning aviation fuel, but the skilled crew had brought it under control.

The crazed determination of the Japanese to destroy the ship using a suicide pilot was hard to fathom. Had the Japanese known that MacArthur was on the ship, they would surely have sent even more of the dreaded kamikaze planes.

At that moment Oatmire was sitting in the mess hall, enjoying his dinner as he read a tattered paperback novel, trying to ignore the flies. He had seen the flies swarming on the Japanese dead ashore, and he had the thought that maybe, or rather more than likely, a batch of the same flies had made their way to the ship, carried on an offshore breeze.

With that thought in mind, he finally surrendered the last few bites of meat loaf and mashed potatoes to the winged pests, pushing his plate away to focus on lighting a cigarette and sipping a mug of coffee. The flies seemed to have the good sense to steer clear of the thick navy coffee, even if Oatmire himself didn't. In fact, he had come to rather like it.

He looked up and saw Major Lundholm across the mess hall.

Lundholm ruled the staff with an iron fist and occupied a space just a step down from MacArthur's inner circle. As his buddy Andy Tatum liked to say, "From Lundholm's lips to God's ears." Of course, in this case Major Lundholm had the ear of General MacArthur and not the Almighty, but that was close enough.

Lundholm seemed to be looking for someone. Oatmire's heart fell when Lundholm's gaze found him and the major began making a beeline for the table where he was sitting.

"There you are," Lundholm said, a note of annoyance in his voice, clearly not happy about having to track him down. "It seems like every time I try to find you, you're either in the mess hall or out on a smoke break."

"Yes, sir," Oatmire said, hoping it didn't sound as if he was agreeing with the major. He started to stand up, scattering the flies and spilling some of his coffee in the process.

Looking annoyed all over again, Lundholm waved him back down. Oatmire knew that he wasn't Lundholm's favorite person, but he wasn't going to cry any tears over it. He didn't much care for Lundholm either. Lundholm had formed some kind of judgment about him and seemed to think that he didn't fit the mold of the rest of the headquarters staff. The major likely would have been happy if Oatmire had not returned from the Leyte invasion, but he had managed to do just that despite the best efforts of the Japanese.

Oatmire should have known better, but something about Lundholm brought out the smart-ass in him. He asked, "Did you come to find out how I liked the meat loaf, sir?"

"Did I—" Lundholm scowled. "No, that's not the reason, Oatmire. You've always got to be the wiseacre, don't you? I came to tell you that you'd better get packing. The Old Man wants a liaison on Luzon, and I couldn't think of a better candidate to march around through the mud and swat at flies."

"Thank you, sir." Oatmire dared to ask, "Luzon?"

"That's where the next big show is going to be, now that things are wrapping up on Leyte," the major said. "I'd have expected that you'd know that, Captain."

"Yes, sir."

"Your launch leaves in thirty minutes," Lundholm said. "Make sure you're on it. It's an awful long swim otherwise."

"Yes, sir. But, sir, may I ask what I'm supposed to be doing once I'm back on shore?"

The major looked around, and then, to Oatmire's surprise, dropped into the empty chair across from him. The major suddenly appeared much older and more tired than he had a moment ago. His shoulders sagged so that he resembled a turtle about to withdraw into its shell. Oatmire felt a pang of conscience, realizing that the major probably had more responsibilities on his mind than the younger officer could ever know. The major frowned at the plate, where a fly was trapped in a pool of the ketchup that Oatmire had added earlier to improve the flavor of the meat loaf. "Here's the thing, Oatmire. The Japanese have taken many hostages in Manila, maybe thousands of hostages by some accounts, most of them American civilians, but a few British and Australians, too. We need someone to negotiate with the Japanese when the time comes."

Oatmire couldn't help but open his eyes wide in amazement. "Why me, sir?"

"It should be obvious by now that you are a man of many talents, Oatmire."

"With all due respect, sir, I don't know anything about hostage negotiation."

"None of us do, Oatmire. It's not a position that the United States Army usually finds itself in. Don't worry, the worst that can happen is that all the hostages end up dead."

The major got up and left Oatmire stewing in his own juices.

His head was spinning. Negotiating with the Japanese? What

could possibly go wrong? The answer was *everything*, which was likely why he'd been given the job. If things didn't work out, they'd need somebody to blame.

He glanced down at his plate, suddenly feeling more than a little sympathy for that fly trapped in the ketchup.

* * *

OVER ON LEYTE, Ernie Pyle was continuing to chronicle what the troops were going through. Rail-thin and much older than the troops he wrote about, Pyle stood out and was easily recognized by the soldiers wherever he went. His folksy piece about Christmas dinner with the boys of the 77th Infantry Division had been read by thousands, if not hundreds of thousands, back home. He didn't sugarcoat things, a fact that had made him beloved by the troops in Europe. He had left Europe to cover the Pacific conflict and found an entirely different situation, despite it being the same war. His reporting painted a truthful picture of "island hopping," a term that sounded breezy compared to the grim reality of it all.

He'd discovered some interesting things around the Pacific, such as the fact that one enemy encountered by the troops was the sheer boredom they faced when they weren't being shot at. This wasn't Europe with its friendly and grateful villagers. There were no adventures in the countryside involving wine and joyrides in jeeps, or the occasional local French girl willing to help a GI feel less lonely. In the Pacific, men might be stationed on a quiet stretch of island where there was no danger of attack, but also precious little to do and nothing to look at but the sea, sky, beach, and coconut trees. Some poor bastards were driven nearly mad by the unrelenting sameness of it all.

Then there was the enemy. Germans were easy enough to understand. They were a lot like Americans except for the fact that they had fallen under the spell of a Fascist madman. You could sit down and share a cigarette or a joke with a former German soldier. But the Japanese were an altogether different enemy.

Pyle wrote, "I've begun to get over that creepy feeling that fighting Japs is like fighting snakes or ghosts." Like most, he also had the feeling that the fight would get even harder the closer that the battle came to Japan itself.

"As far as I can see, our men are no more afraid of the Japs than they are of the Germans," he wrote in one dispatch from the front. "They are afraid of them as a modern soldier is afraid of his foe, but not because they are slippery or ratlike, but simply because they have weapons and fire them like good, tough soldiers."

He also wrote of observing Japanese prisoners, describing the unsettled feeling they gave him even while watching them talk among themselves, even laugh. *What the hell were they laughing about?* Nobody knew.

Then there was that samurai mindset. In one often-reshared account, Pyle had described how a Japanese officer and six men had been surrounded by marines on a beach. Rather than surrender, the officer had shouted orders to his men. All six had bent down and waited patiently as the officer drew his sword and beheaded each man. The marines then shot him dead.

Germans didn't do that. All in all, the enemy in the Pacific remained full of puzzling surprises.

"The Japs are dangerous people, and they aren't funny when they've got guns in their hands," Pyle wrote. "It would be tragic for us to underestimate their power to do us damage, or their will to do it."

In the Pacific in early 1945, nobody could argue with that.

CHAPTER FIVE

When it came to exploring the abandoned fortifications that the Japanese had left behind, you never knew what you were going to find. Patrol Easy came across items that ranged from abandoned rifles to household goods that had been looted from the wealthier Filipino homes during the occupation, finding everything from random silver spoons to teapots.

The GIs also discovered boxes of tinned crabmeat and fish, identified by the labels that Yoshio translated for them, along with bags of rice. Scattered around were a few odd pieces from Japanese mess kits, which Yoshio explained were called *han-gou*.

"One thing for sure, the Nips who left all this stuff behind are either dead, or they're not planning on coming back," Philly said.

Philly inspected one of the crabmeat tins, then held it up to show Lieutenant Steele.

"Honcho, do you think maybe the Japs poisoned these and left them behind for us?" Philly wondered.

"These are sealed cans, Philly. Do you really think the Japs went to all the trouble to can poisoned food to leave for us? No, the Japs ran out in a hurry, is all. Load up, boys, if you have a hankering for seafood."

"How many cans do you want?" Philly asked Deke.

Deke just shook his head. If it didn't have four legs or feathers, he didn't consider it to be food. "If you find any canned ham, just let me know."

"Suit yourself." He held up another can for Yoshio's inspection. "What does this one say?"

"*Tako*. Octopus."

Philly tossed the can away as though it had burned him. "Who the hell eats octopus? I wish they'd left behind something good, like a samurai sword," he said.

"Haven't you got enough of those?"

Philly shrugged. "All right, then how about a Jap pistol?"

Deke shook his head. Many of the men were mad for souvenirs, Philly included. "Just don't set off any damn booby traps."

Deke was referring to the fact that gathering souvenirs could be dangerous. The Japanese seemed to be aware of the American thirst for trophies of war, and more than one GI had fallen victim to a "surprise" left behind by the enemy. Sometimes it was a cleverly hidden trip wire that triggered a mine. Other times it was simply a grenade hidden under a Japanese body, rigged to detonate when the body was moved.

Killing a single soldier with a booby trap wouldn't change the outcome of the war. In Deke's mind, a booby trap was an expression of hatred for an enemy, a last chance to take someone out.

The officers ordered the men to steer clear of the Japanese dead, but the orders were to no avail when there was an Arisaka rifle, Nambu pistol, or especially a sword in plain sight. These weapons were more than the average GI could resist, and some paid dearly when they were lured right into a Japanese trap.

"I remember how I got caught in a booby trap one summer

when I was seventeen," Philly said. "There was this girl named Maria Vinceza, and I couldn't take my eyes off her. I mean, I would walk right into traffic. Once I walked straight into a lamp-post when she went by. It got so bad that my mother thought I needed glasses. Finally getting to second base with that girl made me pretty damn happy, I can tell you."

"Sounds like another tall tale to me," Deke said.

"Believe me when I say her booby trap was as advertised."

Deke snorted. Philly always bragged about what a lover boy he was, but Deke didn't believe half of it.

"That is a different booby trap," Yoshio said, launching into an explanation. That came as no surprise—when other men were playing cards or jawing, their Nisei interpreter could usually be found with his nose in a book, even if it was often a Western novel. "The word comes from sailors who used to catch large birds called boobies in order to eat them. A booby is also an old word for fool. So it is a trap for fools."

"Thanks for that, Yoshio. I think I prefer my definition of booby trap."

Mostly, Deke had not given in to the same temptations as his comrades when it came to collecting souvenirs. However, he wasn't entirely immune, because he did have a thing for knives. One of his prized finds was a beautiful Japanese dagger, more than a foot long, the hilt shiny with gold leaf, the ivory grip decorated with a tiny gold chrysanthemum.

"That is an Imperial Army *tantō*," Yoshio had told him, his eyes showing admiration for the ornately crafted weapon. "It certainly belonged to an officer, and a wealthy one at that."

"I'll be damned," Deke said. Only half kidding, he added, "And here I was about to use it to open cans of rations."

"Please don't do that with such a beautiful knife!" Yoshio blurted, clearly alarmed.

"All right, have it your way," Deke said, and returned the

knife to his pack, wrapping it first in a scrap of oiled cloth. He had kept it there ever since. After all, he had his own custom-made bowie knife to handle just about anything that came his way, from opening cans to chopping brush to defending his foxhole.

But what they found this morning went beyond mere souvenirs.

It had been Deke who'd made the discovery when the damp earth beneath his boots had seemed to shift and give way, revealing a hidden entrance to a dark cave. The rest of Patrol Easy had halted their advance and used their entrenching tools to clear away more dirt until they realized that the cave entrance was big enough to stand up in. Beyond, there seemed to be a network of caves and tunnels. But the cave mouth was as far as any of them were willing to go.

The grim expressions on their faces conveyed a sense of dread as they stared into the abyss. The air that drifted out was foul and tainted with the odor of death and decay, almost tomb-like. Nobody wanted to go down there, but it was clearly something more extensive than the dugout caves they were used to coming across.

"Looks like we found ourselves a jackpot," Philly whispered nervously. "What do you think, Deke? Are these caves just another trap waiting to be sprung? You know how the Japs are."

Deke eyed the dark entryway. "I'm not in any hurry to find out, I can tell you that much."

Lieutenant Steele studied the entrance, then turned to address his men. "All right, listen up. We're going in. We can't just leave a cave like this behind our lines without clearing it first. For all we know, it might be full of Japanese. Keep your eyes peeled for anything that looks like a booby trap. In other words, don't touch a damn thing."

To Steele's credit, he was the first one into the cave entrance.

As they ventured deeper into the tunnels, using their flashlights, the air grew cooler and the walls closed in around them, heightening their unease. Their dim lights seemed to make hardly a dent in the darkness. Rounding a corner, they stumbled upon an underground hospital, with sixteen bunks lined up neatly against the walls, eight on each side, where the tunnel passage had been widened. The bunks had been nailed together out of rough lumber, then lined with thin mattresses that could not have been very comfortable. The mattresses were dirty from use and spotted with brown bloodstains.

Deke shuddered. It was hard to think of a worse place to be lying wounded, in a dark cave in the ground, without much hope of decent medical attention. But his mind stopped short of sympathy. As far as Deke was concerned, the Nips deserved to be miserable. They had killed his friend from basic training on Guam, and they had killed and wounded other good men that Deke had fought beside. He looked over the grim surroundings once more and thought, *To hell with 'em.*

Another area had been dug out of the wall and rigged with electric lights and what looked like an operating table. A few bloody rags covered the dirt floor surrounding it.

"Look at that," muttered Rodeo, taking in the sight of used bandages and medical supplies strewn about the narrow room. "This place has seen some use."

"One thing for sure, the Japs cleared out in a hurry," Steele said. "Looks to me like they forgot to take a couple of their guys with them."

Deke surveyed the bunks, his gaze lingering on the lifeless bodies of two Japanese soldiers sprawled across their beds. The sorry bastards had evidently killed themselves rather than face capture. However, at second glance, there were no weapons evident in the dead men's hands. A more chilling thought was that their comrades had simply killed the wounded that they weren't able to take with them.

Philly noticed the same thing. "I almost feel sorry for those guys," Philly said. "Imagine being killed by your own side. I've got to say, the Japanese mind is hard to fathom."

"Good thing for us that it's not your job to fathom it," Steele said. "Now stay focused, boys. We've got a job to do here and there may be enemy soldiers in this place who are far from dead. Now let's see if there's anything useful in this mess."

As they prepared to leave the hospital wing, Deke couldn't help but glance back one last time at the two lifeless soldiers, their faces far from peaceful in death, but twisted in pain and despair. Perhaps it was no surprise that, for once, nobody seemed all that interested in searching the bodies for souvenirs.

Danilo made his opinion of the dead Japanese clear by spitting in their direction.

They spread out, making their way through the cave and tunnel system. They found more ration tins, these empty ones that had been tossed along the tunnel walls. They even came across a pinup calendar of Japanese women in skimpy kimonos and swimsuits, apparently starlets of film and stage.

Philly gave a low whistle of appreciation. "She's not bad," he announced, studying that month's girl. "But she's no Veronica Lake."

This was no time to debate the qualities of pinup girls. "Never mind that. Just keep your eyes open," Deke said. He hadn't asked to be made second-in-command, but more than ever, he now felt the pressure of making certain that the patrol advanced—and that they didn't all get killed in the process.

Just when it felt as if the tunnel could go no farther, they rounded a bend and the shadowy passageway stretched even deeper into the hillside. Deke looked back and saw the lieutenant giving him a nod. Tightening his grip on the rifle, a flashlight held to the stock, he edged farther down the tunnel. He felt reassured that Danilo was two steps behind him. The Filipino guerrilla had shouldered his rifle and had drawn his wickedly sharp bolo knife—basically a machete. It was clear how he planned to deal with any Japanese they encountered in the dark.

Once again, the tunnel widened. This time there were no hospital bunks, but evidently a makeshift command center. Cubbyholes had been dug on either side of the main tunnel, the cramped spaces filled with rough tables and boxes for chairs, scraps of paper scattered about.

"Hey, Honcho," Deke called out. "I think I found something."

"What is it?" Steele asked, joining him at a small table littered with papers. A pile of ashes on the ground nearby indicated that the Japanese must have destroyed the documents they felt were important and left the rest. Still, there might be something to be gleaned from what the enemy had left behind. The lieutenant called for Yoshio and asked him to take a look.

"This appears to be intel on enemy positions," Yoshio said, having inspected the documents. "I don't know how useful it is, considering that we have already captured some of this territory I'm seeing on the maps. It looks as if they burned anything really useful."

"We'll let the boys back at HQ take a look, just to be sure," Steele said. "Maybe they can make more sense of it than we can. Gather everything up. The Japanese may have overlooked something if they were in a hurry."

"So we turn around?" Philly asked hopefully.

"Hell no," the lieutenant replied forcefully. "We're gonna follow this damn tunnel all the way to Tokyo if we need to."

"Dammit, Honcho. I was afraid you'd say that."

Once again, Deke led the way further into the Japanese fortifications. Given a choice, he would much rather have been forging a path through the green jungle above, even if it meant cutting his way through with his bowie knife.

Deke stared down the narrow, dark tunnel that lay before them. He felt a draft on his face, indicating that there was a fresh-air vent somewhere in the vicinity. However, the air remained stale and heavy with the scent of damp earth.

"Listen up, fellas," he said, his voice firm despite the unease in his gut. "We need to be extra careful going forward. Watch for trip wires."

"Got it, Deke," Philly replied, his own eyes scanning their surroundings with a mix of curiosity and caution, this being the largest enemy fortification that they had explored.

Where had all the Japanese gone? It was possible that they had been sent to defend Ormoc and Palompon, but hadn't survived. Whoever was left had likely taken to the hills.

"Yoshio," Steele called out. "Keep an eye on our rear. We don't want any surprises sneaking up on us."

"Understood," Yoshio responded, his voice betraying a double helping of nervousness.

Who could blame him? Deke thought.

As they moved farther into the tunnels, Deke imagined that the walls were closing in around him, like being inside a boa constrictor. He shook off the sensation, focusing instead on the task at hand. The Japanese seemed to have fled, but there was no way to be certain who—or what—lay hidden in the dark.

The beam of his flashlight reflected off something metallic near the ground.

"Hold it!" Deke shouted, signaling for the others to stop. "Look at that."

Philly squinted in the dim light, noticing a thin wire stretched across the tunnel just inches from his foot. "Good catch, Deke," he breathed, relief washing over him. "That could've been bad."

"Looks like the Japanese left a surprise for us, after all," Deke muttered, carefully stepping over the trip wire. He followed the wire to where it connected to a grenade that had been jammed into the dirt wall of the tunnel. He wasn't eager to mess with it, but if they left the wire in place, it was only a matter of time before someone set it off by accident. "Everybody back."

They retreated along the tunnel. Once they came to a bend that offered some protection, the soldiers hugged the walls beyond the bend while Deke set down his flashlight to illuminate the wire from a safe distance, then lined up his rifle sights on the wire.

"No way he can hit that," one of the new guys said.

"Ten bucks says your wrong," Philly replied.

"Keep your head down," Deke said, and squeezed the trigger.

The bullet cut the wire and the tunnel ahead was filled with a flash and echoing bang. Clouds of dust and dirt rolled through the tunnel, leaving several men coughing and dusty, but it was a lot better than being shredded by shrapnel. Their ears rang. The blast wasn't enough to collapse any tunnel walls, but the grenade would have played hell with flesh and bone.

"All right, the excitement is over," the lieutenant said. "Let's keep going."

Deke moved forward, twice as cautious as before. He had gotten lucky and spotted the wire. He just hoped that the Japanese hadn't had time to rig too many other surprises for them.

He halted when they heard a strangled cry behind them. *Yoshio*. He had been bringing up the rear. In the dark, he must have wandered down one of the side tunnels they had passed. "Where'd everybody go! I'm lost!" they heard Yoshio shout, his voice edging on terror. "I lost my damn flashlight and I can't find my way back!"

"Stay calm, Yoshio!" Steele yelled in reply. "Keep shouting. We'll come get you. Just stay put!"

"Please, hurry!" Yoshio pleaded.

"You two, go get him and be quick about it," Steele said.

Deke and Philly retraced their steps, finally locating Yoshio in a small alcove down a fork in the tunnel. In the flashlight beam, his face looked pale and sweat drenched. "Thank God," he muttered. "I swear, once we get out of this place, I'll never set foot underground again, even if it means a court-martial."

Philly appeared amused. "What's the matter? You afraid of the dark?"

"It's not the dark, it's the ghosts," he said. "This place is filled with them."

Philly's eyes widened. The look of amusement had vanished. Like Yoshio, he had also gone pale. "Ghosts?"

"Spirits of the dead," Yoshio said. "Japanese spirits. *Yōkai*. They cling to this place. They do not want us here."

Deke didn't spook easily, but he still felt the hairs prickle on the back of his neck. "Dammit, you two, that's enough hogwash for one day," he said. "Let's get the hell out of here and get back to the others."

Quickly, they made their way to the main tunnel, where they found the others waiting tensely.

"Dammit, Yoshio. You gave us a scare. Everybody stick together," Steele said. "Don't lose sight of the man in front of you. Understood?"

"Yes, sir."

They continued, with Deke once more leading the way, Danilo and Philly right on his heels. They came to another wide place in the tunnel, this one crammed with wooden crates and boxes.

"End of the road," Deke said. "This is as far as the tunnel goes."

"Good to know," Philly said. "I was starting to think Honcho was serious about this tunnel going all the way to Tokyo."

By now they were deep within the hill, and it was evident that the Japanese had decided this was a safe place for an ammo dump. Crates filled with munitions stretched in every direction when they played their flashlights over the storage area. There were several barrels of what appeared to be fuel stacked neatly next to the ammo.

"What have we here?" Deke wondered.

"Nobody light a match, that's for damn sure," Philly said. "This whole place is a giant powder keg."

Coming up behind them, Lieutenant Steele let out a low whistle. He couldn't help himself. By far, this was the largest enemy ammo dump that they had come across. "Nice work, boys," he said. "We need to get back and report this. Now let's get the hell out of here before anything goes boom."

CHAPTER SIX

THEY CAREFULLY RETRACED THEIR STEPS, with Deke hoping that they hadn't missed any traps that had been set for them. Back at the surface, free of the dark and stifling tunnel, Deke and everyone else were glad to see sunshine and breathe fresh air, even if it was humid and smelled vaguely of the enemy dead decomposing in the ditches and undergrowth. By now they were used to that.

Orders soon came back from headquarters that the tunnel had to be cleared of munitions.

"Why can't we just seal it off?" Philly wanted to know. "We could just pretend we never found it."

"That's too much ordnance to leave there," Steele explained. "If it ever blows, the whole top of this hill will turn into a volcano. There's a village right near here and people will be moving back in now that the Japanese are on their way out."

"Honcho, I've just got to say that clearing out a tunnel doesn't sound like the right job for us," Philly said. "We're supposed to be scouts and snipers."

"But we're the lucky bastards who happen to be here," Steele said.

As it turned out, the job wouldn't be Patrol Easy's to do alone. Word came down that soldiers from the 92nd Bomb Disposal Squad would be called in, with Patrol Easy assigned to help out. What help they were supposed to give a bomb squad was anybody's guess.

It turned out that the "bomb squad" consisted of just two men. The 92nd was stretched thin from being called upon to deal with weapons stockpiles that had been left behind by the Japanese.

"Honcho, the bomb squad guys are here," Philly announced, leading them to where the lieutenant sat Indian style on the ground, studying a map and smoking a cigarette.

"Just two of you?" Lieutenant Steele asked in surprise.

"Our guys are in demand, sir. What can we say?" replied one of the soldiers, a taller man who informed them that he went by his nickname, which was Sparks. His partner was a guy nicknamed Fuze. The men of Patrol Easy looked at one another, not sure that humor was the best quality in a bomb squad technician.

"Don't you worry, sir," Sparks said. "We'll do a bang-up job."

"Maybe you shouldn't put it that way," Steele muttered. "Sparks and Fuze, huh? You guys are a regular couple of comedians. All right, let's get to it. Tell us what to do."

"You got it, sir."

"Listen, there are still a lot of Japs around, so do me a favor and call me Honcho."

"Honcho, huh? I like that, sir. Keeps any nosy Japs from figuring out you're the man in charge. I hear snipers like to target officers."

"You heard right. So don't call me sir again. And you sure as hell better not salute me."

Sparks got the message loud and clear. "You got it, Honcho."

Despite his joking manner, the man seemed to know his job, announcing that the first order of business was to check for any booby traps hidden within the stockpile itself and then take inventory. The stockpile discovered by Patrol Easy was one of the biggest yet, although it was expected that by the time the army got to Manila, there would be even larger ammunition dumps—if the Japanese didn't destroy them first. It could only be supposed that the Japanese had simply run out of time to blow up this underground depot.

The Japanese had evidently planned on letting the advancing soldiers do that job for them. Patrol Easy reentered the tunnel to escort the bomb squad experts. Close to the ammunition stockpile, Sparks and Fuze found several trip wires attached to mines. If Patrol Easy had gone poking around, Sparks informed them, setting off a mine might have been enough to trigger the entire ammunition dump.

"You did good getting out of here alive, fellas," Sparks announced. "One wrong step and you would've been blown so high that you all would've been dancing on the moon."

"Good thing, because I forgot my dancing shoes," Philly said.

"All right, I'd suggest that everybody clear out of the tunnel for now," Sparks said. He held up a pair of pliers and snapped them open and shut. "Fuze and I need to decommission these booby traps before we can start to haul this out of here."

"You sure about this?" Steele asked.

Despite all his wisecracks, Sparks seemed serious and competent when it came to his job. "As sure as I'm going to be, Honcho. When it comes to the bomb squad, we like to say that you only make a mistake once in your career."

"I don't like leaving you boys alone," the lieutenant said. "If nothing else, someone ought to stay down here to watch your back in case there are any Japanese lurking around. They could take you guys out and blow up this whole damn hill."

"We won't say no to that if you can spare a couple of guys," Sparks said. "As long as they're volunteers."

"That's easy, because one of them will be me," Steele said. He turned to his men. "Anybody else?"

Deke found himself stepping forward. Maybe he was a fool, but he wasn't about to leave the lieutenant alone on guard duty. "I reckon I'll hang back with you, Honcho."

"All right, Deke. I appreciate it, but it's your funeral. The rest of you, get the hell out of here until you get the all clear from us."

Not much rattled Deke, but as he watched the two wise-cracking soldiers of the demolitions team prepare to deactivate the devices that the enemy had left behind, he discovered that his heart was pounding. In fact, he was a bit surprised that the lieutenant couldn't hear it a few feet away.

The two bomb squad guys had grown serious, emphasizing the fact that the stakes were high, and one wrong move could be the end for all of them. They worked meticulously, sweat beading on their foreheads as they carefully maneuvered around the Japanese munitions, using their flashlights to catch a glimpse of any trip wires glittering in the flashlight beam.

Meanwhile, Deke pulled his eyes away to join the lieutenant in keeping an eye on the darkness beyond. They were confident that they had swept the tunnel clean earlier, but all it would take was one leftover enemy soldier with suicide on his mind to blow them all sky high. He and Honcho kept their own flashlights off so that they wouldn't be targeted easily if there were any Japanese around.

Deke's heart raced faster with each motion of the demolitions team, the weight of impending danger bearing down on him as if the walls of the tunnel were constricting. He couldn't shake the feeling that something could still go wrong, that their lives hung in the balance. As Sparks and Fuze edged their way through the darkness, Deke silently prayed that they'd make it through this unscathed. He cursed himself for volunteering to stay behind, but there was no way that he was going to leave the lieutenant down here.

"Almost there," Sparks muttered, his voice barely audible. Fuze nodded, his breaths coming shallow and rapid. There was no wisecracking now. In the pale flashlight beam, sweat beaded both men's faces.

"Got it," Sparks whispered triumphantly, holding up the last piece of wire. Fuze let out a slow, shaky breath before breaking into a wide grin.

"Piece of cake," he said, winking at Sparks.

"Let's not celebrate just yet," Sparks cautioned, gesturing toward the tunnel's exit. "We still need to get these babies out of here."

"Right," Sparks agreed, straightening up and making his way back to Deke and Honcho. He addressed the lieutenant. "With your permission, could we get the rest of your patrol down here to help us figure out what we've got in this tunnel?"

"All right. Deke, go fetch the boys."

Under the capable eyes of Sparks and Fuze, Patrol Easy reentered the tunnel to help with the inventory so that they knew what was being dealt with. But first Sparks offered some instruction.

"Unless you want to meet Saint Peter ahead of schedule, don't touch anything that doesn't look right," Sparks said. "You've all got two eyes, so use 'em."

It turned out that there was quite a lot to lay eyes on, not all of it ammunition, but explosive just the same. Fuze wrote it all down as the men called it out to him. They counted eight hundred drums of aviation fuel, nearly five hundred massive five-hundred-pound bombs, assorted mines and smaller bombs intended to be dropped from observation planes, and one hundred bomb fuses, each with enough juice to take off a man's hand—or trigger a massive blast. The larger bombs had been intended for planes flying out of the nearby Japanese airstrip.

The question was, What to do with it all? As the lieutenant had stated before, they couldn't simply leave it. Steele got on the radio and contacted HQ. He was told to salvage the fuel—and blow up the rest. The fuel could be used in American planes in a pinch, but Japanese ammunition wasn't any good in US guns.

Of course, there was no good way for the handful of soldiers in Patrol Easy to roll eight hundred barrels up the sloping tunnel to the surface. They would need some help for that. Quickly, nearly thirty civilian men were rounded up and put to work. It was hot and sweaty laboring inside the tunnel, but the Filipinos were eager to help. They hadn't been able to take part in the fighting, but this much they were glad to do. In fact, a couple of the local men took over and organized the entire effort. Within a few hours, the drums of fuel had been moved to the surface, surrounded by barbed wire to discourage any Japanese infiltrators, and put under guard by Filipino volunteers.

That left the matter of the ammunition stockpile. Orders were to destroy it. Grinning, Sparks announced that he had a plan for that. He and Fuze disappeared deeper into the tunnel carrying detonators and a roll of wire. They emerged half an hour later, just as the sun was starting to go down. The sky was fading to hues of pink and purple. Bats began to flit through the air.

"Well?" the lieutenant asked.

"For maximum effect, I'd suggest waiting until full dark," Sparks said. "Also, I'd recommend getting everyone off this hill."

They took up positions on the next hilltop, soldiers and civilians alike, gathering around as if preparing to watch July Fourth fireworks. A few guards kept watch for any Japanese who might still be on a night patrol. Sparks and Fuze were positioned closer to the tunnel in order to set off the detonator.

Suddenly the night sky exploded in a brilliant cascade of reds, blues, and greens, each fiery burst echoing across the expanse above. Deke watched in awe, and although he had seen his share of so-called fireworks in this war so far, this was something special. For a change, nobody was being blown up in the process. The very ground shook, even this far away. Beside him, Philly let out a low whistle.

"Would you look at that," he said, nudging Deke in the ribs. "Not a bad way to dispose of the enemy's weapons, huh?"

"Couldn't agree more," Deke replied, his eyes never leaving the spectacle unfolding before them. The Japanese munitions detonated in a display of dazzling pyrotechnics.

Sparks and Fuze appeared, their faces illuminated by the explosions, grinning like two schoolboys who had just pulled off an elaborate prank. It was hard for Deke not to smile along with them. After all, they had just successfully dismantled a dangerous cache of explosives without so much as a scratch. Watching it all go up with a bang felt like a just reward.

"Hey, Honcho," Sparks called out, sauntering over to the lieutenant. "What do you think of the show?"

"Damn good job," Honcho told them, clapping each man on the shoulder. "Maybe my country club back home can book you guys to handle the July Fourth show one of these days."

"Wouldn't that be great," Sparks said, an almost dreamy sound in his voice. "Probably a lot less dangerous than what we're doing now."

More than one man felt a pang when Honcho mentioned home, and the Fourth of July, no less. It all sounded so normal, but would they ever get back home to that?

Another explosion lit the sky, a final blast lagging behind the others. Deke had to wonder what any Japanese must be thinking. It sure as hell sounded like the end of the world. He tried not to think too hard about the fact that one wrong step and they might have been inside that tunnel when the ammunition exploded.

Together, they stood and watched as the last of the Japanese munitions went up in a jet of flames. They could only hope that the Empire of Japan did the same—the sooner, the better.

A final echo rolled across the hills, and then darkness and quiet settled over the landscape once again. Even the night birds and insects seemed to have been stunned into silence. Deke knew all too well that the quiet wouldn't last for long.

CHAPTER SEVEN

Deke had been right about things not staying quiet. There was some excitement during the night when Japanese infiltrators attacked the command post. At least twenty enemy soldiers appeared out of the darkness, carrying satchel-and-pole charges. Their intent was to destroy vehicles, and they did just that, rushing silently toward whatever trucks and M8 armored vehicles they could find.

The night was then interrupted by massive explosions. Soon the leaping flames from the burning vehicles illuminated Japanese troops hastening back toward the safety of the forest.

Several GIs opened fire, but it was hard for them to see what they were shooting at. It didn't help that soldiers had come running toward the sound of the fighting, mixing with the fleeing infiltrators. "Hold your fire!" Lieutenant Steele shouted. "I said to hold your fire, dammit! You'll hit our own guys."

Deke obeyed orders—to a point. He spotted a lone Japanese running for the trees, put his sights between the Jap's shoulder blades, and dropped him.

A handful of other infiltrators had been shot—along with a

couple of GIs who had been unlucky enough to get in the way of the retreating Japanese. Another GI had been stabbed through the belly by a Japanese bayonet.

"Six dead Japs," Rodeo reported.

"Good, we'll add it to the tally," Steele replied.

One of the Japanese must have gotten too close to his satchel charge, because the blast had left him wounded, mostly with burns. One side of his face was black and red, and bits of charred fabric clung to his torso. He was trying to crawl away when Deke found him. He pointed his rifle at the enemy soldier and shouted for him to surrender.

But the Japanese soldier had no intention of giving up. Shouting defiantly, he propped himself up on one elbow and waved a hand grenade with his other arm, clearly intending to take out a few Americans on his way to the afterlife. Deke didn't give him the chance to yank the pin on that grenade. He pulled the trigger and put the poor bastard out of his misery.

"Make that seven dead Japanese," he said.

Tired as they were, nobody slept much the rest of the night. The attack had left everybody on edge.

"For all we know, those Nip bastards will be back," Philly said.

He and Deke sat back-to-back in their foxhole the rest of the night, scanning the darkness for an attack that never came.

* * *

ALONG WITH THE constant threat of infiltrators, a few Japanese planes still harassed them. It was hard to say if the Zeros had taken off from Luzon or a hidden airfield that was still managing to operate on Leyte. Small, lightweight, and nimble, these planes were nothing more than a powerful Mitsubishi engine bolted to a wooden frame with canvas wings. With their lightweight construction, the Japanese Zero fighters did not require much space to take off and land, giving them a distinct advantage in a landscape filled with hidden runways.

One plane strafed a convoy that was evacuating wounded toward the beach, killing several and leaving two trucks in flames before it turned on a dime and roared away at what seemed like an impossible speed to the stunned soldiers on the ground. Two US fighters arrived soon after, but they were too late to catch the marauding Japanese fighter plane.

Another time, a Japanese fighter plane swooped down and strafed the troops at Palompon before being driven off by anti-aircraft fire. But it wasn't done. Turning away from the town, the plane hunted down a convoy carrying troops and supplies. The Zero machine-gunned the road and even dropped a bomb, once again leaving trucks in flames and more men dead. Then the plane disappeared as suddenly as it had arrived. The soldiers might have thought the Zero was a figment of their imaginations if it hadn't been for the destruction left behind.

The troops on the ground welcomed the sight of their own planes on patrol because it meant that the dreaded Zeros wouldn't dare to show themselves. Also, the US planes fired on Japanese ground troops and vehicles whenever they spotted them.

Against Japanese positions deep in the hills, another tactic was being applied from the air. Instead of regular bombing, the planes were dropping a flaming substance that set everything on the ground ablaze—trees, abandoned Filipino villages and crops, and hopefully the Japanese hiding in the remote hills.

From a safe vantage point on another hilltop, Patrol Easy watched as the planes worked over an enemy position. They looked on as the ugly, orange fireballs rolled across the forest, flames enveloping anything the fireball touched.

"What the hell is that stuff?" Philly wondered. "It looks like the devil himself threw up."

"Jellied gasoline," Lieutenant Steele said. "They say it's sticky stuff and clings to the trees—and the Japs. They call it napalm."

Steele's description fell short in this case, but he was simply sharing what he knew. Napalm was a mix of molten synthetic rubber, phosphorus, and gasoline, a nightmare dreamed up by the enlightened folks at Harvard University. It had also been used on German civilians during the firebombing on their cities.

"Whatever they call it, I'm glad we're not on the receiving end," Deke said.

War was never pretty, Deke had decided, but there was something about the vast spreading flames that made warfare seem industrial and inhumane. Unlike a bullet or a knife, this kind of mass destruction was something that he just couldn't understand.

"I don't like it," he found himself saying. "It doesn't seem right somehow, killing people that way."

"One thing humans are awfully good at is coming up with new ways to kill each other," the lieutenant pointed out. He sighed. "Imagine if we put half that energy into developing a cure for cancer or the common cold. I know that's wishful thinking. I suppose it's just human nature to fight and kill each other, and it has been since the days when all we had were sticks and stones. But the way things are going with these new weapons, I wouldn't be surprised if we destroy ourselves in the end."

Deke didn't know what to say to that, other than to think that Honcho was probably right. That napalm was nasty stuff. He couldn't fathom what might be worse.

Danilo was one of the coolest customers that any of them had met, but he made a kind of groaning sound while witnessing his beloved countryside being burned up.

They couldn't help but keep watching, mesmerized by the fire falling from the sky, until the planes ended their mission.

Sometimes the planes flying these daredevil missions needed their help. One night the division got an emergency call from several planes that had found themselves arriving in the middle of a naval raid on their base on the island of Mindoro. Unable to land, they had fled toward friendly forces on Leyte. But by the time they reached Leyte, the six planes were running short on fuel. They either had to land or take their chances trying to reach one of the aircraft carriers for a tricky nighttime landing that none of them had been trained to do. The thought of leaving land behind and heading out again over the dark ocean couldn't have been all that appealing.

A makeshift landing field was surrounded by several trucks and jeeps, which shined their headlights on the dirt strip. It wasn't ideal, but it was the best they could do.

One by one the planes made their landing approach. A single stream of enemy tracer fire coming from the hills showed that the Japanese had spotted the planes. A P-51 broke away and strafed the hill until the enemy gun fell silent. It was the last plane to land, joining the group of five P-51s and one B-25 that dropped down and made a bumpy landing on the runway—although to call it that was a stretch of the imagination.

"Boy, are we glad you guys could help us out," one of the pilots said. Maybe it was the harsh lighting from the trucks, but he looked pale and shaken. It was a reminder that, in the end, the planes were flown by guys just like the ones on the ground. Even the most routine day might quickly become a struggle for survival, whether you were in the air or in the lush jungle.

* * *

At times the enemy emerged from hiding to make an organized attack. When this took place, it served as a reminder that the Japanese were far from defeated.

"I sure do prefer when they show themselves and attack us rather than sneaking around," Deke remarked.

"Yeah, it makes it easier to mow them down," Philly said.

Patrol Easy was accompanying the 305th Field Artillery Battalion near Villaba, helping to serve as their eyes and ears while the artillerymen wrestled their heavy guns down the muddy roads. Rain came and went, often in heavy downpours, so that Patrol Easy and most of the artillerymen wore their drab green ponchos. Rain sluiced off their helmets and made a constant din, reminding Deke of rain falling on an old tin roof back home.

There had been rumors that the Japanese were dug in along the ridges, ready with their own artillery. The 305th was being sent to fight fire with fire.

The artillery unit troops still got wet despite their ponchos, sweating through their shirts in the heat and humidity from the physical effort of coaxing their guns through the muddy places. There were an awful lot of those.

The 105-millimeter howitzers were mounted on rubber tires, now so liberally coated in mud that it was hard to tell where the gun began and the road ended. An erudite gunner could have pointed out that the word *howitzer* originated with the Prussian artillery and referred to the mobility of a gun. These guns were not all that mobile at the moment, being bogged down in *Schlamm*—to borrow another Prussian word, this one for mud.

While the artillerymen labored, Deke and the others dealt with the occasional Japanese snipers taking potshots at the column.

"Got 'em, I think," said Deke, firing at a spot where he

suspected a sniper was holed up. At least, the sniper had gone quiet.

Danilo waded into the brush to verify that the sniper was dead, somewhat like a retriever going after a downed pheasant. Deke covered him until he disappeared into the greenery. Danilo soon emerged, dragging a corpse behind him and displaying a rare grin. He deposited the body at Deke's feet.

"One," Danilo said, revealing that he could at least count that high in English. It was a reminder of the emphasis that had been placed on tallying the number of Japanese killed. Even Danilo had gotten in on the act.

"Hell, I don't want him," Deke said.

Nonetheless, Deke couldn't help but study the body with some interest. The dead sniper was a small and compact man, likely around Deke's own age. The ragged state of his uniform and a patchy beard indicated that the man had been living rough. Considering that the Japanese had fled into the hills, the man's appearance made sense.

Philly bent down and quickly went through the man's pockets. There was nothing of interest there, other than what appeared to be a letter with the black-and-white photograph of a young woman folded inside.

Yoshio scanned the letter. "It's from his wife," he announced. "She says everything is fine at home and that he should be careful."

"He ought to have listened to her," Philly said. He glanced at the photograph. "She's not bad looking. Maybe I'll look her up when I get to Japan."

He dropped the letter and photo into the mud, and they walked on.

Their destination was a distant ridge where Japanese troops had been spotted. One of the landmarks that stood out was Bugabuga Hill, a rocky outcropping that rose higher than the neighboring hills, resembling a crooked thumb rather than a middle finger. Raising binoculars to his eyes, Deke could just make out the distant sight of a Japanese battle flag on that peak. Something about it made his blood boil, and he would have liked nothing better than to sprout wings, fly over there, and rip that flag down. As it stood, it was going to be a long slog to get there.

Intelligence reports indicated that these enemy troops were under the direct order of General Suzuki, one of Yamashita's minions. Along with his superior officer, Suzuki had played a role in the Sook Ching massacre in Singapore during 1942—with help from the Imperial Japanese Army's *Kempeitai*, or secret police, employing thousands of civilian males to intimidate the population and quell any resistance. The GIs didn't know it, but they were up against a war criminal.

Along the muddy road, they began to meet refugees from the Japanese occupation of the Philippines. First, the refugees came in a trickle, and eventually there was a flood involving hundreds of civilians. Many had taken to the hills to escape the fighting during the US invasion, but now that the Japanese had themselves taken to the hills where the refugees were hiding, they were once again fleeing.

Deke watched as crowds of men, women, and children flowed against the advancing troops. They were ragged and haggard from living in the hills without enough to eat or proper shelter. Many were sick, struggling to carry young children or a few meager possessions. Some rode skinny cows or ponies. He could tell from their clothes that these people came from all walks of life, because under the mud and dirt some wore dress shoes or the remnants of a suit. They had all been thrown together by this great calamity that had upended society.

The sight would have been heartbreaking, except for the fact that there was no air of sorrow surrounding the Filipinos. Sure, they were exhausted, but they looked overjoyed to see the Americans. A few waved tattered US flags that they had hidden away and held on to all through the Japanese occupation in hopes of this very moment. An end to their suffering at the hands of the Japanese had arrived. They were flowing back now toward the areas that had been liberated by US forces.

"God bless you! God bless you!" cried one elderly grandmother in English. She looked as if she barely had the strength to stand. Deke gave her a chocolate bar, which she accepted but promptly handed over to a knot of small children nearby.

Deke shrugged and gave her another. "For you," he said.

The old woman broke off a piece for herself and once again gave the rest away.

One older man paused to confer with Lieutenant Steele and one of the artillery officers, pointing out exactly where Japanese troops were dug in on the ridges ahead. It turned out that he had even made a rough map that would have gotten him killed if the Japanese had caught him with it. The officers thanked him, and the man shook his fist at the distant hills before moving on.

The road passed through open spaces covered in thick green cogon grass with a few binayuyo trees growing at the roadside. The binayuyo trees with their magnolia-like leaves sometimes had small clusters of fruit that resembled grapes. Danilo picked a handful and prompted Deke to have a taste. The dark-purple fruit was rather sweet and pulpy, almost like a prune or frost-ripened persimmon. The starving refugees were so hungry that they didn't stop at devouring the ripe fruits but also ate the sour green binayuyo fruit out of desperation. Meanwhile, the GIs shared whatever rations they could spare, and then some, with the hungry hordes.

It became more apparent what the refugees had gone through at the hands of the Japanese marauders in the area. The survivors on the road were the lucky ones. As the troops advanced deeper into the territory into which the enemy had fled, they began to pass bodies that had been stabbed to death with bayonets or even partially beheaded. Some of the dead women showed signs of having been raped, their bodies left partially naked. Dead children lay near some of these bodies, indicating that mother and child had been cruelly killed by the Japanese. Clouds of flies and swarms of ants lost no time in descending upon the dead. Though battle-hardened, seeing the dead women and children was too much for some of the GIs, who stumbled out of the formation to vomit.

Deke felt his earlier fury grow. What the hell was wrong with the enemy to do this to civilians who were just trying to get out of harm's way? It made no sense to him.

The intelligence provided by the Filipino who had drawn the rough map simply verified what the officers already knew, which was that the enemy was dug into those hills. It was Deke who spotted them, his eyes being some of the sharpest.

"I'll be damned," he said. "That hill is covered in Japs."

He was pointing toward a ridge to the left of the landmark Bugabuga Hill. Sure enough, large numbers of Japanese could be seen scrambling into fortified positions. It was the most enemy troops that they had seen in one place for some time. They could handle infantry. What was more worrisome was that the Japanese appeared to have several artillery pieces that they were preparing to fire. Clearly, they planned to bombard the advancing American column.

Seeing the threat, officers from the 305th began shouting orders to get their own guns into play. The problem was that unhitching the guns from the trucks pulling them and getting the howitzers into position wasn't a quick task. But to the credit of the drivers and crews, some swung their trucks around so that their guns at least pointed in the right general direction. The GIs on the road scattered to get out of their way.

Deke decided to do what he could to buy them some time.

"How far away do you reckon those Nips are up on that hill?" he wondered.

"A thousand yards, at least," Philly said.

Lieutenant Steele squinted with his one good eye. "More like twelve hundred," he said.

"Yeah, I'd say about that," Deke replied.

He took off his pack and put it on the hood of a truck, then set his rifle on the pack. The Weaver scope mounted on his Springfield was relatively low power—good enough for the closer ranges of jungle fighting, but next to useless at this distance. But you had to work with what you had.

However, he also had something of a secret weapon. The Springfield normally fired a 150-grain round, but he had managed to obtain a few rounds of 180-grain ammunition that was technically a hunting round. The rounds had come from a grizzled master sergeant who had heard of Deke's reputation and pressed them into his hand with the admonition "Use 'em well, son." Deke planned to. Considering that there were four hundred grains to an ounce, the difference in weight seemed minuscule. However, the heavier bullet could shoot farther and more accurately. And hit harder. He still had a few in his pocket, saved up for a special occasion. This seemed like as good a time as any.

Philly was suddenly beside him, glassing the ridge with binoculars far more powerful than Deke's scope. "See that Jap gun about two o'clock from us?"

"I see it," Deke said after a moment, spotting it through the scope. "I'm gonna reach out and give them a poke."

He breathed in and held it. He reminded himself that he was shooting uphill and at a considerable distance. In theory, his bullet could reach that target. In reality, you had to be able to *see* your target. It wasn't like one of the big naval guns where you could fire beyond the horizon. He made the mental calculations, raised his aim a bit, and squeezed the trigger.

At this distance, it took a few heartbeats for the bullet to reach the Japanese target.

"Got him," Philly said beside him.

Deke worked the bolt and fired again.

"A little high and to the right."

"Yeah," Deke said. He worked the bolt, adjusted his aim, then fired again.

"Hit," Philly reported.

Deke kept it up, firing more quickly now that he had the range figured out, targeting first one gun crew and then another. He was dimly aware of the gunners around him hurrying to get into position. Finally, there came the satisfying boom of a howitzer sending a round toward the Japanese. A burst of flying dirt on the ridge showed that the gunners were off target, so they worked to adjust their aim.

One of the Japanese guns got into play, sending a round screeching over their heads. The civilians who were still on the road dashed for cover.

"Get in the ditches!" Steele shouted to his men. "We'll let the big boys duke it out for now."

But Deke was reluctant to leave his position. With more shells beginning to land on the ridge, it was proving harder to spot targets through the flying dirt and smoke. Enemy shells began to land uncomfortably close. One hit a truck nearby and the vehicle exploded. A fearless gun crew—those who had survived the close round, anyhow—worked to get their howitzer unhitched from the burning truck.

"Dammit, Deke, take cover!" Steele was shouting.

Something held Deke in place, however. A moment later, he understood why. The rising sun battle flag that had taunted them earlier from the peak still flew. A knot of Japanese officers had appeared under it and stood watching the fight unfold. For all

Deke knew, it might even be General Suzuki or even General Yamashita up there.

The targets on the ridge had been far, but the officers were even farther. At this distance, it was impossible to target one man, but the Japanese had helped him out by standing close together. They probably weren't concerned about a sniper at this range, but Deke had a little surprise for them involving the heavier rifle bullet.

He made some adjustments, raising the rifle slightly, and then squeezed the trigger. To his satisfaction, one of the distant enemy officers toppled to the ground. The others hurried for cover. It wasn't much payback for what the Japanese had done to these poor civilians, but Deke figured it was a decent down payment.

Finally, Deke ran for the ditch and dove in next to Philly just as another shell exploded nearby. The bottom of the roadside ditch had a foot of water in it from the recent rains, but that didn't stop him from crouching down and getting soaked in the process. The body of a Filipino lay half in and half out of the ditch, killed either by shrapnel or having been a victim of Japanese bayonets. Deke didn't investigate too closely.

"I was watching through the binoculars," Philly said. "You got him, all right. That was some shooting."

"Even a blind squirrel finds a nut now and then," Deke replied.

Philly shook his head. "You and your damn hillbilly sayings. Did you see how those Japs were standing up there like they ruled the roost? These Japs all think they're a bunch of samurai."

"I'm no samurai, I'm just a sniper," Deke said, nodding toward the distant hill where the Japanese officer lay dead. "Then again, which would you rather be?"

The 305th's gunners were giving as good as they got, and maybe even better. The roar was deafening as the crews worked frantically to load a shell, do a quick check of their aim, yank the lanyard, eject the shell, and then do it all over again. They had done this so many times that their motions looked smooth and easy. A cheer went up when they scored a direct hit on one of the enemy's gun crew.

Deke grinned. "Well now, it's good to know I'm not the only one around here who can hit something."

But the Japanese were far from beaten. A Jap artillery round landed in the road, toppling a howitzer and showering the soldiers with dirt and shrapnel.

CHAPTER EIGHT

SHELLS TORE through the air and great geysers of muddy earth erupted all around Patrol Easy as the American and Japanese gunners duked it out. Deke huddled in a ditch, shoulder to shoulder with Philly and Honcho, feeling the ground quake. Overhead, hot shrapnel hissed through the air. The sound sent a shiver down Deke's spine, and he pressed himself deeper into the ditch. There was a time to fight back and there was a time to take cover—which was *now*. He thought of the unlucky bastards manning the guns, exposed to all that flying metal.

Mercifully, the firing began to slow. The duel finally ended when the guns of the 305th had scattered the Japanese troops on the ridge and wrecked most of their artillery.

"Cease fire!" an officer shouted. Slowly, the howitzers fired their last shots and fell silent. The only sound now was the ringing in everyone's ears.

Through binoculars, the artillery officers studied the damage. Deke borrowed the binoculars from Philly and did the same.

Many of the Japanese guns had been destroyed in the exchange. The American gunners had clearly gotten the upper hand, with more accuracy and a higher rate of fire. Smashed and broken equipment littered the slope.

The Japanese infantry that they had seen earlier was now under cover or had withdrawn into the forest lower down on the ridges. This meant that the Americans would only have to fight them later. It was a bit unnerving that the size of the Japanese force they had seen earlier outnumbered their own. The Japanese might be hidden for now, but all those enemy troops were still out there.

New orders arrived from headquarters, and while the orders were not unexpected, they were not what the soldiers wanted to hear.

"We're being told to pursue the enemy," Lieutenant Steele announced. "And that's what we are going to do."

The column moved out. As the road climbed deeper into the hills, it became clear that the field artillery would not be able to continue. The road became more like a muddy track as it rose steeply. The forest pressed in closer, and in places tree limbs reached out and waved in the breeze as if to snatch at the soldiers. Although the ridge where they had seen the enemy was still some distance away, it was hard to shake the feeling that they were walking into an ambush.

"I don't like this one bit," Philly muttered.

"We can agree on that," Deke replied. "I don't like the looks of this place at all."

He kept his eyes on the path ahead, seeing with some trepidation that it continued into the hills. The whole area might be crawling with Japanese troops bent on revenge after the shelling they had taken. Deke had assumed that the Japanese troops had retreated, but he had the disturbing thought that maybe they had *advanced* instead. A few steps behind him, Danilo also scanned the forest, but the Filipino didn't seem any more alarmed than usual, just cautious.

Finally, the time came to leave the field artillery behind. The bulk of the 305th would turn around and make its way back to the road, where it could fire on the enemy again if the Japanese made an appearance. Patrol Easy would have to forge ahead with a platoon of supporting infantry, meaning that there would be no more than fifty men under Lieutenant Steele's command.

It soon became apparent that the Japanese had chosen a perfect natural fortress. What had been the road became little more than a rocky, washed-out trail. It was also perfect for walking into an ambush. However, Danilo seemed to have other ideas about how to reach the area where they had last seen the Japanese.

"This way," he said, offering no further explanation.

Deke and Philly looked at each other, shrugged, and followed in Danilo's wake as he began to cut through the woods, going downhill. The rest of the soldiers followed. At the rear of the column, Lieutenant Steele didn't so much as question the change in direction. Danilo had been with them so long that there was nothing to do but follow him.

At the bottom of the hill, they reached a massive ravine. Sheer rock walls rose up one hundred feet on either side of them, the stone faces wet with the runoff of springs. High above, there was enough flow from a spring or stream to create a small waterfall, the sound of its rushing water echoing off the ravine's walls. The rock face was interrupted by a few plants and shrubs clinging to the rock in clumps, like the badly shaved face of an old man. Deke found the place strangely beautiful in its mixture of rock and lush growth, as if God had swiped a shovel through the hills and then let the greenery slowly return.

Between the rock walls, in a clear space no more than forty feet wide, thick vegetation grew in the bottom of the ravine, so lush and brilliantly green that it didn't even look real. The ravine stretched for nearly half a mile, and beyond that the ground sloped as if rising to meet the tops of the ravine's walls. They could see trees and open sky beyond.

There didn't seem to be any trail, but Danilo plunged ahead without hesitation. The greenery grew to about shoulder height but was free of any large trees or shrubs, as if the space had been clear cut at some point but had since filled in with vegetation. Deke stopped for a moment, taking it all in. This was unlike anything he had seen before on Leyte.

"Where the hell are we going?" Philly wondered.

"To hell if I know. There's no trail to speak of. Looks like a good place to get snakebit," Deke answered. "Then again, Danilo hasn't steered us wrong yet. Keep up."

Deke waded into the sea of green. He found himself holding the rifle above his head like he might do when wading through water, but in this case he was trying to keep it from getting snagged on the ferns and leaves the size of dinner plates. Up ahead, Danilo moved quickly, as if unconcerned about any Japanese ambush.

They passed through the belly of the ravine and began to climb. Soon the walls weren't as high because the ground sloped upward. It became brighter as they left the deep shade of the ravine. They emerged on a ridge that appeared to run all the way to Bugabuga Hill, which looked much closer. Danilo's shortcut had worked.

Danilo didn't wait for them but kept going. There was a good reason for that, which was the fact that they were now exposed. Any Japanese lookouts would spot them quickly. If any enemy artillery had survived the duel with the 305th, then the patrol might be in yet more trouble. Lucky for them, there was still no sight or sound of the enemy. Steadily, they moved closer to Bugabuga Hill. The clouds had not thinned out, and the dark day was already growing darker.

After another hour, they reached the ridgeline where the

Japanese artillery had been dug in. The destruction was impressive, almost as if the ground had been plowed, with empty brass casings scattered across the plowed land like metallic seeds. A few smashed guns were evident, but the Japanese had removed any artillery that was still operational.

What the Japanese had not removed was their dead. Bodies lay sprawled in the holes and ditches where they had fallen, killed by artillery fire. Steele called for a count, and the men came up with fifty-two enemy dead.

"Some of the bodies were in pieces, so we decided to round up," Philly explained.

"Good enough for me," Steele said. He called Rodeo over so that he could contact HQ and make his report. When he got off the radio, he said, "That made somebody happy. They're collecting numbers down there like stamps."

From the ridge they could clearly see the road they had been on earlier in the day. The Japanese had certainly occupied a commanding position. Higher yet was Bugabuga Hill itself, and Deke, Danilo, and Philly made the climb to the summit. They didn't find any Japanese dead; evidently, whoever Deke had shot up there had been deemed important enough to carry away.

"You can see for miles," Deke said. "No wonder the Japanese were up here."

"The question is, Where did they go?" Philly asked. "We sure as hell didn't kill them all."

"I don't think they went far," Deke said.

Danilo didn't seem to have an opinion, but he also seemed to be watching the forests and hills below them warily.

They climbed back down to rejoin the rest of the unit on the ridge. They were still roughly spread out as a column, but Steele hadn't given any orders to move out.

"Come here a minute, Deke," Steele ordered.

He hurried toward the rear of the column. "Honcho?"

"We're losing daylight," Steele said. "I don't want to go any farther and get caught in the dark, and I don't want us to be sitting ducks on this ridge. You know how the Japs love their night attacks. We'll need to dig in before dark."

The men got to work with their entrenching tools, turning the deeper shell holes into defenses for the night. The men kept throwing glances at the forest beyond the clearing at the top of the ridge, half expecting the Japanese to emerge from the trees. The fact that no enemy troops appeared was not reassuring because they knew it was more likely that the Japanese would attack at night, when the darkness gave them cover.

Deke had an idea, which he brought up with Honcho. "What if we get the Japs to attack us?"

"Deke, what the hell are you talking about? I'm damn sure they *do* plan to attack us." The lieutenant showed a rare flash of irritation, a reminder that the weight of the patrol was on his shoulders.

"Honcho, what I mean is, What if we make them come to us in a banzai charge? When we're in our foxholes, waiting for them?"

The lieutenant thought about that. "Now you're making sense. If the Japs come at us in small groups, it's going to be one hell of a night. Death by a thousand cuts. But if they decide to wipe us all out at once—"

"We can mow them down," Deke said, finishing the lieutenant's thought.

Steele nodded. "All right, that's not a bad plan. Here's what we're going to do. Set up our machine guns and a couple of mortars facing down the slope. It's a damn good field of fire, and it's steeper than it looks, which will slow them down if they're trying to run up it. We've got that hill at our backs and it's rugged terrain, so I doubt a large force can come at us from that direction."

The arrangements were made, and the men soon understood their role. Now all they needed to do was encourage the Japanese to attack. It was Philly who came up with a good idea for that.

"Why don't we throw a party and invite the Nips?"

"What the hell are you talking about, Philly?"

Quickly, he outlined his idea. "You know I'm from Philadelphia, right? Independence Hall, the Liberty Bell, all that Revolutionary War stuff. Plus, George Washington crossing the Delaware. Remember that Washington and his boys swooped down on the Hessians so easily because it was Christmas Eve and all the Germans were drinking and partying. What if we can convince the Japanese that we're like the Hessians? Let's make them think we're having us a good ol' time and that we'll be easy pickings."

"It's not Christmas Eve."

"Do you think the Japanese know that? It was a couple of nights ago, so close enough."

Slowly, Honcho nodded. "All right, let's give it a try. We've got nothing to lose."

The men built a large bonfire, throwing caution to the wind. The fire would be big enough to get the attention of any Japanese in the vicinity, if by some miracle they weren't already aware of the American presence. Once the flames were leaping and the sparks were flying, the men joked in loud voices, shouted "Merry Christmas!" to one another, even sang a few Christmas carols. They did their best to seem like they were also drinking, joking with one another about how good the whiskey was. In reality, they weren't drinking anything stronger than some metallic-tasting canteen water.

Although the celebration was phony, it was easy enough for the men to get into the spirit of it. A few men quietly served as lookouts, having crept out from the defenses in order to spot any Japanese activity right away. Deke wasn't much interested in being part of the fake holiday foolishness, but he was glad to be out in the dark, his rifle and knife at the ready.

After midnight, the plan finally seemed to be working. He thought he heard hushed Japanese voices, and even the sound of branches snapping as if a number of enemy troops were positioning themselves in the woods. He hurried back to report what he'd heard to the lieutenant.

"They're coming, Honcho. No doubt about it."

"You guys stay near the bonfire and whoop it up," Honcho said quietly. He also gave an order to bring in the rest of the scouts. "The rest of you get into your foxholes. Hold your fire until I give the order."

Another hour passed without incident, to the point where Deke wondered if his ears had been playing tricks on him earlier. But then came the sound of the shrill whistles that the Japanese used to signal an attack. They heard shouts and moonlight flashed off a sword blade waved by an officer. It was soon apparent that Philly's plan had worked all too well. They could hear the Japanese running toward them up the slope, even if they couldn't see them clearly.

In the blinding darkness, the sound of so many enemy troops rushing toward them, unseen, was terrifying. That all changed when the mortar squad fired a flare that hung above the slope, illuminating the mass of Japanese headed for their position. In the strange, bright, flickering light, the enemy faces looked contorted and enraged, the eyes and screaming mouths nothing more than dark holes under the rim of their helmets. But now, at the very least, they could see the enemy.

"Here they come," Philly muttered.

"Pick your targets, boys," Deke said. "One shot, one Jap."

Fingers on their triggers, they didn't have to wait long for the order.

"Open fire!" Lieutenant Steele shouted.

The machine guns opened up, tracers racing across the open ground. Swaths of enemy soldiers went down as if they had been yanked on by a rope. The mortar squad added to the havoc, exploding shells knocking holes in the Japanese advance. Thinned out, the enemy kept advancing.

Deke aimed and fired, aimed and fired, each shot taking out another enemy soldier. Nobody shouted orders—there wasn't any need. Each soldier's duty was as obvious as the menacing figures rushing toward them. It was kill or be killed.

Speed was the name of the game, each bullet meaning one less Nip who was going to reach his foxhole. On either side of him, soldiers were doing the exact same thing. At this range, nobody was about to miss. He could hear the deep boom of Honcho's shotgun adding to the hell storm of lead being thrown at the Japanese.

Deke realized that he was too busy to be scared, although anyone in their right mind should have been frightened by the sight of the banzai charge. A few soldiers fumbled their clips when they went to reload their M1s, but Deke's hands remained steady. Work the bolt, aim, squeeze the trigger, feel the jolt of recoil against his shoulder, fire, repeat. Again and again. It felt as if he had already been doing this his whole life, and might be doing it until the end of time—or at least until a Jap bayoneted him.

"Enemy behind us!" Yoshio shouted.

Deke whipped his rifle around in time to see a small group of Japanese who were almost on top of them. They were all so intent on the charging Japanese that they might have been completely taken by surprise without Yoshio's warning. He fired at the nearest man. Beside him, Honcho's shotgun boomed again, followed by the crack of Danilo's rifle, and then Philly's. The threat from the rear was neutralized.

There were still plenty of Japs coming up the slope, although the blazing machine guns had done a number on them. But it hadn't been enough. Now the enemy soldiers were thirty feet away, then ten, then right on top of them.

"Dammit!" Philly shouted.

Deke fired point blank at a screaming Jap racing at them with a bayonet. He went down. There were more right behind him. Deke put down his rifle and reached for the .45 in the belt holster. The weight of the pistol felt good in his hand as he unloaded the fat slugs into enemy soldiers no more than an arm's length away. When the pistol ran dry, he tossed it aside and reached for his bowie knife just as a Japanese soldier tripped and fell headlong into the foxhole. Deke made short work of him with the knife. Danilo was doing the same with his long-bladed bolo knife, chopping at the Japanese like he was harvesting sugarcane.

In the foxholes all around Deke, similar battles were taking place, each fight a primitive struggle for survival that was as old and familiar as warfare itself. It was blade against bayonet, fist against boot. Worst of all were the sounds as the firing died away, replaced by the noise of close-quarters combat. Grunts and curses filled the night. The very air seemed to crackle with the grating of rifles being used like fighting sticks and clubs. There was the dull ringing of heavy blows against helmets. They heard the horrible wet sounds of a long blade sliding into flesh, followed by the final sigh of air escaping from a lung or rib cage. Screams of rage mixed with the death cries of those who were being stabbed or clubbed.

Mercifully, the Japanese tide broke and receded. What was left of the enemy retreated down the slope. A few madmen refused to retreat, throwing themselves into foxholes, stabbing wildly with bayonets. A few hurled grenades before dying in a burst of gunfire. One enemy officer flailed around him with a sword, shouting wildly, before he was gunned down, hit by two or three shots almost instantaneously. He spun like a top and fell.

And then the terrible banzai charge was over, what was left of its broken wave draining back down the slope. The rest of the night passed quietly, except for the moans of the wounded enemy scattered across the slope. A few of the GIs had been stabbed or shot, with medics and other soldiers tending to them as best as they could. Not a single GI had been killed outright. The destruction of the banzai charge had been a stunningly lopsided victory.

Deke unscrewed the cap of his canteen and took a drink. Only then did he notice that his hands were shaking. They had been rock steady during the fight, working the bolt action of his rifle smoothly. *So much for nerves of steel,* he thought.

By the time he put the canteen back, the shaking had stopped. With so much adrenaline running through their veins, the reactions of the other men ran the gamut, from blank stares to uncontrollable giggling. Nobody judged or thought much of it —they were all just glad to be alive.

They reloaded and prepared for another attack, but the enemy did not return.

The morning light only verified the destruction. Lieutenant Steele gave orders to make a count of the dead.

"One hundred and sixty-two," Rodeo reported back.

Steele shook his head and found Deke's gaze. "That worked a little too well," he said. "Sure, we got the Japanese to attack us, but they almost killed us all in the process. Somebody remind me not to listen to Deke and Philly next time."

Looking out at so many enemy dead, Deke had to agree. It had been a close thing. "I wouldn't listen to me either," he said quietly.

PART TWO

CHAPTER NINE

If the battle was being slowly won in the mountain ridges and jungle-covered valleys on Leyte, the fight for the Philippines itself was just about to reach its most difficult stage, and Patrol Easy was being thrust into the middle of it.

The Japanese were firmly dug in throughout the capital city of Manila. The troops here were fanatical, including elements of the elite Teishin Shudan, the Japanese special forces. Those tough bastards were the equivalent of airborne troops, and they had seen a lot of action across the Pacific and China. The thought of crossing bayonets with the Americans just made them smile. The Japanese defenders planned to fight for every paving stone of the city streets and make the Americans pay a high price in blood for every block. As defenders, every advantage was theirs.

"When they come, we will be ready," Major Wataru Tanigawa announced with satisfaction, surveying the grounds of the University of Santo Tomas. Although the university was now filled with civilian prisoners deemed a threat to the Japanese occupiers, care had been taken for its outward defense in addition to keeping the prisoners contained. During the last few months, Tanigawa had seen to it that machine-gun nests were placed at strategic locations, fortified with sandbags. Barbed wire surrounded most of the university grounds. Spider holes and hideouts had been prepared for individual snipers. Of course, he knew that the arrival of US tanks and artillery might make short work of these defenses.

Tanigawa did not share it with Sergeant Inaba, but he was less interested in dying than he was in living—or living long enough to put up a good fight. Although he saw himself as a modern samurai warrior, he was also a pragmatist, his attitude being, *Why die for the Emperor when you can make the enemy die instead?* It wasn't a unique attitude; none other than General Patton had expressed something similar in a recent speech to troops in Europe.

To that end, Tanigawa had a trick up his sleeve that he would play when the Americans broke through their defenses at Santo Tomas. After all, he felt that prisoners would serve as better shields than sandbags when the time came. But for now his troops would put up a savage fight.

"*Hai*. We will fight to the last man, sir," said Sergeant Atsunori Inaba. Inaba served as the major's aide-de-camp and had seen to it that the major's plans for the defensive work around the university had been carried out. Some of the work had been done by Japanese troops, but they had relied heavily on Filipino forced labor. Even the prisoners had been put to work, although Tanigawa considered them too lazy to be of real use.

Tanigawa nodded with satisfaction. It would have been easy to mistake Inaba's words for those of a sycophant, but the grim set of his face and his eyes like stone chips indicated that he meant every word.

In many ways, the two men were represented by their weapons of choice. Major Tanigawa rarely went anywhere without his elegant sword, which was also a badge of office for a Japanese officer, while Sergeant Inaba relied on the cudgel at his belt to keep their Filipino slave laborers and American prisoners in line. Both weapons were efficient in their own way, much like the men who wielded them. And both men seemed to understand one another.

"You have done well, Inaba," the major said.

Inaba nodded and bowed, replying with a gruff, *"Arigatō, Shōsa."*

When Inaba stood as if awaiting his next orders, the major asked, "Is there anything else?"

"The prisoners, sir. They wish to speak with you. They have organized a delegation."

The major grunted. "Very well. Make them wait for an hour, then send them to my office."

* * *

TANIGAWA SPENT the hour doing paperwork. It had been a long and circuitous path that had brought Major Tanigawa to his current position. The Japanese officer corps was highly political and favored those from distinguished or aristocratic families—they were fighting for an emperor, after all, not an elected president. Tanigawa hailed from an ancient family with its roots in the samurai class. Although the samurai rank had been abolished during the Meiji Restoration that ushered in the modern, unified Japan, family heritage still loomed large and had created a social class system.

That pedigree had won him a place in the hallowed halls of the Imperial Japanese Army Academy, where he had graduated in 1904, emerging as a young soldier forged in the crucible of discipline and honor. For these young men, the legend of the samurai was still very much alive.

By August of 1937, his destiny beckoned, and he was assigned to the storied Imperial Japanese Army's 7th Division. His unit arrived too late to do more than mop up at the Battle of Lake Khasan against the Chinese in July 1938. The late arrival added a whiff of incompetence. However, fate had other battles in store for Tanigawa.

In 1939, Tanigawa found himself in the crucible of Khalkhin Gol, where disaster struck as they reinforced the beleaguered IJA 23rd Division that was fighting Soviet troops in Mongolia. The battle's grim toll still resulted in a Japanese setback. By August of that year, Tanigawa had been called back to the heartland, tasked with joining the Central District Army, the guardians of Japan's very shores. It was not a prestigious position compared to conquering or occupying Japanese territories. The message seemed to be that Tanigawa had been found lacking as a battlefield officer.

However, destiny's wheel had not turned its last for Tanigawa. He found himself reassigned to the Philippines, eventually overseeing the prisoners in Manila when civilian administrators were found lacking. *Lacking* in the Japanese view meant being too lenient with their Western prisoners.

But Tanigawa was no pencil pusher or paper tiger. In his youth, he had enjoyed hunting and marksmanship and had worked to hone his skill with a rifle. He had often helped train troops personally in the use of their Arisaka rifles. Personally, he favored a beautiful example of a Rigby double rifle that he had hunted with in his youth during trips to Korea. The powerful rifle was more suited to hunting big game, but he had brought it with him to the Philippines.

His position in Manila was not without its perks. He had taken a Filipino mistress, a girl half his age, who seemed willing enough in exchange for money and favors for her family. She was a frequent visitor to his quarters at the university, where he had moved once the Americans landed on Leyte.

Located in the heart of Manila, the University of Santo Tomas was a Catholic university founded in 1611. It was unlikely that the founding Dominican friars could ever have conceived that their university would someday become a prison camp. The university's motto was *Veritas in Caritate*. The Latin translated as "Truth in Charity." There was little evidence of that motto now. The Japanese had taken over the campus and herded in civilian prisoners, so that some of the more educated prisoners joked that the motto should have been "Truly Suffering."

Several of the university buildings were substantial structures built of a pleasant light-colored stone, three and four stories tall. They had once been grand, as befitted a place of higher learning for several hundred young scholars—all men, of course—but since the Japanese occupation the campus buildings and grounds had fallen into decay and disrepair. Clay tiles had gone missing from the rooftops, letting the rain in. Pigeons nested in the window ledges. Weeds and small trees had grown up in what had once been well-tended gardens where students and professors could spend a pleasant hour discussing matters of faith or simply reading.

The university buildings were now bursting at the seams with up to four thousand prisoners, many of them Americans. Through no fault of their own, conditions had become increasingly squalid. The old plumbing of the university was nearly overwhelmed, meaning that a sewage smell permeated the buildings whenever the breeze wasn't blowing, which happened a bit too often on the hottest afternoons.

Water flowed from taps in a rusty trickle. Showering was out of the question, so that the prisoners had to make do with a damp rag to wash themselves down. There was no longer any electricity to power the ceiling fans, which resulted in hot, sweltering days and nights.

In a sense, the lucky inmates were the ones living in huts erected in the university courtyards. At least they had more access to fresh air and felt less confined, although they baked in the midday sun that reached them and slogged through the mud generated by the monsoon rains.

But even being quartered in the courtyard was disconcerting, considering that they were ringed by the high walls, where a few Japanese machine guns were positioned. The guns were a constant reminder that, make no mistake, they were all prisoners. Although the original university had been limited to men, the Japanese captors believed in equal opportunity. Both men and women were held prisoner within these walls. They could mingle during the day but were segregated at night. The grim conditions weren't exactly conducive to any sort of pleasant courtship. Nonetheless, there had been a few pregnancies as the captivity dragged on, proving the adage that love would find a way.

* * *

BACK AT HIS OFFICE, Tanigawa sat awaiting the arrival of this so-called delegation. He had little patience for such things, but he knew that, as the prison administrator, he had to keep up appearances by hearing them out. Making small concessions helped keep the prisoners in line even better than Inaba's cudgel.

Finally, the delegation of prisoners was brought before him. He wrinkled his nose at the smell that arrived with them, filling his office with the funk of body odor. The poor water supply meant that the prisoners had a hard time bathing. Maybe next time he could have Sergeant Inaba throw them into a fountain or hose them down before they were brought to his office.

Tanigawa sat at his desk, wearing an impeccable uniform that only brought the shabby clothes of the prisoners into sharp contrast. A black lacquered stand held his samurai sword, both a symbol of office and a deadly object of beauty. Adding to the martial appearance of his office was the heavy double rifle in a wall-mounted rack. Presiding over it all was a portrait of the Emperor, standard decoration for any Japanese military office.

The delegation consisted of a very tall man with red hair; a balding and worried-looking middle-aged man named Littleton, who always looked as if he'd rather be somewhere else; and one of the Red Cross nurses, a fortysomething woman with the very Irish-sounding name of Catherine Rooney. Tanigawa sometimes found the various heritages of Americans to be confusing. Unlike the Japanese, they were not all one thing—a mixture of Irish, German, Italian, Greek, and a dozen others—and yet they stood united.

He studied the woman, her dark hair contained under a white nurse's cap that had lost most of its starch. Her uniform could not hide her trim figure. She even wore a touch of lipstick in an effort at keeping up appearances.

Perhaps if she had been ten years younger, Tanigawa might have found her appealing. But no, he would stick with his Filipino mistress, who was prettier and much less troublesome. These nurses had volunteered to become prisoners in order to care for the thousands of civilians being held on the university campus. The other prisoners called them "Angels" for what they were doing. Tanigawa called them annoying do-gooders, always complaining about "conditions." Conditions *this*, conditions *that*. Apparently the conditions were never good enough.

He studied the tall prisoner with an indifferent gaze. It was not the first time that he and this prisoner had crossed paths, but Tanigawa wasn't about to show the prisoner that he was worthy of recognition or that Tanigawa knew his name, which he did. *MacGregor.* The major remained seated, which was partly a snub showing that the prisoner had no honor and therefore wasn't worthy of Tanigawa standing to greet him. There was also the egotistical reason that although Tanigawa was tall for a Japanese, the prisoner would have towered over him by several inches. Tanigawa was too proud to allow that.

What the major didn't know about the prisoner—not that he would have cared—was that the man had a Filipino wife from an upper-class family and three boys who had been born in Manila. Before the war, the tall man had been quite a successful businessman and was well known in the city's wealthiest circles. He didn't care for taking orders from the Japanese—or anyone else, for that matter. The arrival of war had meant his status as an American citizen made him an enemy. As Filipinos, a subjected people rather than outright enemies, MacGregor's wife and sons still dwelled at home.

Nearby, Sergeant Inaba made no effort to hide his sneer. He kept one hand on his cudgel, as if eager to use it and cut the tall prisoner down to size.

"Speak!" Inaba ordered.

"Hello, Major," the tall man said in a Texas drawl. Although Tanigawa spoke English, he found the man difficult to understand, with all those vowels stretched out. "You remember me, don't you? Mike MacGregor."

Tanigawa did indeed remember him, this Texan with the Scottish name. He also remembered his previous complaints, which the major found tiresome. Again, he didn't want to give the prisoner the satisfaction of knowing he was recognized, so he asked curtly, "What is it?"

MacGregor's jaw muscles worked as if he was biting back what he really wanted to say. The lack of food had reduced him to bone and sinew, but he was still a strong-looking man. "It's about the food, Major. You see, we don't have enough."

"You have all the food we can spare," Tanigawa snapped.

Nurse Rooney spoke up. "If you don't feed us more, people are going to start dying. They're in very poor health, you see. These are terrible conditions."

There was that word again. Tanigawa just stared at her until she cleared her throat officiously and looked away.

He wasn't quite telling the truth regarding the food supplies. Tanigawa had sold at least half the food allotted to the prisoners. He had to pay for his mistress somehow.

Then again, the situation at Santo Tomas had been steadily worsening even before Tanigawa came on as the prison camp administrator.

For the first couple of years, there had been barely enough to eat. In the last months of 1944 and now early in 1945, conditions had gone from barely tolerable to miserable because administration of the internment camp had moved from civilian Japanese authorities to the military.

It was no secret that Japanese officers despised prisoners, whom they saw as having no honor. Tanigawa was no exception. In their view, a good Japanese, even a civilian, would do the honorable thing and kill him- or herself rather than be taken prisoner. In fact, Japanese soldiers who allowed themselves to be captured were reported as killed, mainly for the benefit of their families, so that they did not have to live with dishonor.

By the time MacArthur's troops landed, the thousands held at Santo Tomas were starving, pure and simple. The Japanese military did not really give a damn, not when they were themselves fighting for survival.

Food rations were cut and given to Japanese troops instead—or sold on the black market, which was exactly what Tanigawa had been doing. Of course, he was sure that his supply officers were already taking their cut before the weekly supply inventory even reached his desk.

Out in the corridor, they heard the muffled cries of a young woman. The prisoner delegation looked over their shoulders in alarm, but the Japanese in the room seemed unperturbed because this sort of incident was now an almost daily occurrence.

Through the door, he saw that some of his men had brought in a Filipino girl. He'd gotten a glimpse of her—young, frightened, her shabby dress torn. Her piteous cries echoed through the halls.

"Aren't you going to do anything about that?" MacGregor demanded, looking out into the hall. He appeared upset enough to run out and try to put a stop to whatever was happening, but the guards at the door moved closer to block his way. His tall frame seemed to shrink in defeat.

"There is nothing to be done about the food," Tanigawa said. "Ration it as best as you can."

"But—"

"Enough!" Sergeant Inaba shouted. "Out!"

MacGregor drew himself up to his full height and glared down at Tanigawa as if he would like nothing better than to tear him apart. However, they both knew he was utterly powerless to do anything. The woman looked just as angry but kept her mouth shut. The third prisoner just looked afraid, wringing his hands.

Inaba shoved MacGregor through the door and the meeting was over.

Echoing through the halls, the girl's cries continued for twenty minutes while the men had their way with her, some laughing as they urged the others on. They ignored the girl's sobbing. Finally, there was an angry shout, a gunshot that echoed throughout the building, and the girl's cries were heard no more.

There was no doubt that the prisoners had overheard the girl's treatment and her ultimate fate, but Tanigawa thought that it should serve as a warning to them. Their guards' latest victim had been Filipino. So far the female prisoners had been off limits to the depredations of the guards, but for how much longer as the troops grew more wanton and desperate?

It was something for the prisoners to contemplate. Maybe next time, Tanigawa thought, they would think twice before complaining.

CHAPTER TEN

TIRED AND EXHAUSTED, the snipers reached Manila. Most of the division was not being sent into combat but was training for the invasion of Okinawa. It wasn't exactly a vacation, but at least they were getting a much-needed break from the front lines.

Deke and the others weren't so lucky. The fight for Manila was going to involve sniper battles, so Patrol Easy was being sent to do what it did best.

Getting to Manila hadn't been easy. First, they had endured crossing the San Bernardino Strait to Luzon, half expecting to be torpedoed by a Japanese sub or strafed by a stray Zero. The sea had been choppy, churned by a strong southerly wind. Yoshio and Honcho were the only ones who hadn't gotten seasick. Deke would always be farm boy first and foremost, so ships never agreed with him. It was a relief to reach dry land again. What followed next was a long truck ride over rough roads to the capital city of the Philippines. The roads closer to the city were paved and had once been decent, but war and neglect had left them in bad shape.

"I wonder what the girls are like in Manila?" Philly said.

"I reckon they're hiding, if they're smart," Deke said.

"Aw, you're no fun," Philly said with a snort. "If you come across any Filipino girls, you be sure to send them my way. They'll thank me later."

Deke didn't reply but gave Philly a sideways look. It was a sore point with him that he'd never been with a girl. He couldn't admit as much to Philly, of course. He never would have heard the end of it. After all, Deke had proved himself to be the tough guy, the hard man, the crack shot, the one who got things done when push came to shove. But it was Philly who'd had all the women, even if you only believed about half of his bragging.

Just about every young soldier had done his level best to lose his virginity before going off to war and possibly getting killed. Even the religious ones sometimes made an exception under the circumstances. Most young men felt that it would have been a shame to die and never know what it felt like to make love. The memory of the event itself would get many a soldier through a dark and lonely night. The topic of conversation among most soldiers alternated between home, good food, sports, and women—they longed for all of them.

Deke felt embarrassed about his lack of experience and wondered if there was something wrong with him. He supposed that his scarred face scared off the girls. Meanwhile, he held on to his secret like it was a gold nugget.

A distant thump of artillery interrupted Deke's thoughts, reminding him that he had bigger problems to worry about.

In the light of the setting sun, they had their first glimpse of the sprawling city. The rich hues of the tropical sun made the white walls of the city sparkle, although the sight was marred here and there by rising columns of smoke. What Manila lacked in height—most buildings outside the city center were only a few stories tall—it made up for in breadth.

Because Deke was a country boy and his experience of cities

was limited, Manila seemed to him like a very large city. He wasn't wrong—the prewar population made it bigger than Richmond but smaller than Rochester. At the heart of Manila was the historic walled city known as Intramuros, which dated back to the earliest days of Spanish colonization. Now the whole place was going to be a battleground.

Lieutenant Steele filled them in. "It's just another kind of jungle, boys," he said. "Except this one has concrete instead of palm trees."

They soon found out what he meant, spending the night in an abandoned house. The place had once been grand, with a walled courtyard, but the inhabitants had long since fled—or possibly had been killed or incarcerated by the Japanese. All the furniture was gone or smashed, so they slept on the cold stone floor. There wasn't any electricity in this part of the city due to the fighting, so they lay listening to the sound of gunshots punctuating the darkness. It was hard to say who was doing the shooting and who was doing the dying, but to Deke's ears, most of the shots sounded like the lighter crack of the enemy's Arisaka rifles. They were of a smaller caliber, but just as deadly in capable hands. Starting in the morning, it would be their job to take on those Japanese snipers.

The truth was that Patrol Easy was late to the game. US troops had crossed the Pasig River into Manila in early February and had been engaged in bloody street fighting ever since. General MacArthur had urged the Japanese to make Manila an "open city" just as he had done when they had invaded in 1941. Basically, this would have meant that Japanese troops would have withdrawn and spared the city from destruction. But the Japanese were having none of that.

Consequently, Manila had been dubbed "the Stalingrad of Asia," an allusion to the bitter fight between the Soviets and Germans for that city. The Japanese had turned nearly every major intersection into a fortress, meaning that US troops often had to demolish the surrounding buildings just to get at the enemy. The Japanese had also fortified several of the taller buildings, turning them into pillboxes and using the higher floors to their advantage as they fired down upon advancing troops.

Because the Japanese had been there for years, they had the home team advantage and knew every street and alley better than the Americans who had come to reclaim Manila. They'd also had the opportunity to turn the city into a maze of defensive positions intended to thwart the American advance at nearly every street corner or storefront.

"Do the Nips really think they can hold Manila?" Philly asked. It was a good question, given the forces arrayed against them. More Army troops were pouring in all the time. The hope of any reinforcements or supplies making it through from Japan also had diminished rapidly.

"They know they can't win," Honcho replied, his tone bitter. "But for the Japanese, it's not about winning. Not anymore. It's about making us bleed as much as possible in the process of beating them."

There was no doubt that it would be a bloody battle, both for the Americans and for the city itself. Again, the Americans were left with little choice except to use their artillery to turn these buildings into rubble. The conquest of Manila wasn't even being measured block by block, but rather by each building and intersection that was leveled or captured.

In the morning, Patrol Easy ate a hurried breakfast and thought about getting to work.

Even so, that work turned out to be different from what was expected and involved an old ally from the past.

During the night, a runner had come looking for Lieutenant Steele. That wasn't all that unusual because runners were how the command post kept tabs on the patrols. Honcho hadn't mentioned what the message was about, which was his prerogative as an officer, but it was about to become clear. He called his men together in the courtyard of the grand house.

"An old friend tracked us down last night," he announced. "It turns out that he wants to pay us a visit."

He then stepped aside as a figure emerged from a doorway. He was a broad-shouldered man wearing the simple brown frock of a priest.

"Father Francisco!" Deke said in surprise, genuinely pleased at the sight of the priest who had fought alongside them on Leyte. He had been a parish priest in Palo, outspoken against the Japanese, until the enemy had forced him to flee for his life into the hills, where he had become a guerrilla leader. They had made his acquaintance not long after they'd hit the beach near Palo.

"It is good to see you, Deacon Cole," said the priest, who shook hands all around, calling each man by name. "It is good to see all of you, my old friends."

"We can always use the help, Padre," Deke said.

"Oh, it is not just me," the priest said. "I alone would not be of much use to you. I have brought along some help."

He then beckoned to several figures who had remained in the shadows of the house. Half a dozen Filipinos emerged, wearing the informal uniforms of guerrilla fighters, which consisted of olive drab shirts, shorts, no shoes, and straw hats. It was an outfit that made sense in the tropical heat. They carried small packs on their backs and wore either bolo knives or pistols on their hips—sometimes both. All six carried rifles slung over their shoulders. Though it was hard to define, they had a different air about them compared to Danilo, who was a man of the forests and mountains. To Deke's eyes, Danilo somehow looked out of place here in the city. He was a man who blended best with deep-green jungles and lush stands of grass.

Due to the similarity of the guerrillas' dress and gear, it

took the GIs a moment to realize that two of the guerrilla fighters were women, a fact that caused the soldiers to exchange glances that involved raised eyebrows and looks of disbelief. In the countryside, the guerrilla fighters had nearly all been men, but here in the city, apparently women had also joined the fight.

Being a female guerrilla held special dangers. If captured, Filipino men would be killed outright by the Japanese, or if they were lucky, sent to a POW camp. Filipina fighters faced a far worse fate if captured—grimmer even than a quick death. Chances were good that they would be forced into service as so-called comfort women in brothels for Japanese soldiers. It was hard to imagine a worse form of hell. For these female warriors, the stakes were high.

"All of the fighters I have brought you are excellent shots, much like you," Father Francisco said. "However, they have had no real training as snipers. All of them also speak English, which will help with their training."

"That's where we come in," the lieutenant told his men. "We are going to give them a crash course in sniper warfare. The idea is that they will know enough to start shooting Japs without getting killed right away. Remember that when you started, you didn't know a damn thing. But first, let's see how well they can shoot."

The courtyard of the abandoned house was too small for what the lieutenant had in mind, so they moved a short distance to an open area that had once been a parking lot, now choked with weeds. At one end of the lot was the massive wall of a barn-like wooden garage. A bit of paint still clung to the wood, but it was mostly weathered and bare after being neglected during the occupation. Business apparently had not thrived under the Japanese.

"That's perfect for you, Philly," Deke said, nodding at the

broad wall they faced. "It's hard to miss the broad side of a barn."

"Aw, stuff it, Corn Pone."

Using a piece of chalk, the lieutenant walked down and drew six circles on the wooden wall. He paused, then added faces—a grim line for the mouths, a single dot for a nose, and two slanted slits for eyes. Although it was a crude caricature, the last feature was intended to make the faces unmistakably Japanese. The Filipinos were certainly grinning at the sight.

"All right, let's see how you can shoot," Honcho said. His welcoming manner turned gruff as he gave orders. "Spread out. Sitting position first. When you hear your number, shoot the target. Deke, you call the numbers. Mix it up, will you? The Japs wouldn't give you a chance to do things nice and orderly, and neither will we."

Deke stood behind the line of guerrillas. A couple had seemed mystified by the sitting position, including one of the women. He got her set up, elbows on knees, bone to bone, the rifle locked in place. He put his hands on her shoulders and adjusted her position slightly, getting her to lean into the rifle more.

"That is Juana," said Father Francisco, who stood nearby. There was a proud tone in his voice. "She is an excellent shot. So is Hector, the last man down."

Deke grunted. Despite what the priest said, he had yet to see them shoot and wanted to see for himself. "If you say so, Padre."

He noticed that the four men held relatively new-looking Springfield rifles with iron sights, no telescopes. He assumed that it was the resourceful padre who had managed to obtain the rifles. Even with iron sights, there was no finer sniper rifle. The two women were armed with Arisaka rifles. These were somewhat smaller than the Springfields and fit the women better. They also fired a smaller cartridge with less kick. That said, they were no less deadly and had some advantages over US weapons. The Arisaka rifle was a quieter shooter with a smaller muzzle flash that made it harder to detect when fired from a hiding place in the ruined city. In the hands of Japanese snipers, the Arisaka rifles had killed far too many Americans. Now the tables were turned and the Arisaka was being used against them.

That thought alone made Deke happy.

"Call 'em out, Deke," Honcho ordered. It was the lieutenant's habit to use a telescope rather than binoculars, which were pointless for a one-eyed man. He raised the telescope to better see where the bullets struck.

"Three," Deke said, matching the lieutenant's gruff tone.

The guerrilla's rifle cracked, but Deke's sharp eyes needed no help to see that the bullet had punched a hole outside the target circle. Inwardly, he groaned. Would the rest of these Filipinos do any better?

"Four! Five!" he shouted in quick succession.

Number four hit the target, a hole appearing in the lower part of the circle. The woman named Juana was in position five. Her rifle cracked, and the bullet struck right between the target's slanting eyes.

Her glance swung toward Deke, giving him a defiant look. He liked her spirit, but one lucky shot did not a sniper make.

They went through a few more rounds, with Deke calling out their numbers, varying the rhythm. Juana kept hitting the target consistently, and the others mostly did.

"All right, let's switch to prone," Honcho said.

When it came to the prone position, Juana knew just what to do. Her marksmanship was even better now, all her shots occupying a space about the size of a buttered biscuit.

When she looked up again with that defiant expression, Deke gave her a nod. He wasn't sure, but he thought he saw a faint smile play across her lips.

After the shooting test, which seemed to satisfy Lieutenant Steele, he gathered the guerrillas for a lecture in the basics of sniper warfare. The GIs had been curious to watch the shooting action, but they had heard this lecture before. They drifted away to smoke cigarettes, except for Deke and Yoshio. Deke had stayed because Honcho asked him to interject now and then. Yoshio stuck around because he couldn't help learning something.

They took a break for chow, then did some more shooting in the afternoon. Then Honcho declared that their impromptu training course was over.

"You're all graduated, as far as I'm concerned," he said. "Starting tomorrow, feel free to get yourselves killed or, better yet, stay alive for a while and make yourselves useful by killing a few Japs."

They all went back to the house, with Patrol Easy staying in the expansive rooms and the guerrillas camping in the courtyard. A watch schedule was set, just in case the Japanese decided to get frisky.

Juana set about cleaning her rifle. Deke drifted over and watched, telling himself that he was curious about the Arisaka. Maybe he had been—at first. He was also impressed by the deft and efficient way that Juana cleaned her weapon. But as Juana deftly went through the steps of cleaning and oiling the weapon, Deke found that his eyes were more focused on her than the Japanese rifle.

She was no statuesque pinup beauty, being shorter and rounder, but she was soft in all the right places. Her hair was dark brown, not quite black, more like the hue of light coffee than midnight ink. Her eyes were a liquid brown like mountain stone after a rain.

Deke was embarrassed when she looked up and caught him studying her. She gave him a frank look in return, her eyes lingering on the scars down one side of his face and neck, the result of the angry, raking claws and teeth of the wounded black bear he had encountered as a boy. Her eyes widened as if alarmed, a reaction that Deke knew all too well. He wasn't pretty to look at. He turned and walked away.

Philly was waiting for him on the other side of the courtyard, a knowing grin on his face. "If I didn't know better, I'd say you were interested in that girl."

"I was seeing if she needed help, is all."

"You know what, Corn Pone? I hate to break it to you, but *you're* the one who needs help. I think it's clear that you've got it bad for that girl."

Deke felt his face reddening, a rare sensation for him. "Like I said, I was just seeing how she was doing with her shooting."

"She's a good shot, all right. I'd say she shot you right through the heart."

CHAPTER ELEVEN

THE NIGHTMARE that was shaping up in Manila, which Patrol Easy and thousands of other soldiers were walking into, was worsened by a rift in the Japanese command structure, its roots in the rivalry between the Imperial Japanese Army and Navy.

Earlier, the overall Japanese commander, General Yamashita, had realized that Manila was not defensible. The city was too sprawling, and the multitude of wooden structures beyond the city center would make it a death trap if any fires broke out. There was also a massive civilian population that only impeded the city's defense. Yamashita had ordered a withdrawal from the city and was determined to make a stand elsewhere.

However, the naval officer who had taken charge of the defense of the city had different plans. Rear Admiral Sanji Iwabuchi, commander of the Imperial Japanese Navy's 31st Naval Special Base Force, announced that he would fight to the end in Manila. They had every intention of making the fight into a bloodbath. His officers and troops seemed to agree with him wholeheartedly. Either that or they were too afraid of being labeled as cowards to speak up.

Although his forces were under the command of the Shimbu Army Group, Iwabuchi ignored army orders to withdraw from the city. The fact that this rogue commander was a naval officer left Yamashita in a bind, because the Japanese Army and Navy were autonomous and did not always cooperate or recognize the command structure the way that the Americans did, even between branches of the service. In the end, despite rivalries and jealousies, Americans and their allies understood that they were all fighting on the same side. Also, there was a clear command structure. For the Japanese, that distinction was not as clear. They were army or navy first, and Japanese second.

Iwabuchi's troops were mostly navy men, more used to ships than street combat, although his forces included the well-trained equivalent of US Marines, and he also commanded a few thousand army soldiers. In the end, it was hard to say whether these soldiers never got the orders to withdraw in the confusion of war or perhaps felt as Iwabuchi did and preferred to make a last stand in the city after working so hard to prepare their defenses in Manila. Major Tanigawa fell into this second category.

There was no questioning Iwabuchi's record as a career navy officer who had commanded several ships, culminating in command of one of Japan's new cruisers. The magnificent ship was sunk by the Americans off Guadalcanal. Iwabuchi survived but apparently felt that he had lost his honor when he had lost the ship. He saw the Battle of Manila as his chance to redeem himself. Unfortunately, he would drag the fate of tens of thousands and the entire city down with him.

In one of his final orders issued to his troops, while communication to his far-flung forces was still possible, Iwabuchi made his intentions clear: "We are very glad and grateful for the opportunity of being able to serve our country in this epic battle. Now, with what strength remains, we will daringly engage the enemy. Banzai to the Emperor! We are determined to fight to the last man."

And so they would. The table had been set for a bloody feast of combat.

* * *

IN THE CONFINES of the University of Santo Tomas, Major Tanigawa had felt the noose tightening. The sounds of fighting had marched closer each day until the US troops were finally spotted.

Watching from the upper floors of the university building, the major had watched them through binoculars. They scurried like rats through the ruins. He thought that the GIs appeared dirty and disheveled. He knew that the Americans had started on Leyte and, after finally winning the fight there, they had pushed on to Luzon and Manila. It was hard to believe that they had defeated crack Japanese troops to reach this point. Despite appearances, he supposed that they must be capable warriors.

Tanigawa lowered the binoculars and gazed around his neat and spacious office. Large windows looked out over the city where the American forces were gathering. His expansive desk was ornately carved. Shelves of books lined the walls, bound in leather. They were mostly works of religion or philosophy, some in Latin, the words unknowable to him, and these antique books did not interest him beyond their beautiful appearance. Not so long ago, this had been the office of the university president, a priest who had been sent to a far less pleasant prison camp than the one for more run-of-the-mill civilians.

Although Tanigawa rarely drank, he had kept a crystal decanter of brandy left behind by the university president as a trophy. There was his own officer's sword, polished to perfection, gleaming on its stand next to the treasured double rifle with its intricate scrollwork. Both weapons were quite valuable, having been passed down through the family. Truth be told, they were the most valuable items Tanigawa owned. Above them, a framed portrait of the Emperor hung proudly on the wall. The room was neat and orderly, everything in its proper place. Just the way Tanigawa liked it. The very idea of the Americans ransacking his office offended him. In his mind, the space within the walls of his office represented Japan itself. He could not stand the idea of this space being defiled.

To guard against that eventuality, Tanigawa had placed a gallon can of kerosene in the corner, out of sight, although now and then he caught a whiff of the strong-smelling flammable liquid. When the time came, he planned to splash the kerosene over everything and set it on fire. He would not let the enemy enjoy the spoils of war. As for the brandy, he would enjoy a glass and then add the alcohol to fuel the flames.

He sighed, his momentary bitterness ebbing as he thought of all the tasks that still needed to be done, for he was a man who welcomed action. He supposed that he had always known that this day would come, but the actuality of the looming conflict now sank in. Tanigawa was no coward. He would fight until the end and die like a true samurai.

He was reassured by the fact that his men were ready. Once again, he ran through a mental checklist of their defenses. Under the direction of himself and Sergeant Inaba, his men had turned the university campus into a fortress, this main building becoming a bunker. Machine guns had been set up on the surrounding streets, the positions well protected by sandbags, to give his men commanding fields of fire down all the approaches to the main building. Barbed wire was strung across the approaches to funnel the enemy into streets covered by the machine guns. Tanigawa had put a great deal of thought and attention into these defenses. They would be able to hold out for a long time against infantry.

However, at this late stage of the game, his one nagging worry concerned the American tanks. Machine guns would be no use against their armored sides. Meanwhile, the Sherman tanks could take their time blasting away at his own positions, softening them. Tanigawa had no heavy weapons at this disposal, aside from a few mortars. There was little he could do against tanks. However, he had issued orders to prepare a supply of satchel charges that his men could use as a last-ditch defense against any tanks, hurling themselves into the tracks and setting off a blast, trading their lives to disable the tanks. In Tanigawa's mind, it seemed like a fair exchange.

But best of all, his ultimate weapon would be the prisoners that he held. The Americans would be loath to see these people killed, considering that many of those held at the university were their fellow Americans who had lived in Manila. When the time came, Tanigawa planned to use the prisoners to his advantage. If some died in the process, then so be it.

He called for Sergeant Inaba, who kept a small office just down the hall from his own. Again, he thought of how much he had come to rely on Inaba, who was ultimately a man of humble origins. In some ways this went against Tanigawa's inclinations, but the usual chain of command had not been possible because first his lieutenant, and then his captain, had caught fevers. The lieutenant had died and the captain remained in the hospital. Inaba had also gotten sick, but he'd proved too tough for the fever. He was also utterly reliable in obeying Tanigawa's orders. He had proved himself to be worth far more than any of Tanigawa's officers.

"Any updates on the enemy's movements?" Tanigawa asked his sergeant, although he had been watching the approaching Americans through his binoculars.

Sergeant Inaba replied, "Our men have not yet engaged them, sir. However, they are not more than a few blocks away at this point." Inaba paused, emotion playing across his features. His face, normally so impassive or twisted into a scowl, literally rippled as he expressed his despair, eyes wide and mouth open, before his features hardened into anger. "I cannot believe we are in this situation. It is like a nightmare."

"It is the situation we face, Inaba. We will fight and die as we must."

"Have you heard from headquarters? We need reinforcements, sir. We do not have enough men."

"We need to keep our heads, Inaba. We will fight with the men we have."

"How long do you think we can hold them off?"

"Until the end, Inaba."

"Hai!" Inaba sprang to attention, his old fire having returned. Tanigawa could always count on Inaba.

"Keep me informed," Tanigawa said. "That is all."

He picked up the binoculars again and turned to the window. He had meant what he'd said to Inaba. They would fight to the end, but not necessarily in this building.

When the time came, he would share his plan with his men. *Until then,* he thought, *let the Americans come.*

* * *

THE GIs already knew what they were up against because they had faced it before when it came to fighting in the Pacific. Back home in America, readers were getting a glimpse of the Pacific War thanks to reporters like Ernie Pyle in his newspaper accounts. If he had written about Patrol Easy, it might have sounded something like this:

ON THE FRONT LINES OF THE PACIFIC

In the unforgiving Pacific islands, where every inch is hard-won, I've come to know these soldiers in some way. They are similar to the men I got to know in Europe, and yet, like the war itself in the Pacific, they are different. In Europe they have mud, and snow, and Krauts. Here there are biting flies, the jungle, and Japs.

Maybe it comes down to the atmosphere. In the thick of the Pacific jungles, where the air hangs heavy with humidity and the soundtrack of war is unrelenting, the soul of the American fighting man shines with an indomitable spirit.

The men of the 77th Infantry Division are the epitome of grit and gallantry, pushing onward through dense foliage and fortified enemy positions. Every step forward is a battle won, every breath a testament to their determination. The sights here are far from the comforts of home—a world away from Main Street, USA—but the brotherhood formed in these crucibles is stronger than steel.

The nights are long, the days unforgiving, but through it all, the spirit of America marches on. Too often it must march through thick jungles or up the steep slope of a hillside covered by a Japanese machine gun. Sometimes the sun beats down, and five minutes later there's a terrific downpour that soaks everyone to the bone.

The boys just pick themselves up and move on. In this theater of war, our boys are writing history with courage and resilience that will echo through the annals of time.

Yesterday I watched as Sergeant James Toll from Missouri shared a brief, rare laugh with Private Eddie Ramirez from New York over a makeshift game of cards. I describe the card game as "makeshift" because the deck was cobbled together from two or three different decks. There was an extra ace, or maybe one was missing—it wasn't really clear, and no one much cared. The card game was simply to pass the time.

"Who's winning?" I asked, sticking my nose in.

"Anybody who's not dead, that's who," Private Ramirez said.

It turned out that they were playing for bullets, not money. The pot kept growing until there was quite a pile of shiny brass cartridges.

Finally, Ramirez seemed to have turned out that missing ace and won the pot, but he was reluctant to rake it all in.

"Better keep some of those bullets, fellas," he said. "No telling when you might need 'em."

Shots sounded nearby. Reluctantly, the men picked up their rifles and returned fire at the Japanese hiding in the bushes. Then they went back to their card game as if nothing had happened.

It's moments like these, in the heart of chaos, that remind us all of the simple joys and the camaraderie that fuels these men.

The other day I came across a group of tough customers. They called themselves Patrol Easy, and they were snipers who counted a few Filipino fighters among their number.

Sniper warfare is a constant here in the Pacific, with the enemy popping out from holes in the ground or clinging to treetops in order to take a few shots at the advancing troops.

Patrol Easy can usually be found at the front of this advance, dealing with the snipers so that the army can continue gaining ground. They also conduct reconnaissance to see what tricks the Japanese have up their sleeves.

These snipers are commanded by a grizzled veteran of Guadalcanal and Guam and now the Philippines named Lieutenant William Steele, a one-eyed officer who carries a shotgun rather than a rifle.

I asked the lieutenant what the best approach was for dealing with these Japanese marksmen.

"Shoot first if you can," he advised. "And if you can't shoot first, then you'd better shoot better than the Jap just did. You're alive because he missed. You'd better not. You won't get another chance."

That's the thing about the advice here, which every soldier takes to heart, whether he's playing cards or hunting snipers, You won't get another chance.

It's a reminder that in the Pacific war, no matter what you're doing, going from one moment to the next is nothing to take for granted.

PYLE MAY NOT HAVE WRITTEN those actual words, but he had written similar ones about so many of the young men fighting in the Pacific. Sure, he was doing his job as a reporter, but it was also clear that he cared deeply about these men who were so far from home.

CHAPTER TWELVE

THEY FOUGHT IN THE STREETS, they fought in buildings, they took up positions on rooftops. But the strangest place that Patrol Easy fought turned out to be a baseball stadium in the heart of Manila.

In happier times, the Rizal Memorial Baseball Stadium, named for a national hero of the Philippines, had hosted the likes of Lou Gehrig and Babe Ruth, playing exhibition games in the more innocent days before the world had been plunged into war. Local baseball fans still spoke of those games with dreamy eyes and a distant smile on their faces. Filipino boys had taken to the American sport with enthusiasm, playing barefoot and barehanded in vacant sandlots across Manila.

But like peace itself, those days were a distant memory. The place now resembled the sort of baseball field where the Four Horsemen of the Apocalypse might pause for a game of catch. Since the start of the war, weeds had grown up and covered the field. The painted scoreboard had faded and flaked, with a few bullet holes showing where the numbers should have been.

Even worse, the baseball stadium was now a fortress, having

been taken over by the Japanese. The concrete structures of the stadium made a solid defensive position. The dugouts had been turned into machine-gun nests. Snipers occupied the stands where fans had once rooted for the home team. A runner trying to steal a base risked being tagged out permanently.

"My best guess is that there are at least a hundred Japanese dug in here," Lieutenant Steele explained. "We have armor on the way, planning to sweep out the Japanese, but they need infantry support. That's where we come in."

"What good is a tank if it needs us?" Philly wanted to know.

"They don't want to get blindsided by some Japs with a sticky bomb," Steele said.

On Leyte and now on Luzon, more than one Sherman tank had been knocked out by these bombs, known by the Japanese as *Shitotsubakurai*, which were technically lunge mines that made use of a high-explosive charge at the end of a pole. It was a simple and effective anti-tank weapon, the equivalent of a bazooka or Panzerfaust, but on the end of a stick.

One fatal drawback for the Japanese using these lunge mines was that these attacks were essentially suicide missions due to several pounds of HEAT (High Explosive Anti-Tank) charge exploding within a stick's length of the attacker.

"I wouldn't touch a tank with a ten-foot pole, but I guess a Jap would," Deke said.

"With all that steel, you'd think it would take more than a Jap with a stick to take 'em out," Philly said.

"When you attack it from the side, a tank might as well be a tin can. All the armor is up front. You know they don't have a lot of visibility inside those tin cans," Honcho added. "We're going to be their ears and eyes, and tell 'em where to shoot."

Orders being shouted to their right came from an infantry company forming up to attempt a frontal assault on the Japanese, hoping to simply push them out of the dugouts and stands. Farther away, tanks rumbled in the background, assembling for the attack. However, it would be the snipers who went in first, scouting out the enemy defenses.

The Americans were entering the stadium from the outfield —from the direction of the third base line, to be exact. One advantage of fighting at a baseball field was that it used familiar landmarks and features. In the annals of military history, it was probably the only time that a combat action had taken place on a baseball field. Somehow, it felt like an affront that the Japanese had taken something as American as a baseball field and cleverly transformed it into a fortress to use against them.

The lieutenant looked around at his team. For days now, Patrol Easy had been working in coordination with the guerrilla snipers that Father Francisco had brought them. Shortly after bringing them the sniper recruits, the priest had moved on to other corners of the city where his faith and organizational skills were needed. Father Francisco held no rank, but among the guerrillas he was as good as a general.

"I don't know where he found these people," Honcho said, referring to the Filipino sharpshooters. "But I'll take another bunch just like them."

After giving the new recruits a crash course in sniper warfare, Honcho grouped his troops into twos or threes, trying to pair at least one of the Filipinos with the more experienced Americans. More often than not, Deke had found himself paired with Juana. That was just fine by him. She was an excellent shot, she didn't say much, and he had to admit that she was easy on the eyes.

Deke wasn't easily distracted; when it came to fighting, he was like a tractor with a stuck gear. He had one speed and one purpose only, ignoring everything else. But when he looked into Juana's soft brown eyes, it was as if he were transported by thoughts of mountain spring mornings, the smell of fresh-baked pies, the music of cool running streams, and something that he longed for but could not identify. He felt a similar warmth in Juana's gaze, like heat off a cast-iron griddle, shimmering in the morning light. Though pleasant, he hoped the distraction didn't get them both killed.

The Filipino snipers had shown themselves to be quick learners when it came to hunting the enemy. Also, they seemed motivated by revenge in a way that was hard for the average GI to grasp, because it was the Japanese who had occupied their country, after all. The enemy had ruined their fields, taken over their homes, stolen their freedoms. Simply put, they hated the Japanese with every fiber of their being.

So far, just one of the Filipinos had been killed when he had tried to run between buildings and had been picked off by a Japanese marksman. Since then, his countrymen—and women—had paid back the Japanese many times over.

The battle for the stadium promised to be a difficult fight, but the Japanese there had to be eliminated. The stadium could not be left as an enemy stronghold while the American advance encircled it.

"Deke, I want you and Juana to get to third base," Honcho said. "See if you can find some cover in those weeds and start picking off the Japs in the stands on that side of the stadium."

Philly laughed. "That's a good one, Honcho!"

"What's so damn funny?"

"I'm not sure that Deke has ever gotten to third base before."

Honcho did not appear amused. "You're a regular comedian, aren't you, Philly? Just for that, you can take the outfield. There are enough bushes growing out there to give you some cover."

Nobody but Philly seemed to have much of a sense of humor considering that they were about to face at least a hundred dug-in Japs. Deke glanced at Juana, who made no sign of having picked up on Philly's joke about third base. He wasn't about to explain.

Besides, he and Juana had barely exchanged more than a few words during the last few days. In the field, they had made do with hand gestures and nods. It was the only communication they needed, and they had made a good team. After that Japanese sniper had taken out one of the Filipinos, Juana had rigged a helmet on a stick to draw the Jap's fire, enabling Deke to spot his hiding place and put a nice fat chunk of lead into him.

There wasn't time for much conversation when you were busy fighting and trying to stay alive. Deke wondered if he even *wanted* to get to know Juana any better. In his experience, combat situations could lead to a very short life expectancy. Maybe it was better not to get attached, but it was getting so that he trusted Juana almost as much as Philly, Yoshio, or anybody else from Patrol Easy.

He pushed any stray thoughts from his mind to focus on the task at hand, which involved shooting the enemy without getting shot himself.

Deke scrambled forward, crawling on all fours. Juana moved behind him, a little off to his left. Somewhere off to his right, he reckoned Philly would be moving into position. A couple of days ago, it might have felt strange being teamed up with Juana instead of Philly. But they seemed able to read each other's minds. She was a natural and a much better shot than Philly.

Deke was developing a theory that women made better snipers, in the same way that female cats were better at catching mice than tomcats. Everybody back home knew that if you had a barn overrun by mice, the thing to do was to get yourself a mama cat and put her in there. Then again, Deke mused, you didn't want to mess with a mean tomcat.

Thankfully, the machine guns that they knew to be in the

dugouts did not open fire, perhaps not wanting to waste ammo on the sparse targets presented by Patrol Easy. Instead, they were going to let the Japanese snipers in the stands pick them off.

The weeds were tall enough to reach above him, but he worried that the snipers in the stands had a good view of anything moving on the infield. The crack of a rifle and the snap of a bullet overhead verified his concerns. He pressed himself lower to the ground and moved more slowly to create less of a disturbance in the sea of weeds. Another bullet whined overhead, and Deke wished that he could burrow like a box turtle into the infield.

After a few minutes of crawling, he reached the vicinity of third base. Fortunately, there was more than brush to provide cover out here. The wing of a downed plane lay in the weeds, having been there long enough that a few vines crept over it. He could see a chunk of the fuselage in the outfield, which might give Philly some cover. Deke couldn't tell if the plane was Japanese or American, and he didn't much care. In addition to providing decent cover, the broken wing also made a good bench rest.

Juana joined him, and they both rested their rifles on the metal skin of the plane's wing, searching for targets in the stands. Deke had the advantage of having a telescopic sight on his Springfield, although Juana had proved herself more than capable with the iron sights on the Arisaka rifle.

Through the scope, the details of the stands sprang closer. A long, deep overhang protected the stands from the elements, but in this case it created shadows that hid the enemy. The baseball stadium had mostly been constructed out of concrete, which is what made it an appealing defensive position for the enemy. The stands themselves were mainly filled with plain wooden benches, draped with patches of weeds and ivy that had grown up during the wartime years of disuse. A small Japanese soldier could worm himself under a bench while having a commanding view of the baseball field. The entire baseball field spread below him, like a shooting gallery. With a rifle in his hands, that commanding view made that soldier a very effective sniper.

The challenge was finding him. Or *them.* There had to be several Japanese hidden away. Maybe even dozens of them. Deke wondered, *Where the hell are these Nips?*

Finally, one of the Japanese got trigger happy and fired. Deke spotted his muzzle flash.

"Got him," he whispered to Juana.

He squeezed the trigger and saw the figure of the enemy sniper go limp.

One of the Jap snipers got the bright idea to shoot back and received a bullet from Juana for his trouble.

Beside him, he heard the *slip-snick* of Juana working the bolt of her rifle. The sound brought a grin to his lips.

By now the rest of Patrol Easy and their Filipino friends would be in position, facing off against the Japanese snipers.

Bases are loaded, Deke thought.

Both sides held their fire, hoping for a target. Deke had to hand it to the Japanese snipers, who had more discipline than he had expected. Maybe they really all were a bunch of damn samurai.

The tense impasse did not last for long. The attack that had been prepared against Japanese positions now began, with soldiers advancing like angry outfielders rushing the mound after a pitch had hit the batter.

Unfortunately, the Japanese had been waiting for this moment. Machine guns opened fire from the dugouts, red tracers slicing the air. A couple of GIs spun and fell into the deep weeds, not moving again. Still more went down, helmets flying off, rifles falling from lifeless fingers. Those who hadn't been cut down kept running forward, but it was a hopeless situation. The intent of the frontal attack had been to rush the Japanese positions and overwhelm the enemy, but it soon became clear that this strategy was mostly based on wishful thinking.

The Nambu machine guns in the dugouts kept up their ruthless *tap, tap, tap* until not a GI was standing. Those who weren't dead lay with their heads buried as deep into the weeds as they could go. Meanwhile, enemy snipers fired from the stadium heights at anything that moved on the baseball field.

From behind the airplane wing, Deke watched it all with a growing sense of rage. The Japanese had turned the dugouts into pillboxes by piling sandbags in front of the entrances, offering just a slit for the machine guns to shoot from. His rifle felt useless against those defenses. Instead, he concentrated on picking off the snipers in the stands. He fired again and again. Beside him, he could hear the sharp crack of Juana's rifle as she did the same.

Normally, each of the snipers had trained to work with a spotter who could call out targets seen through binoculars while also watching out for any threats coming at them from their flanks or rear. But in this case, the two paired off and work like a team, alternating their fire.

They fell into a steady rhythm, Deke firing, then Juana shooting while he worked the bolt of the Springfield. It was like a one-two punch. Any snipers in the stands who made the mistake of revealing themselves paid dearly. The sniper fire from the stands slackened. Back in the day, vendors might have been selling cold beer up there and tossing out bags of peanuts. Now, the Japanese were tossing out lead.

The sun felt warm and he could smell Juana sweating beside him, the honest clean smell of work sweat. It reminded him of toiling in the fields alongside Sadie.

The frontal attack having been neutralized, the Japanese now turned their machine guns on Patrol Easy. Bullets and tracers sizzled overhead, forcing them to keep their heads down. Deke and Juana had to duck behind the airplane wing to keep from having their heads shot off. The situation had gone from bad to worse.

Now what?

Deke tried to take a shot at the machine gunners in the nearest dugout, but that only provoked a burst of fire that raked the length of the airplane wing. They were pinned down, good and proper.

Like an answer to a prayer, Deke heard the rumble of a tank, then another. The cavalry had arrived.

For the Japanese, the tables had turned. The machine guns peppered the steel sides of the Sherman tanks, but the bullets bounced off. Tracer rounds slid off the armor and went flying through the air. The tanks lined up their main guns and fired at the dugouts. Surprisingly, the sandbags had been piled so thick that they absorbed the first few rounds. But the tanks rolled closer and hit the dugout defenses at nearly point-blank range, demolishing the wall of sandbags. The echo of the muzzle blasts and explosions was deafening within the confines of the stadium.

The main guns were more than enough, but the armored unit was taking no chances and wasn't satisfied with simply pulverizing the Japanese. A couple of the tanks were equipped with flamethrowers. They let loose with burning streams of jellied gasoline, hosing down the dugouts with fire. This napalm was horrible stuff, a sort of sticky lava that clung to everything it touched. A few clumps of napalm fell short and hit the field, setting the tall weeds on fire. The breeze fanned the flames and carried the fire and smoke toward the enemy position. Even from the outfield, Deke was pretty sure that he heard screaming as the enemy soldiers were burned alive, either by the flamethrowers or the spreading brush fire.

Faced with the awful threat of the flamethrowers, some of the Japanese ran headlong from positions around the baseball dugouts. The limited visibility from within the tanks meant that some of the enemy had managed to slip away unseen by the tank crews. However, the fleeing Japanese didn't get far because not all the GIs from the ill-fated attack had been killed. They popped up now out of the long grass and weeds, firing at any Jap who made a run for it, taking their revenge.

Deke picked out a runner and squeezed the trigger, hearing the satisfying *thunk* of a bullet hitting home. It was a sound like a ripe watermelon breaking open—or maybe a fast ball hitting a glove. The Jap went down like a lifeless rag doll. Beside him, Juana grunted her approval.

Another Japanese ran to escape the horror of the flames, his tightly wrapped leggings already burning. The motion of his panic-stricken legs only served to feed the flames. Juana swung up her rifle, but before she could fire, they heard the deep boom of a 12-gauge shotgun. The enemy soldier collapsed in a heap.

"Honcho," she said with a wry smile.

They watched as the one-eyed lieutenant racked another shell into the shotgun and waited patiently for the next target. He might have been hunting pheasants.

Once the tanks had finished their grim business, there was still one task remaining for the foot soldiers. What followed next was like a gopher hunt as they mopped up the Japanese still trying to hide in the stands. With the Americans now controlling the infield and outfield, there was nowhere for them to go except off the high upper rows of the stadium. A couple of them tried it and fell to their deaths.

The Japanese rarely left themselves an escape route. There was no plan in the Japanese mind to fight another day. They fought to the death. The American soldiers were glad to oblige them.

Patrol Easy were joined by more GIs for the mopping-up operation. They spread out in a rough line, from the upper rows down to the box seats, and worked their way through to find any Japanese snipers trying to hide among the benches. Sometimes the Japanese leaped up and ran at them, screaming bloody murder in a singular version of a banzai charge. They were quickly shot down. Some put up no fight at all, but remained hidden in hopes that they might somehow escape their fate.

From up in the stands, the soldiers could see the bodies of several dead GIs sprawled in the weedy field where they had been mowed down by the machine guns in the dugouts. None of those American boys would ever be going home again.

As they hunted down the last of the defenders, nobody bothered to ask if any of the Japanese wanted to surrender, not even Yoshio.

CHAPTER THIRTEEN

SMOKE FROM DOZENS of small fires hung like a pall over the city, turning the setting sun bloodred, like a single angry eye squinting at the destruction. In addition to the smell of burning wood, the smoke stank of scorched rubber and sometimes roasted meat. By night, the GIs holed up in the ruins and slept fitfully even when they weren't on watch, wary of any marauding Japanese. There was no electricity across Manila, but the darkness was interrupted by flickering flames and an occasional muzzle flash. The soldiers welcomed daylight, even if it only meant more fighting from one ruined block to another.

That was about to change. A runner arrived at daybreak with new orders for Lieutenant Steele. The soldiers of Patrol Easy were still licking their wounds from the battle at the baseball stadium, but it turned out that they been assigned a special task that took them all by surprise and would be one of their greatest challenges yet.

"Grab a seat," Steele said, having gathered them all to hear what he had to say. Deke and the rest of the patrol, along with the Filipino fighters, could only guess at what they were being asked to do next. Deke glanced at Juana, who was watching the lieutenant intently, ready for anything. She looked up and caught Deke's eye. Her lips were normally set in a grim line, but she gave him a slight smile. Deke did the same in return.

Philly had caught sight of that exchange and stared as if he had just witnessed two lumps of coal suddenly sparkle like diamonds. He opened his mouth to say something that he would probably regret, but at that moment the lieutenant started to speak and saved his bacon.

"We're being asked to do a job that requires some finesse," Steele began. "HQ wants us there because we are good shots, but there may not be any shooting. In fact, it would be better if there wasn't."

Philly spoke up as usual. "With all due respect, Honcho, what the hell are you talking about?"

"I'm getting to that," Steele said. "I'm talking about a hostage situation. Our boys have a bunch of Japanese surrounded at an old university near here, but it turns out the Japanese are holding prisoners there. A lot of those prisoners are Americans, and they are threatening to shoot them unless we give the Japanese safe passage."

"Safe passage where?"

"They just want us to let them go. I'd imagine that they're hoping to link up with the rest of their friends, planning to make a last stand in the old quarter of the city."

"Why should we let them do that?" Philly wondered. "We'll just have to fight them later."

Steele shook his head. "Remember those hostages I mentioned? It all comes back to that. Anyhow, none of that is up to me. Our job is to pick off the Japanese if it comes to that. The brass doesn't want to start shooting randomly with machine guns or artillery. We'd have a lot of dead prisoners then, including

Americans. Some of the prisoners are women, from what I hear."

"Who is going to negotiate with the Japanese?"

He nodded at Yoshio. "We have an interpreter, remember? That's just in case they don't speak English, although we know a lot of their officers do. But don't worry, HQ is sending an officer to lead the negotiations."

"It figures," Philly said. "What's the matter, Honcho? Doesn't anybody trust us?"

"Look at this way, fellas. If any of the prisoners get killed, it's on him," Honcho said. "As usual, our job is mainly to shoot Japs —if we're needed to do that."

Steele explained that the negotiator was slated to meet them at the campus. Within the hour, they were moving through the increasingly ruined city, heading in the direction of the university. Once-proud buildings had been reduced to rubble during the fighting, mostly the result of artillery that was being used to systematically destroy any structure harboring the enemy. So much dust hung in the humid air that the sunlight turned a strange burnished sepia tone, like it was filtering through a faded yellow curtain at Grandma's house.

Bodies of dead Japanese soldiers lay strewn here and there, but there were many more dead city residents, a grim reminder of the price that Manila had been paying. The Filipinos who hadn't fled worked to gather and bury the bodies, but it was hard to keep up. Nobody bothered with the enemy dead. Stray dogs with their ribs sticking out nosed through the ruins, hoping for scraps.

"It looks like the surface of the moon," Yoshio said sadly.

"I haven't been to the moon, but that sounds about right," Deke replied.

Where the fighting had quieted down, bulldozers were at work, pushing the rubble aside to clear the streets so that tanks and supply trucks could advance more easily. Their loud engines and belching smoke only added to the chaotic feel of destruction.

"Keep your eyes open," Lieutenant Steele warned. "There's no telling if there are still a few Nips around."

"They're as hard to wipe out as sewer rats," Philly muttered.

Seconds after Honcho had issued his warning, a shot rang out, targeting one of the nearby bulldozers. Deke literally saw the spark as the bullet glanced off the dozer's heavy frame. Inside the cab of the roaring dozer, the engine noise was so loud that the operator didn't even know that he was being shot at.

Honcho waved at the man to get down, but the operator either didn't see him or didn't know what was going on.

The next shot was right on target, hitting the dozer operator square in the chest. The man slumped behind the controls, and the dozer rolled on as if it had a mind of its own, finally coming to rest against the stout wall of a building, engine grumbling, smoke pouring from the exhaust.

Another shot echoed along the street, but Patrol Easy had taken cover behind some of the larger chunks of rubble. The street-clearing crew had come to a stop, having seen what had befallen the other dozer operator.

"Anybody see where that sniper was at?" Philly called, scanning the remains of the hollowed-out buildings nearby nervously.

"On it," said Deke, who thought that he had seen movement in the empty window of a building that still stood at the end of the block. He put his rifle to his shoulder and the scope to his eye, praying that the sniper gave himself away.

Sharp-eyed Juana had seen something too. "There," she said, pointing, before swinging her own rifle up. She had found cover behind a chunk of concrete not more than a couple of yards from where Deke hid, his rifle resting on a stone block to steady it.

Even through the scope, it was hard for Deke to see any sign of the sniper, because the brownish uniforms worn by the Japanese blended in all too well with the dust-colored buildings, providing nearly perfect camouflage.

But Deke was nothing if not patient. He kept his eye trained on the spot where he thought that he'd spotted movement. He didn't have to spare a sideways glance to know that Juana was doing the same beside him, although her rifle lacked a telescopic sight. Over the last several days, she had done well with the iron sights. Deke's eyes were good, but he was beginning to wonder if Juana was even more eagle-eyed than he was. The thought made him smile.

The enemy sniper made the mistake of firing again. His bullet cracked harmlessly overhead but kept the soldiers pinned down. Nobody wanted to end up in his sights.

Deke couldn't even say that he actually saw the muzzle flash so much as the pressure wave of hot gases leaving the muzzle, creating a split-second ripple against the still backdrop. Looking closer through the scope, he saw a square of the enemy sniper's cheekbone, the sweaty flesh not quite blending in with the sun-dappled ruins in which the sniper hid. Breathing out, Deke put his crosshairs on that spot and squeezed the trigger.

At the same instant that he fired, he heard the crack of Juana's rifle.

The enemy sniper never had a chance. Both bullets hit him at once, flinging him back into the ruined room behind him.

Deke looked over at Juana, who returned his gaze and gave him a nod. Again, he thought he saw a slight smile play over her lips. *My kind of girl,* Deke thought.

"You two make a pretty good team," Philly said. "I've got to say, I'm a little worried that I might be replaced. I always thought it was you and me, Corn Pone."

"Let's face it, Philly," Deke said, grinning. "She's a better shot than you, and she's a whole lot better looking."

Philly laughed. "Is that so? In your case, I'd call that a match made in heaven."

Deke didn't say anything, but he'd been having that very same thought.

The body of the dead operator was removed from the bulldozer. He was carried away with as much dignity as possible under the circumstances. Someone else climbed into the dozer and gave the surrounding windows a nervous glance. The work clearing the streets resumed.

"All right, the show's over, so let's move out," Honcho said. "In case you all forgot, we're expected somewhere else." He paused, looking around at the buildings where any number of snipers might be hiding. "Whatever you do, keep your eyes open."

They moved cautiously through the ruined city, knowing that each empty window or pile of rubble might be concealing one more enemy soldier eager to die for the Emperor while trying to take out an American soldier at the same time.

Deke and Juana led the way, with Philly and Danilo just behind them. Every footstep felt tense as they threaded their way through the streets, dust from the rubble rising up to coat their boots and their trouser legs. As he walked, Deke's eyes swiveled in every direction, looking for any sign of movement. Staying alive from one street corner to the next was starting to feel like a small miracle.

Anyone watching Deke would have been reminded of the way a hunting cat prowls through an alley, every muscle tense, ready to jump sideways or pounce, depending on what emerged from the shadows. But Deke was more than an alley cat; he was more like a mountain lion.

Block by block, they finally reached the university campus. A tank stood by silently, its gun covering the entrance to one of the taller buildings.

"What's the situation?" Steele asked the tank commander.

"That's where the Japanese are holed up with their hostages, sir," the sergeant replied, nodding at the building. "I've got to say, I'd rather shoot at them than talk to them."

"It's new territory for us all, Sergeant," Steele replied.

Steele looked around. Other than the tank crew, who did look itchy to open fire rather than negotiate with the enemy, the only other person around was a dark-haired boy who was keeping his distance from the soldiers. Though dark-haired and with brown almond-shaped eyes, his boyishly handsome face had pale skin and Caucasian features, seeming to combine the elements of both races in a way that surprised the lieutenant and his men. The soldiers were so used to the sight of Filipinos that they had almost forgotten that there were Americans and Europeans who had been left behind when the Japanese first sacked the city.

"Who the hell is that kid?" Steele wondered.

"Aw, he says his father is one of the prisoners inside," the tank commander replied.

"He can't hang around here," Steele said.

"I told him that, but he's still here, isn't he?" The tank commander looked amused. "Now that you're here, I guess it's your turn to babysit that kid."

"So he speaks English?"

"Sure, he speaks it as good as you or me. He just doesn't listen so well." The sergeant added, "Listen, sir, we're gonna roll out. This tank isn't doing much good here, anyhow, because if we open fire, we'll bring that building down on the heads of everyone in it, including the hostages."

"Good point, Sergeant. But are you sure you're that tired of babysitting? What are you going to do instead?" Steele asked.

"We're gonna go shoot us some rats," the tank commander said, nodding at the large gun of the tank.

"Must be some big rats," Steele said.

"City's full of 'em," the tank commander said. "Especially down at Intramuros, the old walled part of the city. That's where the Japanese are planning to make their last stand."

"Happy rat hunting," Steele said.

The tank cranked up, exhaust fumes hanging heavy and the growl of the engine echoing off the stone faces of the nearby buildings. Then the tank rolled out, leaving Patrol Easy to keep watch and wait for the negotiator to arrive from HQ.

Steele looked over at the boy. "Hey, kid. Come here a minute."

The boy approached cautiously, keeping out of arm's reach. "Yes, sir?"

"I hear your father is inside."

The boy nodded. He looked both angry and fearful, which was understandable under the circumstances. Steele was pretty sure there were a couple of tear tracks down the boy's dusty face. "My father is American, but my mother is Filipino. My grandfather is judge of the appellate court. The Japanese took my father prisoner but left the rest of us alone."

Steele could see now that in addition to his American and Filipino traits, the boy's proud bearing hinted at some of the old Spanish blood typical of the city's elite, which an appellate judge certainly was. Right now, it didn't matter if the boy came from the upper classes. This was no place for any civilian, let alone a boy.

"I'm sorry about that, kid. But you need to go home. Your father wouldn't want you to be out here. He'd want you to be home taking care of your mother."

"She's the one who sent me," the boy said. "She wants me to bring him home as soon as the Japanese let him go. Our house was wrecked, so we're living someplace else for now, and he wouldn't be able to find us in this mess. I know this city about as well as anybody. The Japanese don't pay much attention to a kid, so I've been coming and going here for weeks."

The lieutenant rubbed his chin, thinking it over. It was bad enough that he had to cope with grouchy GIs, short-tempered commanding officers, bloodthirsty guerrillas, and sneaky Nips. Now it seemed that he also had to deal with a snot-nosed kid. He sighed.

Philly spoke up. "Honcho, you want me to give him a kick in the pants and send him on his way?"

"No, let him stay." The lieutenant had done a quick mental calculation and didn't like the boy's chances of getting home alive on his own. He pointed to a large rock to Deke's right. "Kid, get down behind that rock and don't you move unless that man there tells you to. He'll keep you alive if anyone can. Understood?"

The boy nodded. "Yes, sir."

"What's your name, anyhow?"

"Roddy MacGregor. My father's name is Michael." The boy paused, then added with a touch of pride, "His friends call him Big Mike because he's so tall."

"All right, Roddy. Keep your head down."

From the open windows, they saw Caucasian faces peering out from the lower levels. Maybe one of those prisoners was the boy's father. The faces of Japanese soldiers looked down from the higher levels of the building. The Japanese soldiers were pointing rifles at them. The Japanese didn't open fire, and neither did Patrol Easy. Instead, the two sides kept under cover, watching one another warily.

"How long do we keep this up, Honcho?" Philly wanted to know.

"Until the cavalry gets here," Steele replied.

"When is that?"

"Whenever they decide to show up, that's when," Steele snapped. "Meanwhile, everybody hold your fire. I see those Japanese in the windows as well as you do, but we don't want to hit any prisoners."

That said, Patrol Easy settled down to wait for this so-called cavalry, which at that moment was several miles away, riding on a bucking steed.

CHAPTER FOURTEEN

Captain Jim Oatmire had ridden in a jeep from the beach to the outskirts of Manila. Although the ride wasn't exactly comfortable, he reminded himself that he had nothing to complain about. Much of the military force descending upon the city had arrived in a beach landing that had been largely unopposed, so different from the reception they had received from the Japanese when landing on Leyte. The Philippines was a nation of islands, and on the island of Luzon, the Japanese had withdrawn inland and awaited the approach of Allied troops. This was going to be a defensive operation. In part, this was why Manila had become a battleground.

"This is as far as we go, Captain," the driver said. Although it was usually the officer who delivered such announcements to enlisted men like the one behind the wheel, the driver in this case seemed to have decided that experience trumped rank. He was an older man who clearly wasn't impressed with Oatmire's captain's bars or neatly pressed uniform.

"What are you talking about?" Oatmire asked. Their surroundings swarmed with activity as army troops pushed deeper into the city, so he couldn't figure out why the driver had stopped.

Unperturbed, the driver nodded at the road ahead—which was largely blocked by rubble and the wrecked, burned-out hulks of civilian vehicles. It wasn't exactly an open road. Oatmire got it then—there was literally no way for the jeep to proceed. Bulldozers worked to clear the debris, but they hadn't made much progress. The only thing that seemed to be getting through was a tank, which was unlikely to give him a ride.

Above the grinding motors of the bulldozers, they could hear a few shots in the distance. The driver didn't appear eager to get any closer to the shooting.

"It's literally the end of the road, sir."

"I can see that. So this is Manila, huh?"

"Not much to look at, is it, sir?"

He had seen postcard images of the elegant old city with its Spanish architecture that General MacArthur loved so much. That picture-perfect city was rapidly becoming just a memory as the war raged. He sighed. "No, it's not."

Oatmire climbed out of the jeep and grabbed his haversack. His only weapon was his sidearm, a fact that the driver noticed.

"Don't you have a rifle, sir?"

"I don't plan on doing much fighting, soldier. No need for a rifle."

"You might change your mind about that, sir."

"I hope to hell not."

"There are still a lot of Japanese around."

"Thanks for the ride," Oatmire said. "You'd better get on back to the beach."

The driver gave him a wave that may have been a half-assed salute, then turned the jeep around and headed back toward the landing area. As the sound of the jeep motor faded, he could hear the thump of artillery in the distance and rifle shots nearby.

Maybe that driver had been right about taking a rifle along. Oatmire looked out at the battered city and thought, *What now?*

Oatmire pulled out his map but quickly realized that he didn't know what the hell he was looking at. The street signs were long gone, and any sort of landmarks on his map were unrecognizable, having mostly been reduced to rubble.

He began picking his way through the city streets, asking for directions to the University of Santo Tomas. Some of the men he asked had no clue; they knew they were in Manila and that was about it, so he kept asking. The areas that he moved through were more or less cleared of the enemy, but not completely. He dove for cover just twice, both times when sniper fire broke out. His clean uniform quickly got dusty, not to mention sweaty.

After two hours of tense movement through the city streets, knowing that each time he crossed open ground, he was making himself a target, he finally arrived at the university.

He soon realized that reaching his destination was only the start of his challenges. It turned out that the university was essentially an island, surrounded by city blocks now controlled by US forces. That much was a relief. Considering that the army had plenty of artillery firepower, the normal course of action would have been to blow the enemy to hell and bury them in the rubble, but that was not an option here. This was because the Japanese held dozens of prisoners hostage. The number of prisoners had been much larger, several thousand at the start of the battle. However, the Japanese had realized that controlling so many desperate prisoners might enable the prisoners to turn on them. Also, they had run out of food and water for the prisoners.

Holding a smaller number of prisoners still gave the surrounded Japanese a powerful negotiating tool. In fact, the presence of the hostages was why Oatmire was here in the first place.

Currently, US forces were surrounding one of the university

buildings, a tall stone structure with architecture that would have been at home in Old Spain. The soldiers held their guns at the ready and kept their fingers on the triggers.

Several of the soldiers covering the building's main entrance were snipers, indicated by the fact that they carried rifles with telescopic sights. Mixed among the sniper squad were several Filipino fighters, including a few women. The presence of the women took Oatmire somewhat by surprise. From their dirty uniforms to the gunpowder grime on their faces, the whole bunch looked like tough customers. Their weapons appeared battered but gleamed with fresh gun oil as if well tended. Oddly enough, there was also a boy hanging around, maybe ten or twelve years old, wearing shorts and a striped shirt, crouched behind a rock next to one of the snipers. He looked more American than Filipino. What a kid was doing here was a mystery. Oatmire decided that one of the first things he'd be doing was sending the boy away. This was no place for a kid.

He noticed that the sniper positioned between one of the women and the boy took his eye away from his rifle scope long enough to assess Oatmire. The man's gray eyes passed over him cooly, his face indifferent. Oatmire noticed that one side of the man's face was covered with a raking scar, but he was otherwise rather handsome in a rawboned way, deeply tanned by the tropical sun. The sniper gave the impression that he'd pull his trigger and deliver a deadly shot with no more thought than he would give to smashing an insect. *Glad he's on our side,* Oatmire thought. Instead of a helmet, the sniper wore an Australian-style bush hat. The hat was not regulation, but Oatmire wasn't about to say anything. That wasn't his role here.

In the windows of the university building, he could see several Japanese with their own rifles at the ready, aimed at the Americans. With a start, Oatmire realized that he was almost certainly in the Japanese sights, and fresh sweat broke out on his forehead.

Nobody was shooting, but for how long? There were itchy trigger fingers all around. He realized that one small miscalculation was going to turn this whole situation into a bloodbath. If that happened, there sure as hell wouldn't be any hostages for him to rescue.

Nobody but the alert sniper had paid any attention to his arrival. "Who's in charge here?" he asked.

A tall lieutenant stepped forward, Oatmire noting with surprise that the man wore an eye patch. The patch looked homemade, as if it had been cut from a scrap of boot leather. Oatmire couldn't help but stare.

"That would be me," the lieutenant said. He didn't offer a salute, which was typical of combat conditions where the gesture would make it easier for Japanese snipers to pick off the officers. "I'm Lieutenant Steele."

"Captain Oatmire."

"You must be our hostage negotiator."

"That's what I've been told," Oatmire said. "It looks as if you have the Japanese bottled up."

"If they didn't have hostages, there wouldn't be a building left, sir," Steele said. "We'd have called in artillery to level it."

"How many hostages?"

Steele shook his head. "I honestly don't know. Too many. Every now and then, the Japanese make their prisoners stand in the windows as a reminder that it would be a bad idea if we start shooting."

"Damn Japs. We're getting reports that they're using civilians as human shields all over the city. Have you talked with them?"

"No, I haven't, Captain. Seems to me like that's your job."

Oatmire nodded, then pulled a white handkerchief from his pocket. He had brought it along for this very purpose. He noted with some disappointment that the handkerchief *had* been white, but the dusty city was already making it dingy. "All right, I'm going to approach them under a flag of truce. Hopefully they won't shoot me."

"Good luck with that, sir," Steele replied. It wasn't reassuring that he sounded doubtful that the white flag was going to do anything but get Oatmire killed. "We do have an interpreter if you want him. Yoshio, come over here a minute."

One of the GIs scurried out from behind a chunk of rubble. Oatmire was surprised at the sight of a young Japanese man wearing an army uniform. He'd heard about these Nisei, Japanese Americans who spoke the enemy's language. Even at headquarters, there were some who didn't quite trust their loyalties.

"Thanks, that will be useful if there are any language issues," Oatmire said. "Some of these Japanese speak at least a little English, but you never know."

"You never know," Steele agreed. He gave him another look. "If you don't mind me asking, how many negotiations have you done?"

"I once bought a used car and got the dealer to knock off fifty bucks. Does that count?"

Steele stared at him for a moment, seeming to wonder if Oatmire was serious or not; then his face broke into a grin and he even gave a short laugh. It had a rusty sound, as if he hadn't had much reason to laugh recently. "And you're the guy HQ sent, huh? Sounds about right."

"That's the army way," Oatmire agreed. He also found himself grinning. "On-the-job training. Any advice?"

The lieutenant thought it over. "Just remember that they're Japs," he said. "They don't think like us. Most Japanese could not care less about dying, and I don't expect that these bastards are any different. Especially the officers. I've got to admit, I'm surprised that any of the hostages have survived. But I guess that they want a bargaining chip."

Oatmire found a low whistle escaping his lips. "That's not much to negotiate with. A bargaining chip, huh? What the hell do they even want?"

"Probably to let them leave here so that they can fight and die gloriously in a last stand somewhere else in the city." Steele tapped his shotgun barrel. "We'll be glad to oblige."

"All right," Oatmire said, squaring his shoulders. "Let's get this show on the road."

"One thing, sir," Steele said.

"What is it?" Oatmire found that he didn't mind any excuse that delayed stepping out into the open, in full view of the Japanese riflemen in the upper floors.

"Maybe you could go alone at first. It's just that I'd hate to lose our interpreter too."

Gee, thanks for that, Oatmire thought. He took a deep breath to settle his nerves, although it didn't help much, and shook out the so-called flag of truce. He realized that he was trusting his life to a dingy white handkerchief. "All right," he said. "I'll call your guy over if I need him to translate. Here goes nothing."

CHAPTER FIFTEEN

FROM THE SAFETY OF COVER, the soldiers watched tensely as Captain Oatmire approached the university building, waving his white handkerchief. He was not armed, having put his faith in the scrap of fabric to keep him safe.

"What do you think the odds are that the Japanese will shoot him?" Philly wondered.

"Fifty-fifty, but I'm not taking that bet," Deke said.

"Me neither," Philly said. "You've got to hand it to that captain, though. He's got some guts."

Deke couldn't argue with that, he thought, watching the officer approach the massive, arched entryway of the stone building. Then again, there was an outside chance that Oatmire was more afraid of failing General MacArthur than he was fearful of the Japanese.

Like the others, Deke held his breath, waiting for the shot to ring out that would send Oatmire toppling into the dirt. If Oatmire had any qualms, he showed no outward sign of fear, striding forward toward the entrance with all the confidence of a door-to-door salesman looking to unload some encyclopedias or vacuum cleaners.

Deke thought that the captain was either a brave son of a bitch or a fool who didn't know he was dead yet. Maybe a little of both.

Instead of being greeted by a gunshot, Oatmire was met by a Japanese officer. Deke was surprised to see that he was tall for a Japanese and neatly dressed, down to the creases on his uniform that looked sharp as a samurai sword—which the officer happened to be wearing at his belt. Although the officer himself was not waving a white flag, the man next to him, a tough-looking fellow who was apparently some sort of flunky, did have one. Other than the sword, which was more like a badge of office for the Japanese rather than a weapon, they were not armed—but there were plenty of Japanese soldiers in the building behind them with weapons at the ready. In an instant, there might be a storm of lead flying at the Americans.

Oatmire and the Japanese officer spoke briefly, then Oatmire looked toward Patrol Easy's position and waved. Apparently he had need of an interpreter, after all.

"That's your cue, Yoshio," Lieutenant Steele said. Then he pointed at Deke. "You go with him, Deke."

Deke was taken aback. There was no way that he wanted to offer himself as a target. Without thinking, he blurted out, "What the hell, Honcho? I don't speak the lingo."

"You don't need to say anything. Some things can be communicated better without words. With all due credit to Yoshio and that captain, I want you to make an impression on the Japanese about what's in store for them if they don't go along with Oatmire. He looks like a damn overgrown Boy Scout. We need somebody to put the fear of God into them. If they don't release the hostages, I want to remind those Nips that the last thing they're gonna see in this world is your ugly mug."

"Good cop, bad cop," Philly muttered. "You are definitely the bad cop."

"You sure know how to make a fella feel appreciated, Honcho," Deke said, then straightened up. He wasn't reassured by the worried look that Juana was giving him. Like the others, she seemed to expect shooting to break out momentarily. She kept her captured Arisaka rifle pointed at the enemy position.

"Should I bring my rifle, Honcho?"

"No, those Japs aren't armed. Leave your rifle here, son."

Deke did as he was told and left behind his rifle and pistol. It felt strange not to have them within reach, almost like he was naked. He did keep his bowie knife in his belt. He figured that was fair enough. Hell, that Jap officer had a damn *sword*.

He followed Yoshio into the open and they joined Captain Oatmire, who was facing the two Japanese. "This is Major Tanigawa," Oatmire said, giving Deke and Yoshio a quick glance. "He's willing to discuss the release of the hostages with us."

Deke looked Tanigawa up and down. Again, Deke was impressed that the enemy officer was tall and well built for a Japanese, even rather regal, with a uniform that was cleaner and neater than the captain's. Although Oatmire hadn't been gone long from headquarters, his uniform was struggling to stay clean and pressed in these combat conditions. The katana sword at his belt added to the major's dignified appearance.

Another damn Jap who thinks he's a samurai, Deke thought, admiring the beautifully crafted sword in spite of himself. It was hard to read the officer's face, which was studiously indifferent. The man would've made a good poker player. His eyes lingered the longest on Yoshio, as if Tanigawa was trying to digest the idea of someone of Japanese heritage wearing an American uniform. His demeanor cracked just a bit, and he almost appeared puzzled by the sight.

The face of the flunky standing beside Tanigawa was much

easier to read. In fact, his thoughts were as plain as the headlines of a newspaper. He scowled, his eyebrows knitting together. He didn't seem to think much of Oatmire or the American Nisei interpreter. Oatmire had picked up on the Japanese flunky's hostility, and jerking his chin at the man, he asked, "Who is this, anyhow?"

Major Tanigawa seemed taken aback that anyone would care about the man who had accompanied him to this negotiation. He barely gave the flunky more than a passing glance before replying, "Sergeant Inaba."

Sergeant Inaba's stare indicated that he would like nothing better than to take out the Americans. At one point the man's eyes slid to Tanigawa's samurai sword, as if contemplating grabbing it and using it on the Americans, white flag be damned.

Same to you, buddy, Deke thought, locking eyes with the man. He touched the hilt of his bowie knife, just to send the Jap a message. The sergeant nodded, seeming to recognize an equal, a slight smile coming to his lips as if he would welcome mixing it up with Deke. Both men squinted as they studied each other, as if lining up the other man across a rifle sight. Sometimes no language was needed to express how you really felt—Honcho had sure been right about that. Deke had to remind himself that their current purpose was to avoid any shooting.

Sounding angry and glaring at Yoshio, the major spit out something in Japanese. The harsh, guttural language grated on Deke's ears.

"What's he going on about?" Oatmire asked.

"He says that I am a traitor," Yoshio explained.

"Yeah? Well, to hell with him," Oatmire said. "Anyhow, we're here to talk about the hostages, not his damn opinions."

Oatmire began the negotiations by making a direct appeal.

"Major Tanigawa, what do we need to do to get you to release these prisoners that you are unlawfully holding hostage?"

Captain Oatmire asked. Then he turned to the interpreter. "It's Yoshio, right? Go ahead and ask him, Yoshio."

Yoshio asked the question. The major replied in Japanese, and Yoshio translated. "He says we can leave the area, for a start. Then he will let the hostages go."

"Tell him we can't do that," Oatmire said. "Tell him he and his men are free to go if they leave the hostages behind."

Tanigawa replied and Yoshio explained, "He says they would require an escort for safe passage."

"An escort? Where the hell does he want to go, Tokyo?"

The Japanese major then startled them by speaking up in passable English. It turned out that the enemy officer had been slyly pretending he didn't know the language. "Not Tokyo, Captain. I only wish to lead my men to join the rest of our troops here in the city."

Oatmire raised his eyebrows in surprise. "I thought you didn't speak English," he grumbled. "If you release the hostages, we could provide an escort."

"Such an arrangement would be amenable to me."

Oatmire nodded. "How many hostages are we talking about here?"

"Many have already been released, but several dozen prisoners remain. They will be released also."

"All right, send them out." Oatmire seemed a bit perplexed that there wasn't more to discuss, as if he had come all that way for not a whole lot. "Once you've done that, come back out and you can be on your way to join up with whomever you want here —with that escort you asked for."

"This is satisfactory to me," Major Tanigawa said.

He offered a curt bow, then turned on his heel with military precision and headed back inside. His sergeant gave Deke one last glare, then followed.

Oatmire stood there, watching the Japanese go.

Deke wasn't as patient. He was antsy to get his hands back on his rifle. Although they had reached an agreement with the Japanese, it hardly felt like a victory. Everything about what had just happened had left them feeling tense and uneasy. Something about the deal just didn't sit right with Deke. "Now what, sir?"

"Now we wait. He said that he's going to release the rest of the hostages." A thought seemed to come to Oatmire. "You've been at this a while, soldier. Do you trust these Japanese?"

"Not as far as I can throw 'em, sir."

"That makes two of us. I'll tell you what. I'll wait here and see what happens. You and Yoshio go back."

"And do what, sir?"

"Get your rifles, that's what. If diplomacy fails, there's going to be some shooting to do."

Deke and Yoshio did as they were told, heading back to take cover in the rubble. Of course, Deke was glad to get his hands on his rifle again. With any luck, he'd have a chance to shoot that Japanese sergeant with it.

"Are we really gonna let them go?" Deke wondered.

"We do what we promise," Honcho said.

"Do you think the Japanese would do the same for us if the tables were turned?"

"Maybe not," Honcho agreed. "But that's the difference between us and them, isn't it? Americans mean what we say. You can take us at our word."

It was hard to argue with that. Even in the midst of a brutal war, whether it was in Europe or the Pacific, the Americans and their allies tried to do the right thing. There was the brutal war fought with bombs and bullets and flamethrowers, but there was also a war for hearts and minds fought by setting an example. So far America and the Allies were winning that war.

Then the lieutenant added an afterthought: "Also, we want

the Japanese to release those hostages, so we really don't have much choice."

Deke felt better now with his rifle back in his hands. "For a bunch of people who like to think of themselves as samurai warriors, they sure don't have any trouble hiding behind prisoners, even ones wearing skirts."

"You've got that right," Honcho agreed.

Several minutes went by, the minutes stretching into an hour. Still, the Japanese had not reappeared. The heat of the sun seemed to amplify exponentially with each passing minute. The scent of smoke, burning debris, and the putrid smell of dead corpses hung heavily in the air. Deke swigged from his canteen to wash away the taste of dust and ash that lingered on his tongue like a sprinkling of the destruction and death that surrounded them. He noticed that Juana had barely moved, her finger on the trigger.

Flies appeared and buzzed annoyingly into their ears and eyes. Everyone tried hard not to think about the fact that these same flies were probably the ones they had seen earlier swarming over the faces of the dead they had passed in the shattered streets. The boy came over and crouched near Deke and Juana, as if he didn't want to be off by himself. Deke couldn't blame him.

Finally, the Japanese began to emerge. This in itself was something of a spectacle because they formed into marching order, as neatly as though they were gathered on a parade ground. It was a strange sight, seeing the enemy up close. So close, in fact, that Deke could see their individual features.

He studied them with curiosity because it wasn't often that he'd seen enemy soldiers this close. They were shorter than the average American by two or three inches, but there was an undeniable physical strength about them, the soldiers being either wiry or squat and powerfully built. Also, these Japanese had been living in comparative comfort compared to the soldiers that Patrol Easy had encountered in the jungles and mountains or damp underground bunkers. Consequently, they appeared relatively strong and healthy, their uniforms clean and even their brown boots polished, contrasting with the lighter-colored laces.

As they formed up, the hobnailed soles of their boots grated in an unsettling manner on the flat paving stones that remained in the courtyard. *Enemy footsteps.* How many times had they heard that scrape of steel on rock in the dark and knew all too well what was coming next? What stood out most of all were the impassive faces of the enemy, all of them with eyes staring straight ahead, as if the Americans were nothing to them at all—or perhaps were not even there. The only other sound aside from the hobnailed boots came in the form of a few harsh, gruff orders. The well-disciplined soldiers obeyed instantly.

There were also a lot of soldiers, at least a hundred men, vastly outnumbering Patrol Easy and the handful of infantry guarding the campus.

Philly gave a low whistle. "Now that I see them up close, I'm glad we didn't have to fight them."

"There were a lot more Nips than we figured," Deke agreed.

"We've got them right where we want them," Philly said. "We ought to just say to hell with it and shoot them all right now. Mow them down. It's now or later, right?"

"Shut up, Philly," the lieutenant said, having overheard. "You talk too much. We're here because of those hostages, remember?"

Maybe the Japanese were worried about that very notion of betrayal coming into the heads of their enemy because it soon became clear that the Japanese weren't taking any chances. Once the Japanese were formed up, there were more shouted orders and their ranks opened like a chunk of firewood being split down the middle. From the college building emerged a dozen prisoners—a mixed bag of men and three or four women.

"Papa!" shouted the boy, who had been watching rapt as the Japanese formed up. Deke and the others had almost forgotten that he was still there.

A prisoner looked up, tall as a drink of water and skinny as a rail. He was six foot four if he was an inch, towering over the Japanese soldiers. The boy had said that his father's nickname was "Big Mike," which made perfect sense. He wore what had once been a business suit, but which was now ragged and hanging loosely on his frame. Clearly, he had lost a lot of weight while being held captive. A reddish beard covered his face, which broke into a smile.

"Roddy!" the prisoner shouted.

The boy started running toward the tall man, who was in turn trying to force his way through the Japanese to reach his son. In a perfect world, it might have been a happy reunion for them both.

But a reunion was not meant to be. "Stop!" Tanigawa shouted, pointing his sword at the man. He wasn't about to listen, but several Japanese soldiers sprang forward and held him. At first it looked as if they might not be able to stop him because he was so determined to reach his son. The difference in height gave an almost comical impression of a giant being restrained by dwarfs. However, the dwarfs appeared quite strong and the giant among them had been weakened by captivity and starvation. Try as he might, he couldn't break free. Still, one of the Japs took an elbow to the nose for his trouble, bright blood spurting. The sight of the blood in the middle of what had started out as an almost ceremonial event was jarring and hinted at more to come.

Sergeant Inaba settled the matter by appearing as if out of nowhere and pointing a submachine gun at the prisoner's head.

"Stop!" he shouted in English. Apparently here was a second Japanese who only pretended not to know the language.

Meanwhile, two Japanese soldiers stepped forward to intercept the boy, who was still running toward the enemy formation. For one terrifying instant, one of them raised his rifle butt as if about to club the boy, but stopped at another warning shout from Tanigawa. Instead of hitting him, they grabbed him and lifted him clean off the ground.

"Let go of my son, damn you!" the prisoner shouted, struggling anew to break free. "Get your hands off him."

The neat Japanese formation began to unravel. Rifles came off shoulders and began pointing toward the US soldiers, whose own fingers were on their triggers. Deke already had his sights lined up on the Japanese officer, Tanigawa.

"Come on," he breathed. He fought the urge to pull the trigger. "Come on."

The situation had quickly worsened and threatened to turn into the bloodbath they had expected from the outset. To his credit, it was Captain Oatmire who stepped forward, putting himself squarely in the middle of everyone's gunsights. He moved toward the soldiers holding the struggling boy.

"OK, it's OK, I've got him," he said.

Yoshio was now right on his heels, shouting something in Japanese. The enemy soldiers glanced at Major Tanigawa, who nodded. They let Oatmire take charge of the boy, who got a firm but gentle grip on his shoulders. "It's all right, kid. You'll see your father soon enough," he said. To the father he shouted over the tops of the enemy's heads, "Don't worry. We'll take good care of him."

"Damn these lying people!" the father shouted, but he allowed himself to be shoved back into formation. He really didn't have any choice.

But Sergeant Inaba had to get in one last blow. He used the

metal butt of the submachine gun to jab Big Mike savagely in the small of his back, right in the kidney. The prisoner cried out in pain and sank to his knees.

"Damn you, Inaba!" Big Mike shouted.

The sergeant just smiled. He raised the weapon as if to smash Big Mike again, but stopped when Major Tanigawa shouted something. It was likely that the major was less motivated by any sense of kindness toward the prisoner who was now on his knees than by a desire to maintain the calm after a melee had nearly broken out. Reluctantly, Inaba lowered the weapon.

The rest of the Japanese got back in formation, sandwiching the prisoners in the middle as neatly as a hot dog inside a bun or jelly inside a doughnut.

"One thing for sure, that boy's father has got a loud mouth," said Philly, lowering his rifle. "He's not afraid of these Japanese."

"In my experience, being a loudmouth can be a health hazard," Deke replied, muttering around his rifle stock. He hadn't taken his sights off the Japanese major, a fact that hadn't gone unnoticed by the lieutenant.

"Deke, lower your weapon, dammit," Honcho said.

"All right," Deke said, taking his time doing it.

He didn't like how this was unfolding at all.

Briefly, Deke had been a prisoner himself during a rescue mission on Leyte. General MacArthur had made the release of POWs a priority, just as he was doing here in Manila, so Patrol Easy had found itself at a remote jungle prison camp. The best way of getting the prisoners out had promised to be from within, so Deke had allowed himself to be captured, posing as a lost GI. He had then helped lead the prisoners through the wire and toward safety, all while being pursued by the Japanese guards and a demented camp commandant with a bow and arrow. It had made for a memorable few days, to say the least.

In any case, Deke could certainly sympathize with how these

prisoners must feel now, with freedom snatched from them at the last instant. It didn't sit right with him.

He wasn't the only one.

"What the hell is happening here?" Honcho wondered aloud. "This wasn't the deal. They're supposed to let the prisoners go. Dammit, Oatmire, go talk to him."

CHAPTER SIXTEEN

TANIGAWA NOW STOOD at the head of the Japanese formation, calmly watching as Captain Oatmire approached him again. This time there was no charade about the need for interpreters. It had already become clear that the officer spoke English.

"Major Tanigawa, what the hell is going on?" Oatmire demanded.

Tanigawa gave him a cold smile. "Insurance policy," he said. "I think that is the expression that you Americans would use."

"That wasn't the agreement," Oatmire complained. He felt his temper spike and struggled to keep it under control, knowing that it wouldn't make the situation any better. "We didn't talk about any damn insurance policies."

Tanigawa just shrugged. "Do you wish for the release of the prisoners or not? I have let most of them go. These few will be released once we reach our destination."

Oatmire marched back to Lieutenant Steele with the bad news. "I hate to say it, but these Japs have us stuck between a rock and a hard place."

"That's putting it mildly," Honcho said. "I would've said they had our nuts in a vise."

"Well, that too," Oatmire admitted. "Dammit, I feel like my first hostage negotiation didn't go so well. I must have missed something."

"Captain, the only mistake you made was trusting these lying Nips in the first place," Steele said.

"No kidding," Oatmire said, sounding disgusted.

"Not your fault, you know. You were simply making a good-faith effort. I've got to say, I don't like it any better than you do, but at this point, I don't think we have much of a choice except to go along with what Tanigawa wants. We'll escort them to wherever they want to go, and then we'll see that the prisoners are released."

"All right," Oatmire agreed. Although he outranked the older man, he wasn't about to order around the lieutenant or his veteran combat patrol. "Sounds like the only choice we have."

"I'd suggest that we just keep one thing in mind," Steele added.

"What's that, lieutenant?"

"The Japanese have already lied to us, so chances are that they'll do it again. Knowing that, let's both of us be on our toes in dealing with them."

Right before they moved out, Sergeant Inaba barked an order and several of the Japanese soldiers fixed bayonets. Their intent seemed to be to use the bayonets to prod their prisoners along. If anyone was too slow or caused trouble, such as trying to make a run for it, the Japanese clearly meant to stab them in the back.

The icing on the cake was a soldier who carried a Japanese flag next to Major Tanigawa at the front of the column.

"It looks like they're having a damn parade," Deke muttered.

"All they need is a marching band," Philly agreed. "Just who the hell do they think they are?"

"They're proud bastards, I'll give them that," Deke replied.

With the Japanese now formed up in marching order, Patrol Easy and the Filipinos formed a loose ring around them, and both groups moved out into the city. Tanigawa had not announced his destination, but from the pace he set, it was clear that he knew where he was leading his men.

The surrounding city was a mess, a labyrinth of burned-out cars everywhere, along with broken buildings and scattered bodies, mostly of Filipino civilians, not to mention a few dead dogs. Overall, it was far from a pleasant or encouraging sight. The smell of the dead in the warm sun mixed with the odor of raw sewage and the acrid stink of burned rubber. It all made Deke long for the greenery of the jungle. This manmade jungle was far worse.

As the soldiers moved through the city, the only living beings they passed seemed to be other combat troops, mainly American soldiers and a handful of Filipino guerrillas. They watched the procession with curiosity and puzzled expressions. For the Japanese, having an American escort forming a loose ring around them had proved to be very smart, because they would not have lasted long otherwise, surrounded by trigger-happy GIs. Even with the hostages, their chances of making it so much as a block wouldn't have been very good.

"Ain't this a hell of a thing," Deke said as they walked along beside the Japanese. "Who would ever think we'd be babysitters for a bunch of enemy troops?"

"Yeah, it doesn't make sense to me," Philly agreed. "You know that we're just going to have to fight these sons of bitches later, and if not us, then some other poor bastards will."

"I don't think we have much choice," Deke said, nodding at the prisoners. They walked with their heads down, picking their way through the rubble. If any of them slowed down too much, Inaba or one of the other Japanese was quick to shout at them. So far they had refrained from jabbing the prisoners with bayonets. Even Big Mike appeared cowed, walking along with his head bowed. They could see him plainly because he was literally a head taller than the surrounding Japanese.

Tagging along with Patrol Easy was the prisoner's son, who had insisted on following them. The nightmarish cityscape they passed through was no place for a young kid.

"I wish to hell that kid would go home," Deke said. "He doesn't have any business being out here."

"If that was your father being herded along, would you go home?" Philly wondered.

"I don't reckon I would."

"There you go. What makes you think that kid is any different?"

The boy appeared to sense his tenuous position because he kept well away from the soldiers. He seemed to be afraid that if he got too close, they would yell at him to go home. However, the shattered streets they were passing through wouldn't have been safe for him to travel alone. They began passing more and more civilian bodies, including women and children. Several of the injuries to the women and their torn or missing clothes indicated that they had been molested. They passed the body of a young woman, her shirt ripped open, revealing that one of her breasts had been cut off.

"Who the hell does that?" Philly wondered.

Nobody had a good answer for him. Juana went over and tugged the young woman's shirt closed, then put a handkerchief over her face to keep off the flies. It was as much dignity as she could give the young woman in these circumstances.

It was becoming clear that the Japanese were killing anyone they could, including Westerners. Not all the bodies belonged to

Filipino civilians. One of the dead appeared to be a heavyset middle-aged Caucasian man wearing linen suit pants and a dress shirt sliced to ribbons by bayonet cuts. The shirt had once been white but was now soaked in uneven stripes of blood. This victim appeared out of place alongside the others.

"Another American?" Philly wondered aloud.

"If he was running free around the city, instead of being a prisoner, he must be a German," Honcho said. "Allies with the Japs. They've corralled everyone else."

"Good riddance, then," Philly said.

There had been a surprising number of Germans in Manila, most of them there in some kind of business capacity. There were also a small number of German Jews who had escaped Nazi Germany just in time, scattering to whatever far corner of the world would take them. The Japanese had not cared about their religion and consequently considered these refugees to be on equal footing with the other Germans. The presence of a German population was a problem that would have to be dealt with once the city was secure. Right now, US forces had more immediate concerns.

The heat beat down, humidity seeming to add extra effort to every motion. Deke forced himself to stay alert. There was no telling when the enemy might try something. Also, there were more than a few trigger-happy GIs wandering the streets who would have been happy enough to avenge the death of a buddy by opening fire on the Japanese soldiers. If someone from their own side opened fire, Deke wanted plenty of warning. He also wasn't going to lift a finger to defend the Japanese if that happened, although it wouldn't bode well for the prisoners within the enemy ranks.

"The Japs say they want those prisoners as insurance, but what do you really think they want with those women nurses?"

Deke wondered, having seen what the marauding enemy had done to the Filipino women.

"The thought crossed my mind. I just hope to hell they don't kill the rest of the prisoners as soon as they get where they're going," Philly replied. "You can't trust these damn Japanese."

"Don't let the boy hear you say that. He's upset enough as it is."

After the boy stumbled over a bayoneted body and stared down at it in horror, Lieutenant Steele waved him over. "Stick close to me, kid. We don't want to lose you in all this mess."

Shaken by what he had seen, Roddy did as he was told and did not stray far from the lieutenant's side. As for the boy's father, Big Mike was too far away to communicate with his son. Once or twice when he did try to speak up, he only earned himself a rifle butt slammed painfully into the small of his back. That was better than the point of a bayonet, at least. But where the Japanese were concerned, he might be pushing his luck. It was clear they had little patience for their prisoners.

Deke had to hand it to the Japanese—they were quite disciplined, marching in tight order while still managing to herd the hostages along. There were a dozen hostages, mostly men, but among them, Deke counted three women who looked to be in their late thirties or even their forties. They had a no-nonsense appearance, not about to be confused with beauty queens, although one of the younger nurses had on a touch of lipstick. All three wore nurses' uniforms, and he was amazed at their bravery.

He'd heard about these Red Cross nurses who had volunteered to help the prisoners, in turn becoming prisoners themselves. Now, instead of being released, they had either volunteered to be hostages or the Japanese had decided that female hostages gave them more negotiating power. He caught a glimpse of the nurses' faces and saw no tears there, or even fear, but only a calm defiance.

From time to time, Deke locked eyes with the Japanese sergeant he had traded threatening glances with during the negotiation phase. Again, the Jap kept giving him what he must have thought was a mean-eyed scowl. Deke wasn't impressed.

You don't know the half of it, fella, he thought. His finger itched on the trigger, and he was more than eager to simply take out the Jap, but that wasn't going to be possible under the circumstances. For now, they would just have to put up with him.

The group marched for nearly an hour across the city. The distance they covered wasn't impressive, because the condition of the city streets made for slow going. In a few places, the Japanese had to march around obstacles rather than pick their way through. Once or twice, the rubble from collapsed buildings completely blocked the wall like a rockslide in the mountains back home. Maneuvering around it all took extra time.

Meanwhile, artillery boomed and echoed off the barren walls of the remaining intact buildings that still lined the streets. Rifles cracked and flamethrowers vomited fire into basements and dugouts, flushing out any hidden Japanese defenders. Those who fled the flames were instantly shot, and those who stayed were burned alive. Of all the weapons of war wielded by the soldiers, the flamethrower was the most horrible, a nightmare as much as it was a weapon. The sickly-sweet smell of roasted flesh drifted on the afternoon breeze. Once smelled, that odor could never be forgotten.

Tanigawa's unit somehow managed to ignore the fate of their comrades and kept moving. Their destination soon became clear as the old walls of Intramuros came into sight.

"I'll be damned," Honcho muttered. "So that's where they're headed. Rumor has it that every Japanese soldier left in the city is holing up in there to make a last stand."

"Looks like these boys want to join them," Deke agreed.

Intramuros was the original walled city of Manila, walled like a medieval European city against whatever threats the surrounding countryside and seas posed. In the distant past, there had been raids by Muslim pirates against the Spanish and, of course, the constant threat of insurrection by the Filipinos themselves, who didn't always appreciate being under the Spanish bootheel. On occasion, a warlord had risen up and found his forces broken against those thick walls.

As Honcho had stated, this walled city was where the remaining Japanese in Manila had decided to make their stand. Not only was this the oldest quarter of the city, but it was basically a fortress in its own right, offering cover for house-to-house and street-to-street fighting, where the defenders would enjoy a distinct advantage. Every inch of ground would be hard-fought inside the walled city.

There were several gates into the city. Once they reached one of these gates, the Japanese called a halt. Major Tanigawa detached himself from his men long enough to approach his escort. He was still carrying his double rifle. The expensive hunting weapon with its ornate filigree and finely checked stock looked out of place in the rough surroundings, considering that most other weapons were dull, battered, and scratched. In comparison, the submachine gun that Sergeant Inaba carried appeared completely utilitarian, to the point that it looked as if it had been welded together out of scrap metal. But Deke had seen those Type 100 submachine guns in action and knew that a quick burst could practically cut a man in half. The weapon was just as brutal as it looked.

"This is our destination," Tanigawa announced. "We will join our comrades here."

"That's as far as we go, then," Steele said. "We'll take those prisoners off your hands now."

Tanigawa did not reply but shouted an order in Japanese. His men began to move through the gate, still surrounding the prisoners. He still had not acknowledged the lieutenant's comment regarding the prisoners.

"Hey!" Honcho yelled. "What the hell is going on here?"

Tanigawa continued to ignore him as his men trooped inside the old city.

Deke and Philly raised their rifles, but Lieutenant Steele shouted, "Hold your fire! You'll hit one of the hostages. Maybe the bastards will release them once they're inside the city walls."

Deke did not lower his rifle. He had Tanigawa in his sights and his finger on the trigger. All that he needed to do was put slightly more pressure on the trigger—

"Deke, do not fire that rifle!" Honcho shouted. "You'll get every last hostage killed."

"I ain't gonna hit anybody but that Jap officer," he muttered around the rifle stock, fully confident of where his bullet would go. He didn't take his finger off the trigger.

"Do not fire. That's an order!"

Slowly, Deke lowered his rifle, watching as the Japanese got farther away, becoming smaller targets. The snipers' opportunity had passed.

Honcho's hope that the Japanese would release the hostages at this point turned out to be wishful thinking. Even with their weapons trained on the Japanese, there was nothing they could do except watch in anger and frustration as the enemy troops moved inside. Suddenly the neat ranks of Japanese fell apart as the men at the back of the column spun around and sprayed fire at Patrol Easy and the Filipinos.

Deke noticed how that damn Inaba stood in the middle of the pack of Japanese, so close that Deke could see the maniacal grin on his face as the man hosed down everything in sight with his submachine gun. Deke and the others hit the deck, dodging bullets. Deke and the others put their rifles to their shoulders, ready to return fire. They hesitated, fearful of hitting the hostages. Meanwhile, short bursts from Inaba's weapon kept them pinned down. Deke pressed his face into the dirt and dust, his mouth filling with grit as the fat slugs ricocheted around him.

"Hold your fire! Hold your fire!" Honcho shouted. "You'll hit the prisoners!"

The lieutenant wasn't the only one yelling. They heard the boy give a heartrending shout: "Papa!"

But Big Mike was likely too far away to hear and too close to the enemy gunfire. They had a final glimpse of his tall figure before he and the other hostages were spirited away at muzzle-point.

Helplessly, they had no choice but to watch while the Japanese slipped away into the city, taking the hostages with them. The enemy fire slackened and Deke straightened up, keeping the rifle to his shoulder, hoping for at least a parting shot, but no good target presented itself.

He lowered the rifle and spat some of the grit from his mouth into the dirt.

"Dammit all. Now what?" Honcho wondered, clenching and unclenching his fists in helpless anger.

The lieutenant seemed to be thinking out loud, but Deke went ahead and answered.

"We go after those lying bastards, that's what," Deke said.

PART THREE

CHAPTER SEVENTEEN

IN THE RUINS of Intramuros at the heart of the old colonial city, the final battle for Manila began. Most of the Americans knew that it was only a matter of time before they ground the enemy into defeat. However, the lives of the hostages now hung in the balance.

Like the others, Deke had watched with anger and disbelief as the Japanese disappeared into the ruins, using their human shields to keep them safe.

"What a bunch of yellow-bellied cowards," he said. "They're hiding behind prisoners, including a bunch of damn women."

"They're Nips," Philly pointed out. "What else do you expect?"

Deke hawked up some of the dust that had been collecting at the back of his throat and spat. His own saliva tasted like bitter bile. In situations like this, one of the best things he could think to do was to shoot something. His gray eyes flashing, he looked around for a target. He didn't see anything stirring among the rubble, which only added to his frustration.

Somewhere in the surrounding walled ruins, the Japanese

were ready to make their last stand. While Patrol Easy was mainly focused on liberating the hostages that Major Tanigawa had taken, they would face more challenges. It wasn't just Major Tanigawa and his band, but several thousand die-hard Japanese soldiers that he had joined for this final struggle.

The simplest approach would have been to shell Intramuros into rubble, indiscriminately destroying every building in sight. However, the artillery units had been informed that there were American hostages within those walls. Lieutenant Steele and Patrol Easy were being given a very narrow window to find those hostages before the shells came raining down again.

Honcho wasn't sure there would be enough time. He went in search of the artillery commander to beg him to hold off long enough to give Patrol Easy a chance to do things their way.

"Dammit, I'll give you until lunchtime tomorrow," the unhappy colonel grumped when Lieutenant Steele explained the situation. He chomped on a cigar and glared at the lieutenant as if holding off on an artillery barrage was a personal affront.

"Sir, that's just not enough time. Hell, we don't even know where the Japanese have taken these hostages."

The colonel did not look sold on the idea, especially when it was coming from a mere lieutenant, so Captain Oatmire spoke up. His uniform was still clean enough that he was obviously not a combat soldier. He introduced himself as MacArthur's liaison, which was something of a stretch. Still, the fact that he had come from headquarters gave his words extra weight in this situation. What he lacked in rank he hoped to make up for with clout. "Colonel, I have direct orders from General MacArthur to get those hostages to safety."

Honcho gave him a sideways look. He knew that what Oatmire was saying wasn't entirely true, but the colonel seemed to buy it hook, line, and sinker. "All right, I'll give you a few more hours. Dammit, I'm not happy about it. I won't have those Nips sneaking away again. If that's not good enough for MacArthur, then by gum he'll have to come down here and tell me in person."

"Thank you, sir," Oatmire said.

As they walked away, Honcho said, "That went better than I expected. If I didn't know better, I would have believed you when you brought up that bit about MacArthur."

"I'm pretty sure you're not gonna go running to headquarters and tell them any different. Anyhow, believe me when I say that the last thing any career-minded officer wants to do is get on MacArthur's bad side."

"It seems to me maybe that's just what you did, to get sent out here."

"Come to think of it, you might be on to something."

They returned to find Patrol Easy and the Filipino snipers waiting for them, plus the boy that had somehow latched on to them. Steele had mixed emotions about dragging the boy into this mess, but they were too deep into the city to send him home. Considering that the place was a war zone, he would never make it home.

The lieutenant looked around at the faces, which were tired and dusty. Hell, when was the last time that any of them had washed, slept, or eaten something that hadn't come out of a ration can?

Even Deke, who was as lean as a locust fence post and usually took about as much abuse as one of those weathered posts without complaining, looked a bit gray around the edges. They would all have to get some decent sleep tonight, if the enemy let them.

To Honcho's surprise, he saw that Deke wasn't constantly scanning the surroundings, as he was wont to do. For a change, he was in a halting conversation with Juana. Then again, the Filipino girl was hardly a talker herself. They both knew just a few words of the other's language. However, she seemed to understand Deacon Cole well enough.

Realization dawned on the lieutenant. Deke and Juana? He always counted on Deke to be as tightly strung as the short strings at the top of a guitar neck, a crack shot and cold-blooded hillbilly killer with a chip on his shoulder *because* he was a dirt-poor hillbilly farm boy, and an ugly, scarred one at that. Deke played one note, like constantly plucking that tight guitar string all the time. But maybe there was another side of him, after all. A rare smile crossed the lieutenant's face. *Well, I'll be damned.* To be fair, he should have seen this coming. If you put a red-blooded man and a woman together, something like that was bound to happen, even in the middle of a war.

He found himself facing the dilemma of many officers in that he loved these grimy goddamned men, had even come to respect and appreciate the Filipino fighters, but he had no choice but to order them back into the meat grinder of battle. Their work here was far from done and the clock was ticking. The ruins of Intramuros beckoned, possibly waiting to swallow them whole.

"Now what, Honcho?" Philly wondered.

"Now we go after the bastards and free those hostages, that's what. Let's move out."

* * *

THE CHASE BEGAN. This old, central heart of the city literally existed within walls entered through several gates interspersed along those walls. The gate that Patrol Easy entered through now was called the Gate of Saint James. Deke thought the gate was a wonder, unlike anything he had seen before, intricately carved in stone, featuring a warlike sculpture that intrigued him.

He couldn't have known that was an image of Santiago Matamoros, or Saint James the Moor-killer—patron saint of Old

Spain. He was depicted crushing Muslims, traditional enemies of the Spanish Catholics, under his horse's hooves. Above it all presided the royal seal of Spain. There was certainly no ambiguity here. This gate and stone carving were a projection of long-ago colonial power. The weathered carvings seemed so ancient and foreign, however, that any meaning was lost on the average American soldier.

If the soldiers hadn't been so tired or more given to consider the philosophical nature of things, rather than trying simply to avoid getting shot, they might have reflected on how history simply repeated itself, war and violence being the common denominator. Like Mark Twain once said, history might not repeat itself, but it often rhymes.

* * *

THEY WEREN'T the only ones preparing to enter the city. Ahead of them, a rumbling Sherman tank bulled its way through the rubble. When it couldn't go around the chunks of rock and scattered timbers, or even a twisted bicycle or two, it stubbornly went right over top of them. The presence of a tank always made foot soldiers feel better, like a big brother backing you up with a baseball bat.

"We'll let those boys go first," Steele said, referring to the tank. "If there's a welcoming party, I'd rather have a tank crash it than us."

"Honcho, I like how you think," Philly replied. "Maybe those boys can track down those Japs for us?"

"Don't push it, Philly."

Ahead of them, the sturdy Sherman tank squeezed through the gate in the walled city, its steel flanks nearly scraping the stone. Not so much as a single rifle shot greeted its arrival.

The question was, Where had the Japanese gone? They had

last seen Major Tanigawa and his men slipping away through the city before being forced to temporarily retreat. Deke was reminded of rats scurrying to hide when the door of a corncrib back home was flung open. Unfortunately, the rats in this case were herding prisoners. Both the Japanese and their hostages had simply melted into the landscape.

The tank and the GIs parted company, with the tank having to keep to the more open areas of the streets so that it could navigate between the piles of rubble. Patrol Easy struck out in the direction where they had last seen Tanigawa's contingent. There was no sign of them anywhere. How could they have disappeared so quickly?

It was Danilo who spotted it, just when they were feeling lost. A Red Cross nurse's cap hung from the branch of a shattered street tree. This was the best kind of breadcrumb that they could have hoped for. In fact, Deke guessed that one of those brave nurses had done this on purpose, leaving them a sign to follow.

"Aqui!" Danilo shouted.

The Filipino guide raced ahead, Deke and Philly trotting after him like hunting dogs with a whiff of the quarry in their noses. Danilo was as tough as monkey meat left to dry in the sun. However, Danilo was such a creature of the mountains and jungle that he looked out of place in the ruined city. But he was adapting, as they all were. Manila was just a stone and concrete jungle, after all.

They were reminded of this fact as they picked their way cautiously through the ruins. The shelling that had already taken place had left the city a mess. Deke moved down what must have once been a street, with the tall stone facade of a building to his right. Each block of stone must have weighed hundreds of pounds, all of it joined together with thick layers of mortar. No wonder the building still stood when the shelling had ripped its surroundings asunder.

If the street had once been paved, it was hard to tell because the surface of asphalt and cobblestones now resembled a freshly plowed field. Deke was reminded of the fact that he sure as hell didn't want to be here when the big guns resumed firing.

The sun was still up, casting long shadows across the rubble. Although the artillery barrage had been suspended for now, much of this inner city had already been severely damaged by shelling and aerial bombardment.

He walked under an overhang of corrugated metal with holes punched through it by shrapnel. Deke had a passing thought that he hoped the flyboys had also gotten the message to hold off—the last thing they needed were bombs falling around their ears.

It was shadowy under there, but the shrapnel holes let daylight filter in. To his left, where the plowed street was located, more tangles of sheet metal clogged the area. The big, corrugated sheets lay every which way, resembling metallic leaves blown into piles by storm winds. The whole mess smelled of burned metal, charred wood, cordite, and unpleasant whiffs of hidden corpses rotting in the warmth.

Deke kept his eyes peeled because there were so many potential hiding places for the enemy. It was the perfect environment for an ambush if Tanigawa's men intended to slow them down—or wipe them out. He had the unsettling thought that one hidden Jap with a machine gun or a grenade could have cut them all down, especially if he was willing to die himself in the process. That never seemed to be an issue with the Japanese.

"Easy, easy," he called to Danilo. He struggled to summon a word from his limited Spanish vocabulary. *"Cuidado."*

But the tough guerrilla guide was too intent on pursuit to listen. Deke cursed under his breath and hurried after him.

Leaving the tunnel of corrugated sheets behind, they emerged into an open area that appeared to be a city square. That's when they caught their first glimpse of Tanigawa's group.

Danilo whooped and fired a shot, which set the events that followed in motion.

Although they were strung out, the problem was that Tanigawa had nearly one hundred men with him, each determined to die like the good little samurai they imagined themselves to be. Several still herded the prisoners along with bayonets. As soon as Danilo fired, a handful of Japanese soldiers turned to fight a rearguard action, meeting their pursuers with gunfire. Deke realized that they'd been foolhardy and had badly overreached. They were so outnumbered that if the Japanese had decided to fight in force, they might easily have wiped out their pursuers. To make matters worse, Patrol Easy was basically moving in a straight line because they had all been so eager to follow Danilo.

"Spread out, spread out!" Lieutenant Steele managed to shout, right before the deep boom of his 12-gauge shotgun echoed between the buildings.

The Japanese returned fire, bullets whining and ricocheting off the rocks and rubble. Up ahead, the main force of the Japanese kept moving. Tanigawa seemed to have a destination in mind.

Deke crouched behind a stone block—not a moment too soon, it turned out, as a bullet struck the stone and sent chips flying. The enemy's smaller-caliber Arisaka rifles had a sharper, higher-pitched report, making the shots from their side sound like a crackling fire.

Briefly, he looked around to check the position of the others. Honcho was not far behind, in the process of shoving the boy's head down. The stupid kid had apparently been curious to see what all the shooting was about.

Philly crouched right behind him, sharing the stone block for cover. But where was Juana? He didn't see her right away and felt a momentary pang of concern, right up until he glimpsed her taking cover behind a tangled pile of corrugated metal sheets. He checked himself, wondering why he cared so damn much. But now wasn't the time to ponder that.

"Ready?" he asked Philly. "I'll shoot right, you shoot left."

"Yeah."

"One, two, three!"

Both men popped up, shooting at the Japanese. They got off two rounds each, working the bolt in between. Lucky for them, the enemy troops also had bolt-action rifles. Deke squeezed off a third shot at a Japanese who was turning his rifle in their direction.

"Got one," Philly said. "You?"

"One, maybe two."

But they hadn't gotten all the Japanese, who were soon returning fire. More bullets hit the stone that they were sheltering behind. Lucky for them, it would have taken an artillery shell to get through that block. Off to one side, Honcho's shotgun boomed again.

"They're falling back," Honcho shouted. "Let's go!"

They had taken out some of the rear guard, but more peeled away to replace their fallen comrades, and in greater numbers. The sniper squad was at a disadvantage because they relied on precision rather than firepower. Undeterred, the Americans pressed forward as best as they could, firing, advancing a few feet, taking cover, then doing it all over again. Deke shot a Japanese, whose arms flung wide as dramatically as a dead man in a movie. Two more took his place.

Clearly Major Tanigawa was prepared to fight a battle of attrition and didn't care about the losses of his own men if he could slow down his pursuers.

What transpired was a running battle through the ruined

city streets. The Americans continued to advance, but it was slow going.

"Look out!" Yoshio warned.

He had spotted something to one side of their route through this no-man's-land. One of the Japanese soldiers they had shot wasn't quite dead. He lay wedged between two chunks of concrete, grasping a grenade to his chest.

Yoshio shouted something in Japanese at the soldier, probably encouraging him to give up. But by now Yoshio should have known that surrender was not the Japanese way.

I guess he's got to try, Deke thought. Even though Yoshio was clearly wasting his breath.

It wasn't clear whether the wounded enemy soldier intended to blow himself up or throw the grenade at the nearest American. Deke didn't give him a chance to make up his mind. He squeezed the trigger and put another bullet in him. The body twisted with death throes and then the grenade went off, the noise ringing in Deke's ears. Some wet gore spattered on the rocks and on his trousers.

Philly swore and wiped at his face, which had a splash of blood across it.

"You all right?" Deke asked him.

"Not mine," he said, wiping his lips with the back of a grimy hand. He spat. "Dammit, I've got some of that Jap's blood in my mouth. I hope to hell he wasn't diseased."

They moved on, stepping around the dead soldier's mangled body. Deke didn't give a second thought to shooting him—it had been them or the Jap.

"Keep after them," Honcho shouted, then ran ahead, outpacing even Danilo, who seemed to have a kind of death wish, evidently determined to be the first to reach the Japanese column. He had found a wounded Japanese soldier among the rubble and had finished him with a quick swipe of his wickedly sharp bolo knife.

It was becoming clear that the Japanese were making for a large building across the square. It looked like something official, like one of the government buildings that Deke had seen on his visit to Washington, DC, before shipping out. Neoclassical was not in Deke's vocabulary, but that was the architectural style that they were looking at. There were elements of Rome in there, and Greece, with some Spanish colonial mixed in. The solid stone building was a brooding presence over the rubble-strewn square.

The formidable building would make a good fortress. The Japanese were making a beeline right for it.

"That's the legislative building," Honcho explained. Despite the quick pace, he hardly sounded winded. "The heart of the Filipino government—at least until the Japanese came along."

The Japanese reached the broad stone steps and surged between the tall pillars. Deke caught a glimpse of the red-haired American, who was looking back, as if still hopeful of rescue. Then he was gone, forced within the shadowed entrance with the other prisoners.

It turned out that Tanigawa's men were not the first ones there. Rather, they were joining Japanese forces already in position. Emphasizing this fact, a Nambu machine gun opened fire from the rooftop, tracer rounds suddenly burning even brighter than the scorching sun.

"Down, dammit, everybody down!" Honcho shouted.

More fire poured at them, every window seemingly occupied by a Japanese soldier with a rifle. It was becoming clear that the Japanese had let them approach this close so that they would enter the killing field.

Honcho fired his shotgun, but it was only adding to the noise, the 12-gauge useless at this range. More machine-gun fire swept around the Americans and Filipinos. Entire hunks of stone went flying, and the whine of ricocheting bullets filled the air. Improbably, an alley cat had been mousing in that no-man's-land and streaked away, leaving the humans to their fate.

Patrol Easy got down low in the rubble, dodging the enemy bullets by some miracle. Their luck wasn't going to last long, however. The Japanese machine gun was giving them the worst of it.

"Deke!" Honcho shouted.

Deke knew just what to do. He brought the rifle to his shoulder, resting his arms over a chunk of what had once been a building. A bullet struck the stone, but he ignored it. He could just see the tops of the machine gunners' helmets above the parapet of the legislative building.

That Nambu was spitting bullets and tracer rounds like a fire-breathing dragon. But all that Deke needed was one bullet. Well, maybe two.

He put his crosshairs on one of those helmets and fired, feeling the satisfying punch of the powerful rifle against his shoulder. The .30-06 round split the top of the Jap's head like an ax blade pops apart a chunk of firewood. He slumped over the gun, blood sizzling on the hot barrel. The second machine gunner did his duty, pushing aside his dead comrade and getting behind the Nambu. Deke lined up the sights again, and the Jap thought his last thought before the top of his head was likewise blown off.

Now that the machine gun had blessedly fallen silent, the GIs and Filipinos ran for better cover than that offered by the rubble. Japanese bullets nagged at them, but the soldiers weaved as they ran, managing to dodge the gunfire.

They reached the shelter of a stone building overlooking the square.

Panting, Philly looked back at the heavily defended legislative building and said, "That's gonna be a tough nut to crack."

Deke spat out a mouthful of dust. "That ain't no nut, city boy. That's a damn cannonball. Good luck cracking that."

Nearby Honcho was looking around with concern. "Anybody see where that boy got to?"

"Last time I saw him, he was hightailing it over here with the rest of us," Rodeo said.

"Well, I sure as hell don't see him," Honcho said. He raised his voice and called, "Roddy, where the hell are you?"

They all looked back toward the no-man's-land of the city square that they had just navigated, but the boy was nowhere in sight.

CHAPTER EIGHTEEN

RUNNING FOR HIS LIFE, Roddy made a fateful last-minute decision not to stick with the Americans. They seemed intent on getting away from the Japanese, running for cover, which seemed to Roddy to be completely the wrong direction. They should have been running *toward* where the prisoners were being held. Thanks to the immortal perspective of youth, he didn't think that any of the bullets were meant for *him*. His only thought was *I've got to get my father back*. He hadn't figured out how he was going to do that but had acted on impulse. He now felt as if the whole weight of rescuing his father had fallen on his thin, young shoulders.

He veered left, hooking back toward the hulking legislative building. The storm of bullets followed the soldiers but left Roddy alone, as if he had just managed to swim out of a riptide.

He was small enough that the Japanese didn't see him making his way through the rubble. That was what saved him in the end. He paused, hiding, and studied the landscape around him to pick out a path to take. Even his young mind recognized that a frontal attack on the huge building wasn't going to work.

Instead, there had to be a back way, or a side way. It didn't really take a military genius to understand the situation. After all, young boys knew about such things from their own games of chase and war. You outsmarted your enemy by finding their weak point, which was just what he set out to do.

Although his mind vaguely registered the fact, he didn't realize just how much danger he was in. At any moment a Japanese sniper might spot him. The machine gun atop the building might open fire again once its crew had been replaced. His short life might be over in an instant.

But he was in too deep to go back, entirely on his own in this no-man's-land of a battleground. He had no choice but to stick with the plan that he had set for himself.

Little did young Roddy know that he was on a collision course with the Japanese.

* * *

BACK IN THE shadows of the bank building, Lieutenant Steele announced that they were going to send out a search party for the boy. In their hearts, Patrol Easy knew it was the right thing to do, but that didn't mean they were happy about it.

"Let's face it, that dumb kid is probably dead," Philly pointed out. "He had no business being with us in the first place."

Deke glanced at Juana, who was normally stoic. He knew that, like Honcho, she had grown fond of the boy in the short time that he had been part of their patrol. She looked stricken at Philly's words.

"Shut up, Philly," Deke muttered out of the corner of his mouth.

Philly looked as if he wanted to say more, but he glanced at Deke and went quiet.

"Look, fellas, I don't like this any better than you do,"

Honcho explained. "But I don't like the idea of leaving that boy out there if there's any chance he's still alive. What are we going to do, get his father away from those Japs and then break the news to him that we got his son killed?"

It was a valid point.

In the end, Deke and Philly volunteered to look for the boy.

"I thought you said the boy was as good as dead?" Rodeo said.

"If Deke wants to go look for him, that's good enough for me," Philly said. "Besides, somebody's got to keep him from getting his crazy cracker ass shot off."

Rodeo wasn't convinced. "Are you sure it's not the other way around? Seems to me that most of the time Deke is the one saving *you*."

Philly did his best to look indignant. "Are you being serious right now?"

Juana wanted to go along to help look for the boy. Deke's first instinct was to say no, but then he thought better of it. He realized that he somehow felt protective of Juana. He wondered where in the hell that feeling had come from. She was as good of a soldier as any of them. Maybe even better than most. Juana was tough, reminding him of his sister, Sadie. What would Sadie have said if Deke had tried to keep her from doing something because he thought it was too dangerous? Hell, she would have belted him in the gut, that was what. He was sure that Sadie and Juana were cut from the same cloth.

Grinning at Juana, he nodded. "We'll take all the help we can get with the Japs so close," he said.

Deke glanced at Danilo, but their Filipino guide didn't meet his eyes. This was uncharacteristic of Danilo, who was usually up for anything. However, it was clear that the city unsettled him. Danilo preferred the mountains and jungle to the dusty rubble and the stinking burned wreckage of vehicles and buildings. His element was the natural world, not these choked city streets. Deke knew just how he felt, but a soldier couldn't always choose his ground. Besides, how terrifying it must have been for that boy to be out there on his own. If he was out there, Deke knew that he had to at least try to get him back.

Juana pointed them in the right direction. "This way," she said. As it turned out, she had been one of the last to see the boy, just when he had taken off on his own. Fortunately, the machine gun on top of the legislative building remained silent. Even the snipers they had spotted before in the windows seemed to be giving them a break.

Then again, nobody thought this was going to be easy. There was a lot of ground to cover if they wanted to find the boy. Deke just hoped that the boy wasn't already dead.

* * *

WHAT THE SEARCH PARTY—AND Roddy—couldn't have known was that at that very moment, the Japanese inside the legislative building were preparing a patrol led by Sergeant Inaba to counter any attacks on their flanks or rear—the exact approach routes that the boy's mind had conjured. Ideally, Inaba would be able to leave pairs of soldiers in the outlying rubble as forward observers, or the equivalent of outposts, to detect any approaching threats.

Sergeant Inaba carried his submachine gun again, while one of his men carried an Arisaka rifle with a telescopic sight. Inaba was hoping against hope that his sniper would have a chance to use it against the American sharpshooters. Such was his confidence in the superior abilities of Japanese troops that he had no doubts that his sniper would prove to be the better shot. He took twelve experienced soldiers with him, more than enough to handle any enemy patrols they encountered.

"Move!" he admonished his men. *"Ugoku!"*

Major Tanigawa stood nearby, looking on with approval as Sergeant Inaba organized his men. The major's samurai sword hung from his belt, and he held his prized double rifle in his hands. Although it was not a military weapon, it was perfect for this kind of urban fighting, able to get off two quick shots that would pack quite a wallop, considering that he was using a cartridge designed for big game.

"I feel like I am about to go on a hunting trip!" he said, a rare grin touching his face.

Inaba nodded at his superior officer, then led his patrol into the smashed ruins surrounding the building where the Japanese were planning to make their last stand.

The battle had reached the point where it went without saying that they didn't plan on taking any additional prisoners, whether they were American GIs, civilians, or boys. As for the hostages they had taken, they were still alive, but at a command from Major Tanigawa, that would no longer be the case.

Inaba looked forward to that moment.

"We will split up," the major said. "That way, we will cover more ground. Take some of the men and make sure that the *gaijin* are not hiding in the rubble or the alleys on the far side of the square. If you run into trouble, I will bring up the rest of the patrol."

"Hai," Inaba said, and began to lead his men forward, finger on the trigger, ready to shoot anything that moved.

* * *

NOT THAT FAR AWAY, Roddy picked his way through the ruined square. He wore gray dungarees and a red-and-white-striped shirt, which hardly helped him blend into the strewn rubble and debris. He passed wrecked vehicles and a handful of bodies. He knew better now than to look at them too much, but he couldn't resist staring with fascination at the bodies.

Most were dead Filipinos, although a few were Japanese. The clothes of the dead Filipinos were shredded and sometimes pulled open as if they had clawed at themselves in pain. It was hard to know how they had died. Some of the bodies of the women were bloody in places that his innocent mind found hard to fathom. One thing for certain, whether the dead were Filipino or Japanese, the buzzing flies had found them all. As for the smell—he walked away quickly, gagging. He didn't know it then, but it was an odor that he would never be able to forget. He hoped that he wouldn't end up the same way. It seemed a horrible way to be dead, lying out here in the open.

He felt sorry for them all, mostly for the kind and friendly Filipino people, but also a little for the dead Japanese. There had been at least a few Japanese soldiers during the occupation who had been easygoing enough, even kind, at least toward harmless kids. You could never paint every Japanese soldier with the same brush. Roddy was still of a tender age, and like the innocent boy that he was, he had listened in church enough to believe that there was good in all people, at least deep down. He didn't yet know that this wasn't true. In particular, the Japanese occupiers overall had shown that they were capable of cruelty in ways that were hard to understand.

* * *

EVEN THOUGH HIS father had been imprisoned, his family had remained relatively insulated from the worst that the Japanese had to offer. From time to time, an officer and a couple of soldiers appeared at their door, politely asking the names of all who lived there, including their two servants. Roddy hadn't felt much fear or anger toward the Japanese, but really just boyish curiosity, being more interested in the rifles that the soldiers carried and the pistol on the officer's hip. Any boy found weapons fascinating. The Japanese had been polite rather than threatening. The Japanese soldiers had never given them any trouble after his mother provided that information, made courteous apologies, and quickly left.

But times hadn't always been easy, and they had steadily gotten worse. They were sometimes allowed to visit their father at the university compound, and Roddy recalled how his father had asked his mother what had become of her diamond stud earrings.

"My earrings?" she'd said vaguely, touching her bare ears as if in surprise, when they all knew very well that she never went anywhere without them.

"The ones I bought for you in Brisbane before the war," he'd said, looking at her with sad eyes, as if he had already guessed the truth.

Tearfully, his mother had admitted that she had traded them for a two-pound can of dried milk. Roddy hadn't had any idea that the food he and his brothers were eating had been so dearly bought. Years later, Roddy would wonder what else his mother had given up to provide for and shelter her family. One by one, their family heirlooms and the pretty objects his mother had collected had quietly disappeared.

More than once, his mother had pointed out that they were lucky because they still had at least *some* money. Anyone with money in American banks—the Philippines was a US territory, after all—had no access to their saving because the banks had been closed, their assets possibly gone forever. However, their family connections had meant that his father had ended up keeping their money in a Filipino bank managed by one of his mother's distant relatives. There just hadn't been much of it, considering that his father had been unable to conduct any business after the Japanese arrived.

Despite the fact that his mother did what she could to insulate her children from the realities of war, the threat of the Japanese was always there, and sometimes Roddy had tempted fate. There was nothing playful about the Japanese, and their patience with *gaijin* children went only so far.

He recalled seeing a truckload of American and Australian POWs stopping in his neighborhood on its way through the city. This in itself was unusual, but it was a hint that Allied forces must be slowly closing in on Manila, if there were now new prisoners being taken or old ones being moved out of the way of advancing forces.

One of Roddy's pretty young neighbors had passed by, a Filipino girl in her late teens or early twenties, and one of the Australians had tipped his hat to her in a gallant gesture. The Japanese had responded by using a rifle butt to knock him unconscious. Roddy and his friends did their best not to react, because the Japanese guards were watching them and would have beaten them if they showed any sympathy for the poor prisoner.

Another time, he and his friends had been playing spy by lingering outside the local Japanese headquarters and keeping track of how many vehicles came and went, writing down the numbers in a little notebook. The information didn't have any point or use. The boys were just playing at being spies, but if they'd been caught gathering that information, the Japanese surely would have killed them without mercy.

One of the stranger things that the Japanese had done was to seize every toy pistol that they could find. Playing cowboys and Indians was a favorite game, and a toy six-shooter was a boy's prized possession. It turned out that the toy guns had also become popular with Filipino guerrillas and even thugs, who used them against unsuspecting Japanese soldiers who couldn't tell the difference between a toy gun and the real thing. Owning a toy gun became a very serious crime.

Roddy had come to realize that there was nobody prouder than a Japanese soldier, men who considered themselves superior to any of the civilians. They had been pumped up by their own propaganda. They certainly didn't look superior to Roddy, especially compared to his tall father. The Japanese were short, often bowlegged, and many wore thick eyeglasses. But they were the ones with the guns, which was all that it took to make them superior.

In the distance, he heard a Japanese shout, which made his mind snap back to the present. He had better pay attention if he wanted to help his father and not get caught.

Working around toward the rear of the legislative building, he found himself in a kind of alley at the back of the structure. The alley was now choked with debris, including chunks of stone and broken tree limbs, from the various bombardments that Intramuros had already suffered. There were long rows of trash cans and piled boxes, indicating that the alley would have been used by the service staff who came and went through the back rather than the formal front entrance, or for taking deliveries.

On the other side of the alley stood a stone wall and beyond that another tall building, creating a kind of manmade canyon. The only way in or out was at the ends of the alley. It was a promising way into the building, and as far as Roddy could tell, it wasn't guarded. He felt his spirits soar at his good luck, wondering if he had so easily found a way into the building, but he stayed cautious, creeping forward.

His hopes were soon dashed. Peering above a chunk of stone, he spotted the Japanese patrol moving toward him. He counted a dozen of them, all with rifles, looking this way and that. Apparently they had recognized the alley as a weak point and were on the lookout for any interlopers.

With a start, Roddy recognized their leader as the sergeant who had been at the university when the hostages were brought out—his father among them. Instinctively, he knew that this man was trouble. He had a cruel hatchet-like face with a perpetually angry expression.

There was no way that Roddy could avoid the Japanese patrol if he stayed where he was. He looked around for someplace to hide, where he might be able to tuck himself into the rubble, but unless he could shrink himself to the size of a mouse, he was out of luck. He looked again at the Japanese. They were close enough now that if he made a run for it, they might spot him. What should he do? He ducked down again, trying to make up his mind, feeling his heart hammering. He wished that he was older, bigger, stronger, and that he had a rifle like the GIs. He thought of the lieutenant with his shotgun and that soldier with the scar—either one of them could have licked these Japs in a minute.

But Roddy had only himself.

What would his father do in this situation? His father would fight back, that was what.

Roddy remembered one time when he had gotten into a fight with an older boy who had been picking on one of his friends. He had come home with a torn shirt and a bloody nose, having gotten the worst end of things. But the older boy had gotten the message that Roddy and his friends weren't worth picking on. He had fully expected to get in trouble for fighting. His tall, red-haired father had towered over him, scowling down at Roddy.

Tears of anger and frustration that he'd held back in the wake of the actual fight had found their way out when recounting events. Roddy had wiped the tears away using the back of a hand with scraped knuckles from an ill-timed punch that had managed to hit a patch of gravel instead of the bully's face when

Roddy had briefly gotten the upper hand as the boys grappled on the ground.

His father had heard him out and then put a reassuring hand on his shoulder, saying with a sad smile, "It's all right, son. Sometimes you have to stand up and fight for what's right, even when you know you're going to lose."

Roddy's hand went to his pocket, where he kept one of his most-prized possessions, a barlow knife that had been a Christmas present from his father. He clenched the pocketknife, reassured by its heft, but knowing that it was still a puny weapon. But it was all he had. There wasn't any other choice. The Japanese soldiers were coming closer. He was cornered.

Desperate now, he slowly began to draw the knife from his pocket—

When he felt the touch on his shoulder, he started to jump up and would have cried out if strong hands hadn't pulled him down and clamped over his mouth.

"Whoa now, pardner," a voice whispered in his ear. "We're on the same side."

Roddy turned his head enough to see that it was the sniper with the scar who had grabbed him. Roddy recalled that his name was Deke. Roddy nodded, the sniper nodded back, and the soldier released his grip. Somehow the GI had managed to slip this close to the Japanese without being seen.

"They're coming," Roddy said. "Aren't you going to shoot?"

"There's too many of them," Deke said. "They haven't seen us yet, so what do you say we skedaddle? Do me a favor and try not to get lost this time."

Keeping low, they beat a hasty retreat down the alley. The sniper moved as silently as smoke, and the boy did his best to follow just as quietly. Some distance away, the others were waiting for them. Roddy saw now that it wasn't the whole patrol that had arrived, but only Deke, Philly, and Juana.

"Look what the cat dragged in," Philly said. "I thought for sure that you were dead."

"He doesn't need to hear that right now, Philly," Deke snapped. "Besides, if you haven't noticed, there's a passel of Japs headed our way."

That seemed to get Philly's attention. "Huh, you don't say?"

Sure enough, the Japanese had come back into view, prowling down the length of the alley. Lucky for the GIs, they still hadn't been spotted.

"Think we can take 'em?"

Deke shook his head. Juana didn't look convinced either. "Too many. One of them is Sergeant Inaba. I'd recognize his ugly mug anywhere. As much as I'd like to shoot that son of a bitch, I don't like our chances. We need to get this kid the hell out of here anyhow."

"I'm not afraid of those Japs!" Roddy blurted.

"I like your spirit, kid. But let's see if we avoid getting killed today."

They began to beat a hasty retreat, but they had delayed too long. A shout came from the direction of the alley. They had been spotted. Moments later, a rifle shot rang out. The bullet went too high, but it made an unsettling twang as it split the muggy air. Another bullet shot struck a chunk of concrete and ricocheted with an off-key note not unlike the sound made by plucking a bent saw blade.

"Move it!" Deke shouted, although it wasn't necessary. The four of them quit trying to be stealthy, keeping low and under cover, and started running for all they were worth.

A spray of bullets pattered viciously on the rocky moonscape around them, but nobody slowed down. To Deke's relief, the boy didn't have any trouble keeping up. He was running like a jackrabbit. Deke dodged and weaved, trying to make himself a difficult target, helped in part by the uneven ground. The others did the same.

Juana spun around and fired a shot at the Japanese. Not to be outdone, Deke did the same, but it was like spitting into the wind. The Japanese were running now, shouting encouragement to one another and sounding to Deke's ears like baying hounds with the scent of quarry in their noses.

Thankfully, the bank building loomed into sight. The others sheltering there heard them coming and started firing at the Japanese. One of the soldiers who had been firing a submachine gun dropped, bringing some welcome relief from the storm of gunfire following them.

As the covering fire from the bank building increased, it became clear that the tables had turned. Now it was the Japanese who were in trouble. Another soldier dropped. To Deke's disappointment, it was not Sergeant Inaba who had taken a bullet.

The Japanese stopped their advance and began to fall back, keeping to the cover offered by the rubble.

Deke led the way into the shelter of the building, the boy in tow. He turned to get off a couple of shots at the retreating Japanese, but once again they had scurried away into the rubble just like rats. At this point he couldn't pick out Inaba anyhow. Settling his score with the Japanese sergeant would just have to wait.

Lieutenant Steele was waiting for them. "Good job, you three," he said, then turned his attention on the boy. "Listen up, kid. Don't go wandering off. You need to stick with us. I don't know what happened out there or what you were thinking, but don't let it happen again. Do I make myself clear?"

The boy gulped. "Yes, sir."

"Good." The lieutenant turned to the others. "Now that we

know the Japs are launching patrols from their hidey-hole there, let's see if we can catch a few of them on their way out."

CHAPTER NINETEEN

To call the massive legislative building a hidey-hole was just the sort of understatement that a good GI found humor in. To call it a fortress was more accurate. The tall, brooding building commanded the ruined city square. Though quiet and still, the square was deceptive in that anyone who dared to cross it found himself under the enemy guns. A few desperate civilians tried to get across in hopes of finding safety, but they found themselves at the gates of heaven instead.

Even stray dogs weren't safe—they watched one pick its way across the square. A shot rang out from the Japanese bastion and the dog went down, spasmed, and was still.

"Those sons of bitches shot that dog," Deke said, incredulous. He'd always had a soft spot for dogs, even these strays that seemed to plague Manila. "What the hell is wrong with them?"

"I'd make you a list, but I don't have enough damn paper," Philly grumped. "Besides, maybe we ought to thank that dog. It was a good reminder that if we try to cross that square, the same damn thing will happen to us. The whole damn place is a big damn Japanese shooting gallery."

"Damn," Deke added, just in case Philly hadn't said the word enough times.

The legislative building was far too formidable for Patrol Easy to launch a direct attack on the enemy position. They needed to find a way to take down the enemy forces holed up inside the legislative building without putting themselves in too much danger. Lieutenant Steele was right that if they could catch a few of the Japanese out in the open, away from the cover of the building that the enemy had turned into a fortress, so much the better.

No sooner had they escorted the boy to safety than they set out once again to deal with the Japanese. Keeping to the cover of the buildings that still stood, Patrol Easy worked its way toward the rear of the legislative building, Deke leading them to where they had found the boy and encountered Sergeant Inaba's patrol. With any luck, they might catch the patrol out in the open. This time Deke had more firepower with him, so he hoped that the outcome would be different.

Attempting to stay out of view of the Japanese so as not to lose the element of surprise, they moved away from the square and followed streets one block away. However, he soon grew confused in the back streets that they passed through because they all looked the same. It was odd that he'd never felt lost in the jungles or mountains that they'd fought through so far, but the city was something altogether different.

He wasn't the only one who seemed to feel this way. Even Danilo, who was so adept at navigating the forests of the Philippines, just looked at Deke and shrugged. He appeared as lost as Deke felt.

After taking a wrong turn that led them away from the square, rather than closer to it, Deke had to admit, "This damn city all looks the same to me."

"This way," said Juana, stepping forward to take the lead.

Instead of feeling miffed, Deke had to admit that he felt grateful.

Juana, a city girl who was somewhat familiar with the layout of Intramuros, suggested using the tunnel-like alleys that ran between the buildings. Even the boy seemed to know the way, and at one point he and Juana conferred briefly about which direction to take.

These alleys had been used since the Spanish colonial times. If the brooding stone walls could have spoken, what tales would they have told? No doubt these walls had seen their share of murders, thievery, and liaisons over the centuries. Dark and narrow, the alleys provided a sheltered route that enabled Patrol Easy and the Filipinos to work toward the rear of the legislative building without being seen. Their success depended entirely on the element of surprise.

It was risky, considering that at any moment they might go around a blind corner and run smack-dab into the Japanese, who could be planning to ambush *them*, but it could be their only chance at getting close enough to the building without drawing heavy fire from the enemy defenders within.

Cautiously, they made their way through the dark and rubble-strewn alleys until they reached a point directly behind the legislative building. Like city alleys everywhere, the sides were lined with trash cans, many of them knocked over, their contents not smelling very pleasant in the heat. An alley cat raised its head and glared at them as if considering holding its ground as they approached, then thought better of it and ran down the narrow crack between two buildings, dragging half a fish skeleton with it.

Clumsily, Philly's boot kicked a garbage can lid, making it skitter and clang along the cobblestones.

"Dammit, Philly!" Lieutenant Steele muttered. "Watch where the hell you're going."

If there were any Japanese around, there was a good chance that they had heard that. They all went on high alert, straining to listen. Of course, the city itself was far from silent, with the constant thump of artillery and the crack of small-arms fire, most of it in the distance.

Sure enough, they could hear faint voices and even a few footsteps nearby, the sound of hobnails crunching through gravel or grinding on pavement, indicating that the Japanese were on the move. However, the confusing echoes in the narrow alleys made it hard to tell which direction the Japanese were taking. They were out there, but where?

"I hear them, but where the hell are they?" Philly wondered.

"I reckon they're wondering the same thing about us," Deke whispered harshly. "They sure as hell heard us. Now kindly shut your piehole or they'll find us before we find them."

This was going to be a game of cat and mouse. It was entirely possible that the Japanese had already guessed that the Americans were there. Would Patrol Easy get the drop on them, or would the Japanese turn the tables?

The end of the alley loomed, a partially collapsed brick wall that created a dead end. Cautiously, they looked out over the open ground between the end of the alley and the steps of the legislative building in the distance.

Deke motioned for Juana and Philly to stay put as he climbed the broken wall. He reached his destination—a shattered window near the top level that had been previously boarded up with wooden planks. He quickly pulled out his bowie knife and began to pry them off one by one, doing it as quietly as he could under the circumstances. He was still worried about where that Japanese patrol that they'd heard earlier had gone. He just hoped to hell that they hadn't managed to circle back and were coming down on Patrol Easy through the alley.

He was soon at a point where he could look over the square.

Peering out, he saw several Japanese soldiers standing guard on the upper floor of the building. His finger itched to get on the trigger and take some of them out, maybe wreak a bit of havoc, but what he saw next made him freeze. The Japanese patrol that they had heard was almost directly beneath him, having a smoke break. He could plainly see Inaba, the only one of the bunch who was looking cautiously around them, clearly on high alert.

Deke glanced back at the others, signaling that he had seen something. He quietly made his way back down the crumbling wall to his fellow soldiers and whispered his plan. They would throw a few grenades and hope for the best. There was no way for them to climb the wall quietly enough to bring fire to bear on the Japanese.

And so they did just that. Rodeo had the best arm, so he threw the first grenade, then Philly, and finally Honcho following up with a third grenade.

Three blasts in quick succession followed. *Crump, crump, crump*. The wall didn't do much to muffle the blasts, explosions echoing through the alley and shaking loose bits of mortar from above. The mortar pattered on their helmets, the sound as loud as the inside of a drum. Deke wore the bush hat as usual, so the chunks rained down across the brim, though he scarcely noticed because of the terrible ringing in his ears. Those grenades had packed a wallop, that was for sure.

"Go! Go!" Honcho shouted, the need for any kind of quiet gone, and their group swarmed up the pile of bricks, ready for anything, aware that the Japanese were on the other side.

Taking advantage of all the chaos caused by their grenades, not worried about how much noise he was making, Deke led the charge up the broken wall. As he scanned for movement from their vantage point on top of the ruined wall, Deke looked down and saw just what he had hoped for—the torn bodies of Japanese soldiers on the ground. However, there should have been *more* dead Japanese.

Deke lowered himself down the other side of the wall. Philly was just behind him, and Juana behind *him*. Honcho and Rodeo stayed on the wall, ready to offer covering fire. So far there hadn't been any sign of any surviving Japanese.

Deke darted out from behind cover without giving it a second thought, rifle at the ready. He stepped over one of the dead Japanese, the shrapnel from the grenade having eviscerated the man. He didn't waste time looking, other than to ascertain that the Jap was dead. Deke's eyes went everywhere at once, looking for targets. It seemed as if the grenades had been grouped a little too close together, the shrapnel missing some of the Japanese patrol. There weren't enough bodies, and Inaba wasn't among the dead.

"Where the hell did the rest of them go?" Deke wanted to know. "There were more than three Japs, I can tell you that."

"Look awake, everybody!" Honcho shouted.

They soon got their answer. The dust shifted as if the rubble was coming alive. Sergeant Inaba suddenly appeared. He and two more Japanese had managed to camouflage themselves in the rubble. Armed with his submachine gun, Inaba sprayed bullets at the American snipers. Deke quickly took aim and was about to fire a shot at Inaba's chest to bring an end to this episode, when something stung him in the upper arm, above the elbow. That was what it felt like—a sting, as if a hot, metallic hornet had found him. Somewhere in the back of Deke's mind, he realized that he'd been shot.

He didn't have time to assess how badly he'd been hit—at any rate, his arm still worked, which turned out to be a good thing. He was going to need it. He swung his rifle up, trying to get it into play against the Japanese sergeant.

But he didn't have time. Another danger had appeared.

A figure emerged from behind Sergeant Inaba, looming out of the drifting dust and debris left by the grenade blast. It was Major Tanigawa himself, armed with his double rifle. He was leading a handful of troops toward the fight.

Where the hell had he come from with those other troops? Deke wanted to kick himself for not spotting the major earlier—and those reinforcements.

They were so close that Deke got a glimpse of Tanigawa's eyes, glittering like wet basalt in his dusty face, as the man glared at them from his position in the moonscape of the ruined city square.

Though meant for hunting big game, Tanigawa's rifle was more than adequate for a combat role. Tanigawa's rifle fired twice, the two shots so quick that they were almost one. Near Deke, one of the Filipino snipers cried out and went down.

Just when it seemed like Tanigawa had gained the upper hand with his powerful rifle, Juana appeared out of nowhere and threw a grenade at him. The explosion shook the ground as Tanigawa was thrown off balance. His fancy rifle went flying, and the major fell to his knees before throwing himself onto the ground as more shots whipped over his head.

Taking advantage of this opening, Deke aimed carefully and prepared to fire a shot at Tanigawa. Deke's heart pounded, the sound of gunfire and explosions echoing in his ears. The Japanese were advancing quickly, their relentless attacks threatening to overwhelm the small US patrol. A bullet snapped past his ear, forcing him to flinch. By the time Deke was ready again, Tanigawa was scurrying away with his rifle, getting under cover.

It was hard to say how long the savage fight lasted. Time seemed to slow down as shots were exchanged no more than a few paces apart, stabs of flame from the muzzle flashes cutting through the dust left by the grenade explosions. Another one of the guerrillas fell, but Deke was only vaguely aware of that from the corner of one eye. All his attention was focused on the Japanese.

Bullets ricocheted off walls and debris as fighters on both sides dodged and weaved to avoid being hit, leaping for cover and diving behind chunks of stone or sections of brick still clumped together with mortar. Close as the fighting was, they never reached the point of hand-to-hand combat. They were fighting a brawl; it was the gunfight at the OK Corral all over again, bullets flying, every man for himself.

Deke had a glimpse of Captain Oatmire, helmet gone, sweaty hair plastered to his head, firing his .45 at the Japanese.

Just as quickly as they had appeared out of the dust and smoke, the Japanese faded away to regroup. There were more than before—Deke could see them gathering for a counterattack, more of the enemy clad in their brownish uniforms streaming from the legislative building. Several dead men were similarly clad, but the enemy hadn't gotten the message.

"These Japs just won't quit," Philly complained, taking cover behind a pile of rubble. "It's like they don't care how many men they lose."

"Same old story," Deke replied grimly, aiming and firing again at the distant targets, all the while keeping his eyes open for Tanigawa or Inaba. At that moment they were nowhere to be seen. He was beginning to think that they were more like ghosts or phantoms than men, seeming to appear or disappear at will. "When did the Japanese ever care about that? All they care about is winning at any cost. It doesn't matter how many of them die."

Deke became aware of the pain in his arm and glanced down at the wound, noticing that blood was running down his arm. He didn't find much relief in the fact that it was a trickle rather than a torrent. Along with the pain, an awareness that the blood was leaking out of him hit him hard. A sudden wave of weakness nearly caused him to drop his rifle, and he stumbled.

Philly looked at him with concern. He reached out to steady Deke. "Dammit, you're hit."

"It's nothin'," Deke responded, shrugging off Philly's hand. There was no rear to go to, anyhow, no medics to call for help. His only choice was to keep fighting. He cursed under his breath but pushed through the pain and moved forward with his rifle again.

The brief respite did not last long, no more than a few minutes. The window for retreat narrowed and then closed. More Japanese troops streamed from the legislative building, coming to renew the attack. Deke got off a couple of shots at them, dropping one man and missing another due to his weakened arm, but the enemy troops were multiplying like ants. It was clear that Patrol Easy would be outnumbered.

"There's too many of the bastards!" Philly shouted over the chaotic sound of gunfire. "We need to get out of here."

"Dammit," Deke muttered. He hated to give an inch of ground to the enemy, but he knew that Philly was right.

More Japanese soldiers poured out from the ruins of the buildings, making it clear that they were outnumbered and outgunned. Deke kept shooting, taking down as many enemies as he could, but Philly was right—they couldn't keep this up forever.

Lieutenant Steele seemed to have arrived at the same conclusion. "We need to fall back!" he shouted.

One by one the GIs and Filipino guerrillas began to peel away and return to the alley, which turned out to be their best escape route, giving them cover from the Japanese onslaught. First, they had to pass the bodies of the dead enemy that had been torn by the grenades, then climb the tumbled brick wall, all the while coming under direct enemy fire. Bullet strikes raised puffs of brick dust the color of blood. One of the Filipino fighters was dead, and they left his body behind. Juana and Rodeo were on either side of the wounded Filipino fighter, half carrying and half pushing him up and over the rubble wall.

Soon only the lieutenant and Deke were remaining. The Japanese kept coming, bullets flying at them as the enemy fire increased.

Two of the enemy got close enough to launch their own version of a banzai charge, howling with rage as they screamed toward the two Americans. They were so close that Deke could see how their faces were twisted into contorted, angry masks.

Deke shot one. Beside him, Honcho's 12-gauge boomed and the second attacker flew back as a handful of buckshot hit him.

There were more Japanese coming behind them. Honcho racked another shell into the chamber and fired.

The enemy continued their advance relentlessly, firing indiscriminately. The zip of Japanese lead cut through the air. Deke hunkered down behind debris and tried to steady his breathing as he took aim at an approaching soldier. He squeezed the trigger just as a nearby explosion rocked the ground beneath him. The damn Japs had thrown a grenade.

His shot went wide, the bullet whizzing past the Japanese soldier's head.

Honcho grabbed Deke's shoulder and shoved him toward the wall.

"Deke! We need to get out of here!"

Finally, with a heavy heart, Deke turned and started scrambling up the brick wall. The lieutenant struggled up the half-demolished wall behind him. Deke might have stayed, but he knew that Honcho wouldn't go without him.

At the top of the wall, Philly had taken up a position to offer suppressing fire with his rifle, not that it seemed to be slowing down the Japanese. Juana was up there, too, firing, working her rifle bolt, then firing again.

Deke tried not to feel like a scared rabbit or a kicked dog running with his tail between his legs. The Japanese jeered at them as they fell back, taunting them with shouts of victory.

Deke gritted his teeth and kept moving. People talked about defeat having a taste, something bitter, and they'd be right. He could taste it now, like something he'd bitten into that was spoiled and rotten. He spat. A split second later, a bullet hit the same brick that his spit had struck.

Then he was up and over the wall.

As they regrouped farther away from the Japanese, Lieutenant Steele barked orders for them to establish a new defensive position. They set up behind some partially destroyed walls, using whatever cover they could find in the rubble-strewn streets.

They braced themselves, ready for it, expecting the Japanese to come over the remnants of the wall and pour down into the alley. A grenade flew over the wall, then another, the Japanese returning the earlier favor. The blasts echoed ruthlessly between the alley walls, shrapnel shrieking. By some miracle, nobody was hurt.

But no soldiers followed. For whatever reason, the Japanese had decided to break off the attack. Maybe, in their minds, a handful of Americans just weren't worth the effort. They had bigger fish to fry.

Lieutenant Steele stood up. He had taken shelter behind a miniature landslide that seemed to be made up primarily of broken doors and garbage cans. Something dark, foul-smelling, and wet clung to the knees of his fatigues.

"All right, show's over," he announced. "Let's get the hell out of here and find some shelter for the night. Those Japanese will be on the prowl."

* * *

If the Japanese had broken off their attack against the Americans, it was only because they had easier targets to occupy their attention.

Major Tanigawa and his men moved out, but not before Sergeant Inaba asked, "What about the American soldiers?"

"Never mind the Yanks," Tanigawa said. "If they return, we shall teach them another lesson."

For the Japanese, teaching that lesson had come at a cost. Inaba did not point out that Tanigawa was stepping around the bodies of the men slain by grenades. He had been fortunate in being out of range, although some of his patrol had not shared that good luck.

A few more bodies lay scattered in the rubble, killed in the melee with the Americans. Ultimately, they had been driven off.

Inaba thought that was too bad. He had wanted another crack at the sniper, the one with the scars on his face. But it was not to be. No matter—they had sent the Americans running like beaten dogs.

During the initial American attack, he and Tanigawa had gone back to the legislative building to organize the counterattack, hurling their men at the small American force. By the time that they could rejoin the attack, the Americans had retreated, climbing the wall at the end of what appeared to be an alley running between the larger buildings on this side of the street. Running like the cowards they were.

Major Tanigawa did not seem interested in pursuing the Americans, so Inaba had little choice but to do as he was told. Also, he suspected that the major was correct. The patrol that had been probing their position was not strong enough to pose any real threat or storm the legislative building itself. It was only a matter of time before US forces reached them in greater numbers, or unleashed their air force or artillery against Japanese positions.

"Major, where are we going?" Inaba could not help but ask.

Major Tanigawa smiled. "Hunting," he said.

* * *

MAJOR TANIGAWA LED his men into the city, shooting any civilian on sight. Others were put to the bayonet. Whether the victim was gray haired, or a woman or child, didn't matter. Anyone they caught was slain. These civilians were only trying to flee the fighting and get themselves or their families to safety.

Even soldiers who ordinarily would have shown restraint found themselves driven on in their killing spree by the officers and by their fellow soldiers.

When they'd finally had enough, the major brought his men back to the legislative building. His troops were now in a bloodthirsty mood, and their eyes fell upon the prisoners, under guard by a few men that they had left behind.

"Should we finish them off?" Sergeant Inaba asked. "These prisoners have troubled us long enough."

The major shook his head. "Not yet," he said. "They may still have some value to us. As long as we have the prisoners, the Americans may wait to shell this building."

Inaba nodded. As usual, the major was thinking two steps ahead of him. *"Hai!"* he said.

"Make sure the men eat well," the major said, referring to the captured foodstuffs they had found. "Allow them a few bottles of sake. One way or another, this fight will end tomorrow."

CHAPTER TWENTY

As the light began to fade, Patrol Easy moved to hole up for the night in the ruins of an old house. Perhaps the house had once been grand, but the stucco facade was now scorched and cracked, ravaged by war in addition to the neglect brought on by the years of Japanese occupation. It might even be said that the battered house very much resembled the mood of the snipers.

Currently, the dwelling's chief attribute was that the house had thick walls and barred windows that would keep out enemy infiltrators during the night. In a sense, the house was a small fortress within the walled city itself.

Compounding the soldiers' exhaustion was the fact that the fight for Intramuros had not been going well. The Japanese had sworn to fight to the last man, and so far they were living up to that pledge. The code of the samurai warrior seemed to beat in the heart of every Japanese in this city. For them, there would be no surrender. The battered army troops were getting frustrated by their losses. Consequently, it was only a matter of time before the full brunt of the US Army's massive artillery firepower was brought to bear on the city. If they hoped to rescue the hostages, Patrol Easy was running out of time.

Inside the temporary shelter of the house, the patrol was licking its wounds, both literal and figurative. The Japanese enemy had chewed them up royally today, seemingly always one step ahead of them, as if reading their minds. It was not only frustrating; it had been costly to life and limb, with one of the Filipino snipers having been killed and one wounded. Deke himself had suffered a minor wound—he knew that it could have been much worse.

They all felt battered after today, but they could not yet give up. Tomorrow they faced a stark reality. They would have to find the hostages early in the day or watch as the old walled city was obliterated along with anyone inside it—hostages included.

Why were they even bothering? It was a good question. Of course, the boy's father was one of the hostages, but that wasn't the only reason to try to get them back. It was just the idea that the hostages were somehow an extension of home. Also, the Japanese had tricked them and gone back on their word by not releasing the hostages. When Deke thought of that snake Major Tanigawa and his henchman Sergeant Inaba, he felt himself getting angry all over again.

If the soldiers and even their tireless guerrilla allies appeared disheartened, their young guide looked the most dejected of all. Maybe he had started out the day with a sense of adventure, but seeing men die had cured him of that. It seemed to be sinking in for the boy that war was a deadly business. Like most boys his age, he'd probably been caught up in the excitement of it all. Because of his age and his relatively wealthy family, he had been sheltered from the worst of the war. Not any longer. For better or for worse, he had been forced to grow up a great deal in a single day based on what he had witnessed.

Honcho opened rations and handed them to the boy, along

with a spoon. Franks and beans—the finest tinned rations a soldier could expect. "Eat up, kid. You're gonna need the energy."

"Yes, sir," Roddy said. At first, he picked listlessly at the food, but then hunger overcame exhaustion and the sound of the spoon could be heard scraping against the empty metal can. As if by magic, chocolate ration bars appeared next to him on the stone block that was serving as the boy's seat.

Honcho watched him eat for a moment, then said, "Hey, kid, you know what? Your father would be proud of you."

The boy smiled in spite of himself and perked up. "Thank you, sir."

"I thought I'd tell you that since he's not around to say it. But don't you worry, kid, he'll tell you that himself soon enough."

Roddy nodded and tackled a chocolate bar. The Hershey's tropical bar or D ration was chalky, engineered not to melt in the heat, and while they weren't exactly candy, they would somewhat satisfy the sweet tooth of a hungry boy. The kid deserved a whole lot more, like maybe an ice-cream sundae, but this was the best they could do in these conditions.

Deke realized that the lieutenant had an easy way of talking with the boy, who couldn't have been more than ten years old. The lieutenant reached down and mussed the boy's hair. It was such an automatic gesture that it hinted at Honcho having done this before, maybe back home, to a young nephew—or maybe his own son. Deke realized how little any of them really knew about the lieutenant. He had never mentioned family of any kind, but now Deke wondered. They lived and fought elbow to elbow, yet they all managed to keep some part of themselves private, especially officers, who naturally kept apart from the enlisted men.

Each man had a different way of handling the war. There were men who preferred not to think about home or the future because those were only distractions from the business of being a soldier. Some men, like Philly, talked constantly about home, women, food, baseball, or whatever else came into their heads. You couldn't blame them—it was their way of dealing with being thousands of miles from home and being shot at to boot.

Deke preferred not to share anything too personal. Hell, now that he thought about it, Philly was probably the only one of the bunch who even knew he had a sister. Then again, it wasn't hard to guess at Deke's background or his nature. There was no hiding his Appalachian accent or those hard gray eyes that resembled ice chips when looking down the barrel of a rifle. He couldn't hide the scars on his face and body, either, although few knew the story behind them.

Never one for deep thoughts, Deke turned his attention to his rifle. It was dusty and battered with fresh scars on the wood and new scratches on the barrel. Still, he had managed to keep the precious scope from being broken. Beat up as it was, the rifle looked pretty much like he felt.

He dug his cleaning kit out of his haversack, broke down the rifle, and set to work. When he had finished, he felt better, as if he had also somehow managed to clean out the grimy parts of his mind. Though the wooden stock was battered and the barrel was scratched, the rifle still managed to gleam with deadly intent.

Deke spread his blanket on the stone floor, and Juana did the same beside him. The rest of the squad was nearby, either having something to eat or focusing on cleaning their weapons.

Nobody said much, and even Philly was quiet for a change. They were all exhausted from a hard day of fighting and from the losses that they had taken at the hands of the Japanese. The final fight in the alley had been short and vicious before they had been forced to beat a hasty retreat. The boy curled up near Honcho and was asleep in minutes. There was no electricity, but

Deke had found a candle in the ruins and dancing shadows soon lit the interior walls.

"Déjame eso," Juana said, nodding at the bloody bandage on Deke's arm. He had learned that Juana, like many Filipinos, could switch easily between languages. Spanish had been the language of the land for three centuries. Then English was taught in schools during the American era, which explained Juana's fluency. She also spoke Tagalog with her fellow guerrillas. Hardly any Filipinos had bothered to learn Japanese, in part because the occupiers were so hated.

"Leave it be," he said, starting to pull away. "It's just a scratch."

Juana just shook her head and reached for his arm to unwrap the bandage, which was stiff with dried blood. Tipping water from her canteen, she wet the end of a rag and dabbed at the wound. The injury was just an annoyance; come to think of it, Deke realized that he had gotten banged up much worse than that doing chores on the farm or hurrying to get the hay in before a rain, ignoring the rough twine from the heavy bales cutting into his hands until they bled or the deep scratches on his arms. And, of course, the claws and teeth of that enormous bear had done a lot more damage than the Japanese, nearly killing him as a boy.

The wound began to bleed again, which wasn't a bad thing, the fresh flow of blood carrying away the dirt and dust so that a clean scab would form. Juana put a fresh bandage on the wound and bound it tightly. It hurt like fire, but Deke was so captivated watching her work that he didn't so much as make a sound.

"You are a good man," she said.

"If you say so."

But was he? Deke had often wondered about that. The last few months had forced him to question everything he knew about himself, and humanity in general. He had proved himself to be a very capable soldier, even a skilled killer, but neither of those things meant that he was a good person. He missed seeing the good in people, including the good in himself.

Normally, he might have disagreed with Juana, but tonight he didn't mind hearing her words. Just five kind words spoken in truth the way she saw it. They were like a salve to all his wounds, physical and mental.

"I do say so," Juana said. "And when I say something, I mean something."

All he said in return was, "Thank you. You're not so bad yourself. A lot of girls wouldn't pick up a gun to fight, but you did."

"Of course I want to fight," she said, her voice going hard, sounding indignant. "Life has been very hard for the people of the Philippines. *My* people. First, the Spanish came centuries ago. Then the Americans came in my grandparents' time. The Americans have been good friends to the Philippines, teaching us what freedom meant. We lived under your Constitution. But then came the Japanese. There were no more rights. Never has there been such cruelty."

"We'll help you beat the Japanese," Deke said. "But after the war, it sounds as if the Philippines should be run by Filipinos."

"I could not agree more."

She surprised him then by reaching out to take his hand. They had never touched before, at least not in this way. Her skin was rough, like a farmer's hand. He was reminded of his sister Sadie's touch, rough but gentle at the same time. It was a touch with heft and strength behind it. He squeezed her hand.

Later, he couldn't have said how they both knew what to do next. Something unspoken passed between them.

Picking up their blankets, they moved deeper into the house, away from the others, giving themselves some privacy. If any of the others saw them leaving, they pretended not to notice.

The candle provided a soft light. In a corner of an unoccupied room, they once again spread their blankets on the stone floor. For a while they simply sat studying one another, their shoulders touching, a kind of electricity building between them. The very air seemed to crackle. Deke found his head spinning as if he'd just had a drink of Old Man McGlothlin's moonshine back home. Being this close to Juana felt intoxicating.

There was enough light that he could see her upturned face, her closed eyes and slightly parted lips. Deke didn't have much experience with the opposite sex, but he knew one thing for sure. Here was a girl waiting to be kissed.

"Deke," she whispered.

"Juana." He exhaled her name like he was breathing out to take the longest shot he had ever taken. In a sense, it was. They kissed again, and he felt himself melting into her. Their hands wandered over each other, slowly at first and then more desperately.

"Mi soldado," she murmured. *"Mi guerrero."*

Like any inexperienced young man, Deke had always worried about what to do that first time he made love, but everything happened naturally and urgently. Afterward, they lay sticky and spent under a blanket despite the warmth of the tropical night. It was the part that came after that was harder, at least at first. Deke ran through several emotions ranging from embarrassment about giving in to his urges, to wanting to go off by himself to process what had just happened, to the desire to do it all over again—but that wasn't going to happen because he felt pleasantly limp as a shoestring and empty as a sack turned inside out.

Deke had often imagined what it would be like to be with a woman, and now that the veil of mystery had been lifted tonight, he decided that it was everything he had imagined—and then some. He was glad that he had waited to find someone whom he cared about rather than running off to the whorehouses like some of the boys had done back in Hawaii. With his scarred face and body, he had doubted that he would ever experience a night such as this without having to pay for it. Juana had given him a great gift tonight.

She murmured something and wrapped herself around him, soothing his restless mind. They heard the occasional thump of artillery or the rattle of a machine gun beyond the walls, but that all sounded far away and they felt safe enough in this house, with their armed companions on watch in the next room, isolated for a few hours from the war. Juana's steady breathing soon indicated that she was asleep. Deke closed his own eyes, then slept deeply.

But the Japanese wouldn't leave him alone, even on this night of all nights, haunting his dreams. He kept seeing the enemy snipers shooting at them, hearing screams as men went down around him. Deke tried to shoot back, but in his dream there was always something that wasn't working right. Sometimes his rifle wouldn't fire. Other times his finger couldn't even pull the trigger, as if locked in rigor mortis.

All the while the grinning face of an enemy sniper taunted him through the rifle scope. Again and again he felt the terror of imagining enemy crosshairs on him, helpless to get out of the way, his heart hammering in his dreams. Even as the noose closed around the enemy, the Japanese seemed to grow more powerful.

He woke in the morning because he felt Juana's eyes on him. Her face lay inches away, the two of them breathing the same air. He stroked her warm body under the blanket, pleased that his fingers worked just fine despite the unsettling dreams.

It was already light, dawn filtering in through the shattered windows. In a few minutes Honcho would be rousting everyone for another day of war. They still had those hostages to rescue. Time was running short for these prisoners. But for now it was just the two of them. Just as with Honcho the night before, he realized how little he really knew about Juana. Did she have any family? What had her life been like before the war?

Finally, he wondered if what they had done together now joined them in some way. At the same time, he knew that this one night might be all that there would be for them. It had been a sojourn for them both, a renewal, a reminder that they were young and alive. It was all so distracting, given the business at hand.

"Juana, I—" he began.

But Juana was having none of that. She touched his lips to silence him. "Do not think of me today," she said, as if she had read his mind. "That will get you killed. *Muerto*. Think only of how true your bullets will fly. I know your heart, *mi guerrero*."

"We're still chasing those damn Japs—"

"No mas," she said. "That ends *hoy dia*. Today you will know victory, *mi soldado*. Today you will kill our enemies."

Reluctantly, Deke disentangled himself from Juana's arms and slipped out from under the blanket. Juana did the same, and he got a quick, glorious glimpse of her naked body. They dressed in the dim light, the candle having melted down until the wick lay sputtering in a puddle of wax, signaling the end of the dark night, and he felt his old resolve returning like the rising sun itself.

The night with Juana had renewed something deep within him. His eyes glinted as he bent to blow out the candle and then reached for his rifle. Deke's sense of determination had returned stronger than ever.

He decided that Juana was right. The fight would end today, one way or another.

CHAPTER TWENTY-ONE

THE SUN ROSE on another hot and muggy morning. Instead of the promise of a new day, the rising sun revealed a city that was a battleground. In the distance, they heard scattered gun shots and the boom of artillery like the thunder of an approaching storm. Normally, birds would have greeted the new morning, even in the city, but their singing among the shattered trees had either been drowned out by the sounds of war or the winged songsters had done the smart thing and fled.

Patrol Easy had been surprised by the arrival of a messenger from headquarters. He was a slight young man, a real bantamweight built for speed and stealth, the perfect candidate for messenger duty, or what in army slang was called a "carrier pigeon." He had come to remind them about the looming deadline for the artillery barrage to resume. The colonel hadn't bothered with a written message, considering that what he had to relay was short and to the point.

"The colonel says you've got two hours. He says that after that, he's going to open fire no matter what."

"All right, we'll take what we can get," Lieutenant Steele said. "Did you run into any Japs getting here?"

Helmets were all the same size, and the runner's seemed far too big for his head to the point that only his nose, the whites of his eyes, and his bright white teeth were visible from the hidden depths under the helmet brim. "Maybe I did, and maybe I didn't, but dead men tell no tales," the messenger said with a grin, brandishing his carbine. Then he slipped out the door and was gone.

Philly watched him go. "Do me a favor, Corn Pone. Next time I complain about anything, remind me that I could be a carrier pigeon instead."

"Aw, you'd complain even if you got hanged with a new rope."

"Sounds about right."

Deke stepped outside the house where Patrol Easy had sheltered for the night and took a deep breath. The damp morning air smelled of dust, rotting vegetation, and the faint hint of bodies decomposing in the ruins. He longed for the clean smell of mountain air, redolent of green leaves and high-country meadows, or at the very least, the earthy aroma of freshly plowed fields. The mountains were what he yearned for, but battle-torn Manila was what he had.

He turned to the wall and relieved himself. The smell of warm urine mixed with the other pungent smells of the ruined city. The boy, Roddy, sat on a chunk of stone in the morning sun and gnawed at one of the chalky tropical chocolate bars, using both hands in a way that reminded Deke of a chipmunk attacking an acorn. Danilo came out, leaned against the wall just beyond spattering distance, and lit a cigarette, oblivious as the contents of Deke's bladder streamed down the wall and puddled in the dust. Rodeo was relieving himself nearby, all of them so used to living in proximity that they didn't give bodily functions a second thought. Besides that, wandering off to relieve yourself might put you in enemy crosshairs.

Deke realized that was something else he missed—privacy. The only real private space a soldier had was between his ears.

He buttoned up his khaki trousers and turned to find Juana offering him a hot cup of coffee, something of a miracle in these circumstances, but Juana and the other guerrillas were always resourceful. They had built a tiny, smokeless fire under the portico of the grand house.

He gave her a grateful nod, and she gave him a shy smile in return, which Deke answered just as bashfully. He found it funny —neither one of them had been all that shy last night. This morning, returning to the reality of a war zone, last night seemed like a dream. Had it actually happened? He realized that Juana's smile was all the proof he needed.

For the others, it probably hadn't been any secret what he and Juana had been up to off by themselves. Nobody said a word about it, except for Philly, who gave him a smirk and said, "I guess you didn't get much sleep last night."

"What's that supposed to mean?"

Something in Deke's eyes wiped the smirk off Philly's face. "Uh, nothing," Philly said. "Forget I said anything."

"That's what I thought." Deke sipped his coffee and added, "You know I ain't one to kiss and tell."

Philly grinned. "Unlike me, you mean?"

"If the shoe fits."

Deke sipped more coffee, watching as Juana delivered another cup of java to Lieutenant Steele and then to Captain Oatmire. Honcho looked more tired than any of them, every last one of his years showing. Maybe it was Deke's imagination, but he could have sworn that when Honcho took off his helmet, there was yet more gray hair.

Although he found it hard to take his eyes off Juana, this wasn't the time to dwell on what had happened last night, wonderful as it had been. Today, Deke knew that they had to get the hostages out. They were out of time because the artillery barrage was set to begin again. It was now or never.

And Deke finally had a plan.

But he was going to need a little help. This wasn't something that he'd be able to do alone. He approached the lieutenant and told him as much. Still looking tired, Honcho nodded. "All right, let's hear it."

Deke made his way to the center of the group as all eyes turned to him.

"Gather round, y'all," he said. "I think I've got an idea to outfox these Japs."

"This I've got to hear," Philly said. "Although I'd much rather hear about last night."

"Watch it, city boy."

"Who, me? What did I say?" he asked innocently.

Honcho interrupted before things could get ugly. "All right, Deke. That's enough suspense. Let's hear about this plan of yours."

Lieutenant Steele was more than willing to hear him out. What Deke proposed was simple enough. He wanted the patrol to make a frontal attack, but more as a diversion. Meanwhile, he and Philly would slip away and come at the legislative building from the side, hopefully taking out the machine gunners again. Once that machine gun was knocked out, it would clear the way for Patrol Easy and the Filipinos to advance. Deke and Philly would continue to pick off any Japanese they could get in their sights.

If they got Sergeant Inaba or Major Tanigawa in their sights, so much the better. But that was almost too much to hope for. If he wanted to find Inaba or Tanigawa, he might have to go looking for them.

With that in mind, he continued to explain his plan to the others.

"Meanwhile, we'll be working our way around to the back of the building," Deke added. "When we went that way searching for the boy, we saw what it looked like back there. There's a kind of alley and lots of doors and windows. The Japanese can't have blocked them all, and they don't have enough men to watch every inch of the place. Also, we know that they're using at least one of those back doors to leave the building to go out on patrol. They'll be worried about the attack out front. We might have a shot at getting inside and then finding those prisoners to get them out."

"In other words, a two-pronged attack. Knock on the front door, and meanwhile go in the back," Honcho said. He thought it over, then nodded. "It could work. All right, then, let's saddle up and get it done."

It was a bold plan, considering that the Japanese holdouts outnumbered them. The key would be taking out that machine gun. Deke was going to need to get in position to take the shot, and he'd require not a little bit of luck along with it.

"There are a lot more of them than us," Philly said.

"When has that ever stopped us?" Deke pointed out.

They gathered their gear and prepared to get going. The sun was rising higher above the city skyline, the heat of the day already growing. A haze of smoke and dust turned the sun blood-red. Although it was the cooler season in the Philippines, it promised to be another warm and muggy day with enough humidity to make you feel as if you had just stepped out of a shower. Off to the west, a few dark clouds were already building, threatening a downpour later in the day.

The only one who didn't have a role that morning seemed to be the kid, Roddy. He was moping around like a lost puppy. They couldn't send him home, not through a dangerous war zone, but they couldn't simply abandon him here with bands of Japanese soldiers on a killing spree, targeting any civilians they found.

From the bodies they had seen among the ruins, they knew that the Japanese had no qualms about killing children.

"Stick with me, kid," Honcho said. "When the shooting starts, I'll want you to hang back."

"Give me a gun," the boy said. "I can fight."

"I know you can," the lieutenant said. "I like your spirit, kid. But what I really need you to do is carry our canteens. We'll be no good today without water."

Roddy nodded glumly, apparently not thrilled with the idea of being a water boy. "Yes, sir."

However, Honcho wasn't done assigning him duties. "Also, you are going to help us by watching our rear and making sure no Japanese sneak up on us."

"Really?" Robby seemed to understand the importance of what he was being asked to do, gun or no gun. He nodded somberly. "Yes, sir. I can do that."

"You be ready—give a shout at the first sign of any Japanese. But keep your head down and stay out of sight. With any luck, we'll get your dad back today. I sure as hell don't want to tell him that his son stuck his head up and got himself killed."

The boy seemed glad enough to do his part, smiling and squaring his shoulders, pulling himself up to his full height. He was ready to prove that he was as much of a soldier as any of them.

For the briefest of moments, Deke and Juana found themselves alone. This morning their missions would take them in different directions.

Deke turned to her and said quietly, "Listen, Juana. If I die, I want you to know that I . . . that I—"

Juana shook her head and touched a finger to his lips, silencing him. "No dying," she said, then added a few words in Tagalog: "*Makinig sa akin, sundalo*. Only winning."

Lowering her hand, she went to join the other Filipino fighters.

Standing nearby, Philly had overheard the exchange. "I like how she thinks," he said. "But if you do get killed, can I have your bowie knife?"

"Sure you can have it." Deke touched the hilt and grinned. "Just as soon as you pull it out from between your ribs."

"Very funny," Philly replied.

Deke pantomimed drawing the knife, and Philly pretended to double over with an imaginary stab wound. Both men suddenly looked younger than they had in months, more like overgrown boys, the weight of war momentarily lifted.

Honcho spoke up: "I'll be damned, Deke. That's the best mood I've ever seen you in. Maybe you ought to get laid more often."

"Wha—" Deke reddened.

Honcho went on, "Now, if you two are finished playing grab-ass, how about we go shoot us some Japs?"

* * *

TWENTY MINUTES LATER, Patrol Easy found itself back at the open square, looking out at the rubble-filled space. The landscape was becoming all too familiar to the point that Deke longed for some greenery, which made him feel most at home.

Aside from a few trees shattered by bombs, there wasn't a stick of vegetation. The acrid smell of smoke and gunpowder hung in the air, along with a whiff of sewage and worse, a reminder of the violence that had taken place. The taste of dust and grit lingered on Deke's tongue as he breathed in the aftermath of destruction. Every now and then the sound of a distant explosion and the rattle of machine-gun fire could be heard, another reminder that the war was still raging.

Presiding over the space stretching before them was the legislative building. The building stood tall and imposing, its exterior marred by bomb blasts and pockmarked by bullets. However, the thick walls looked impenetrable and forbidding. The Japanese flag flew boldly from the parapet. They could see Japanese soldiers in some of the window openings, waiting for them. One soldier broke discipline and fired a shot that whispered overhead, causing Deke's spine to tingle.

"I guess it was too much to hope that the Japanese moved out during the night," Deke said.

"That would mean we'd miss all the fun," Philly replied.

Honcho glared at the enemy flag. "If the sight of that flag isn't a sharp stick in the eye, then I don't know what is," he said. "One way or another, that flag is coming down today."

Honcho glanced at Captain Oatmire, who simply nodded back in agreement. He was letting the lieutenant call the shots, which in Deke's mind was the smart thing to do.

Then again, bringing down that Japanese flag might be easier said than done. The enemy was still firmly entrenched in the fortresslike building.

Deke realized that his plan would have worked better under cover of darkness, but they had learned that the night belonged to the Japanese. Whether it was on land or at sea, the Japanese had extensive training in night fighting. They knew what tactics worked best, and they had practiced nighttime combat. Most of their deadly banzai attacks came at night, taking advantage of the cover of darkness. Whether the Americans wanted to admit it or not, these night tactics added to the fear that the Japanese inspired in their adversaries. Americans preferred to fight by the light of day.

Here in the morning light, there was no point in trying to be stealthy. The Japanese were certainly on watch and likely had spotted them as soon as they'd entered the square. Adding to the lack of surprise was the fact that Danilo had spotted a stray dog chewing at something in the ruins. Manila, like most of the Philippines, had no shortage of the smallish, short-haired mutts that roamed the streets of cities and towns. The ownership of these dogs seemed to be loose and fluid. Consequently, the dogs had been left behind whenever civilians fled, and hunger made the animals desperate, sometimes roving in packs that had become a danger to the wounded or to children. When civilization faltered, it didn't take long for nature to return to its natural state.

Danilo was nearest the dog and shouted at it, but the starving animal had responded by turning and growling at him, standing guard over whatever it had turned into a meal. Nobody wanted to think too much about what the dog had been eating. The poor beast was probably mad with hunger or possibly rabid. Danilo raised his rifle and fired a shot that struck close enough to the dog that it finally ran off.

"If nothing else, that will wake up the Japs," Philly said.

He was right about that. Moments later, a burst of fire from a Nambu reached toward them, causing Patrol Easy to dive for cover.

"See, what did I tell you?" Philly said, hugging a concrete block as tracer fire passed overhead.

"When you're right, you're right," Deke agreed.

"OK, now's the time," Honcho said. "Deke, you and Philly break right and see if you can work around their flank. I'll give you a few minutes, and then I'll let the Nips know we're here."

Deke did just that, keeping low, using the rubble and debris for cover. So far he didn't think that he and Philly had been spotted. They kept moving, going as fast as they could to get around to the eastern side of the legislative building. They were running out of cover, however. If they tried to cross the last hundred feet or so of open ground, they would surely be seen.

"There's not enough cover here for a rat," Deke complained.

"That's being generous," Philly said, eyeing the ground. "I would have said there's not enough cover for an ant."

As if on cue, Patrol Easy opened fire on the legislative building, starting to advance toward it in a frontal attack. The Japanese inside the building quickly returned fire. There were a few rifle shots and then came the deadly *peck, peck, peck* of the Nambu from the top of the building.

"Go!" Deke urged, and scrambled across the open ground. Philly followed right behind him.

They covered the distance without anyone shooting at them and got to cover on the other side.

Deke was feeling good about his plan so far, at least until he ran into the Japanese outpost that had been hidden in the rubble. The Japanese gave a shout and opened fire. Deke raised his rifle and picked off one of the men, but that only made the three remaining soldiers that much more cautious. They took their time returning fire, choosing their shots and keeping Deke and Philly pinned down.

With a sinking feeling, he realized that his plan to surprise the Japanese by circling around the building had just fallen apart. Meanwhile, he could hear the deep boom of Honcho's shotgun and the crack of rifle fire as the rest of Patrol Easy kept the Japanese occupied toward the front of the legislative building.

Now what? he wondered.

CHAPTER TWENTY-TWO

INSIDE THE FORTRESSLIKE LEGISLATIVE BUILDING, Tanigawa felt the noose tightening. The morning had dawned quietly, the first hour or two passing peacefully, until the flurry of fire from the square that signaled a fresh attack. There was also gunfire from one of the outposts, indicating that the attackers were also trying to flank them.

Going to the window, he glanced out and enjoyed the view of the early-morning sun, even as it lit the ruins. He couldn't have said how, but he knew with certainty that this would be his last morning. He took a deep breath and enjoyed it, feeling calm in the knowledge. It was how his samurai ancestors would have greeted the dawn before a final battle.

He felt that he had served the Emperor well. He knew that a few officers might opt for *seppuku*, the traditional suicide ritual of the samurai warrior. He would not judge others for taking that course of action. His route was simply different, planning to die with honor, fighting to the last.

He was already dressed, but he took a moment to straighten his uniform, tugging at the creases, rewrapping the puttees around his calves, using a thumbnail to rub away a crusty spot of mud. There were a few splashes of dried blood here and there, but that couldn't be helped. He combed his hair and carefully donned his officer's hat.

Tanigawa studied the sword in its holder on his desk. He stood up and buckled it to his belt, feeling complete.

Although there was no mirror to check his appearance, he could see his reflection in the window glass. Perhaps it was better not to be able to see himself too closely. He grunted in satisfaction.

Yesterday's rampage through the city streets had been a necessary bloodletting, an act of revenge. But today they were not facing helpless civilians. The soldiers attacking them were determined and skilled. The Japanese officer was well aware that if he killed these American soldiers, then there would only be more. Also, he was sure that the Americans had artillery, but had not been bringing it to bear, perhaps to protect the hostages still held by the Japanese.

He had decided that they would not hold these hostages for much longer. They had served their purpose. To that end, he summoned Sergeant Inaba, who he was sure would be glad to carry out the order. Quickly, he explained what he had in mind.

"Shoot the men, spare the women," he said.

"Hai," the always dutiful sergeant replied. If Sergeant Inaba was surprised by the fact that he wasn't to shoot the nurses that had annoyed them so much, he didn't show it.

Once Inaba had left to carry out his orders, the major reached for his double rifle and balanced it over his shoulder, as he might have done if going out for some hunting.

When they left the university where he had been living for more than a year, he knew that he would not be returning and that where they were going, there would be no use for the few more-precious items that he owned, such as his radio and his books. He had not taken much more than his weapons and the uniform on his back. It had been his best uniform, at least. One way or another, he planned to die in it. All that remained unsettled was the when and how, but he knew that it would be soon.

The morning sun had risen, orders had been given, the die was cast.

* * *

MEANWHILE, the hostages were making their own plans.

Mike MacGregor looked around uneasily at the room where they were being held, a dozen of them, the female nurses alongside the men. The thought of being nothing more than a bargaining chip felt demeaning.

He was not a man who was used to being told what to do. Before the war, he had been one of Manila's leading businessmen, managing both a stock brokerage and an import-export business. Of course, the connections offered by his wife's family had helped establish his business, but ultimately he was a capable businessman known for his honesty.

If he was sometimes abrupt or drove a hard bargain, he blamed it on his Scottish roots—his grandfather had immigrated to the United States just in time to serve in the Confederate army and had ultimately settled in Texas after the Civil War, looking for a bit of peace and wide-open country, giving rise to subsequent generations of tall Texans with odd Scottish names. However, MacGregor had also inherited his grandfather's restlessness and wanderlust, eventually finding himself in the Philippines, seeking to make his own name. He had found success and started a family.

Now here he was, a prisoner of Imperial Japan. But not for much longer, if he could help it. MacGregor had reached his limit.

"How much longer do you think they'll keep us?" one of the nurses wanted to know.

"As long as they want to," said one of the men, who looked haggard and gray. Clearly, all the fight had gone out of him, and the man had resigned himself to his fate.

They all looked worse for wear, not having been fed properly since their arrival in the legislative building. They'd barely had enough water to drink. Their latrine facilities consisted of a filthy bucket in the hall. A single soldier stood guard beside the door. Judging by the shooting outside, the other two guards normally posted there had been needed to help defend the Japanese position.

The guard was a middle-aged Japanese, stocky and heavyset. He seemed to be one of the lowest-ranking soldiers, which, given his age, indicated an indifference toward military life. At this point in the war, the Japanese were rounding up every man that they could up to age forty-five for the regular army. Rumor had it that males between the ages of fifteen and sixty were being drafted in Japan, at least for national defense duties. *Barely much older than Roddy,* he mused. The draft apparently included young women. In Japan, with the Allies slowly closing in, there were no longer any civilians, only soldiers.

Anyhow, this guard had probably been judged too old for the physical activity of combat. Even so, MacGregor knew better than to underestimate the man. His appearance was typically sloppy, but he always managed to have a gleaming bayonet on his rifle. He was a mean son of a bitch who treated the American prisoners like dogs. In fact, guarding prisoners appeared to be his singular military talent.

The only Japanese who was worse to them was Sergeant Inaba. Fortunately, they had not yet seen his ugly face today. MacGregor wasn't in any hurry to see him. Having grown up in

Texas, MacGregor was convinced that lately Inaba had taken on the air of a cattleman sizing up steers for slaughter.

They didn't know what the Japanese ultimately had in store for them, but it didn't take a military strategist to figure it out. Some wanted to take their chances and hope for the best, but MacGregor didn't plan on giving them a choice. He stood, drawing himself up to his full considerable height.

"I don't know about the rest of you, but I want to get home to my family. If we don't try something soon, we might not get another chance."

MacGregor hadn't bothered to keep his voice down. One benefit of this particular guard, at least from the prisoners' perspective, was that the man didn't know a word of English. Consequently, they could plot to their hearts' content within earshot of the guard. A few of his fellow prisoners stirred or looked up at him in alarm. "What are you doing?"

"Getting us out of here, that's what."

"The Japanese might have something to say about that," Nurse Rooney said. Her prim appearance signaled that she was a rule follower, even if those rules came from their captors.

MacGregor nodded at the window, toward the sound of gunfire. Clearly, an attack was taking place against the Japanese stronghold. "It sounds to me like they have their hands full right now."

"But for how long?"

"Look, there's one guard in the hall," he replied. "You know as well as I do that the Japanese plan to shoot us. It's now or never."

"We don't have any weapons," Nurse Rooney pointed out.

It was true that the Japanese had taken the precaution of emptying the room of anything that might make a handy weapon. They had, however, left behind several heavy, rather uncomfortable wooden chairs for the prisoners to sit in. Based on their own physical dimensions, the Japanese probably hadn't considered these chairs to be weapons, but MacGregor was far bigger than your average Japanese soldier.

"Get up," he said to the nurse, who was sitting in one of the chairs.

"I beg your pardon?"

"I said, *Get up, woman!*" MacGregor barked.

Promptly, the nurse jumped to her feet.

MacGregor was surprised when Littleton stood and went to the door. The balding, middle-aged man had always come across as too timid in MacGregor's book, but he seemed to have reached the same conclusion that this might be their last chance.

"I'll call our friend in," Littleton said.

"All right. Get ready, everyone."

MacGregor stood against the wall closest to the hallway, just inside the door. He hefted the chair over his head.

His fellow prisoner went out in the hallway and made some fuss, gesturing for the guard to come into the room. From the angry noises made by the guard, it didn't sound as if he was eager to comply. Finally, he shouted something irate and stomped into the room, bayonet at the ready.

Too late, he either sensed MacGregor behind him or felt the rush of air as sixty pounds of hand-carved chair descended in his direction. The guard started to turn, but not before MacGregor hit him with the chair.

The man went down as if he'd been poleaxed.

MacGregor sprang on top of him and delivered two swift punches for good measure. They hadn't been necessary, but they sure felt good.

Littleton picked up the guard's rifle. Clearly, it wasn't his first time holding a weapon. He no longer looked so tired or defeated. It was amazing how holding a rifle gave a man hope and power over his destiny.

"Let's go," MacGregor said.

He started toward the stairs, his plan being to lead them down, but just as quickly he realized that wasn't going to work.

They could hear the Japanese on the stairs below, sounding as if they were coming up, maybe hauling ammunition to the machine gunner on the roof—or coming to finish off the prisoners. MacGregor glanced down and spotted Sergeant Inaba coming up the stairs.

The only way to go now was up. "Follow me!" he said.

He didn't have a plan. Maybe, just maybe, they could overpower the machine gunners and barricade themselves up there, hoping that the Americans could finally somehow overwhelm the Japanese defenses.

They ran up the stairs, MacGregor taking the steps two at a time, the group getting spread out because some of them were weak from the lack of food and water.

There was a shout from below—they had been spotted. A bullet cracked up the stairwell, then another. Littleton fired back and, judging by the shout of pain that followed, had managed to hit one of their pursuers, buying them precious minutes.

MacGregor's long legs quickened the pace, taking the stairs three at a time.

More shots came from below.

* * *

Deke and Philly needed to improvise, now that their plan to get around behind the legislative building had been blocked by the Japanese outpost.

Deke looked around and saw the bank building where the patrol had found cover yesterday. An idea began to take shape. Without any sort of heavy weapons, they would have to do what snipers did best—pick off Japs. There was no time to waste. He looked over toward the rest of the patrol, who were being kept pinned down by the relentless fire from the Nambu machine gun on the roof of the legislative building. The machine gunners had gotten smart and piled up more sandbags, making them a difficult target from ground level in the square. If he and Philly could take out that machine gun, the rest of Patrol Easy might just have a fighting chance. To do that, they were going to have to get up higher.

"Come on," Deke said. "Let's get up on the roof of that bank building."

Philly had also seen that the chances of their original plan working had fallen apart. He nodded, seeming to have read Deke's mind. "If we can get up there, it's gonna be like a shooting gallery for us."

"That's the idea."

They scurried away through the rubble, shots chasing them. Some of the Japanese jeered, evidently thinking that Deke and Philly had turned tail and run—which in a sense they had. However, Deke was a strong believer in living to fight another day. *The Japs think they've got us licked, but we'll see about that.*

Reaching the front door of the bank building, they scrambled inside. El Banco de Manila featured a grand lobby with marble floors, tall Doric columns holding up the vaulted roof, and gleaming counters of polished wood with glass partitions separating the well-dressed clerks from the even-better-dressed customers. Tall windows, covered in ornately wrought iron bars that provided both security and beauty, filled the lobby with the sort of sunlight that encouraged scrutiny. Normally it was the sort of setting where Deke never would have felt comfortable in a million years. But now it was a war zone.

The marble floor was strewn with dust and broken glass from windows shattered by bomb blasts, though the ironwork remained. Birds flitted under the tall ceiling and had even begun to nest at the tops of the columns. Nature asserting itself where humankind had faltered. A puddle of congealed blood spread across one corner, evidence that someone had died there, and badly.

He had to admit that the sight of the ruined bank lobby didn't make him feel sad. He hated bankers. After all, it had been a greedy banker who had foreclosed on their family farm at the rat-tail end of the Great Depression, just before the war. This place was far grander than the local bank that had stolen the Cole family's land—which meant the bankers here were likely that much greedier.

"This place has seen better days, that's for sure," Philly said.

"Maybe there was a run on the bank," Deke said.

"I'll say. Hey, I wonder if there's still any money in the bank vault? If we had a grenade—"

"Come on," Deke said. "There's no time for that. Let's find the stairs and get up to the roof."

They started toward the rear of the lobby. Outside, they could hear the firing as Patrol Easy took on the Japanese. However, Deke heard another sound—boots crunching on glass. He froze, then signaled Philly to do the same.

"What?" Philly whispered.

As if to answer his question, the sound of footsteps came more clearly now. Then they heard the guttural sound of Japanese speaking among themselves. Someone kicked something across the floor, making it hop and bounce. One of the soldiers laughed. Judging from the sounds, it was a small band of Japanese, maybe three or four men. Deke realized that the enemy soldiers were also headed for the stairs. The sons of bitches probably had the same plan that he and Philly did, which was to get to the roof for the commanding view that it offered. If the Japs got up there, Patrol Easy wouldn't stand a chance. They would be sitting ducks, picked off from both directions.

Deke and Philly spread out, moving as quietly as they could across the broken glass on the floor, both finding cover behind the tall stone columns. Deke pressed his rifle against the cold, hard stone and waited.

The Japanese soldiers rounded a corner and came into sight. There were three of them, moving quickly, weapons at the ready. Maybe Deke and Philly hadn't been as quiet as they had hoped and the sound of crunching glass had given them away.

Deke fired at the soldier on the left. Inside the confines of the lobby, there was a distinct sound of the bullet hitting flesh and bone. The soldier went down. Philly's rifle cracked and dropped the soldier on the right. That left the man in the middle, who managed to get off a wild shot that ricocheted off the column that Deke was taking cover behind.

Deke worked the bolt and shot him, Philly's bullet coming in a split second later. Hit twice, the Japanese soldier went down. They waited a moment, just to make sure no Japanese had been lagging behind.

"Coast is clear," Deke said. "Let's go."

"You don't have to tell me twice," Philly said.

They scrambled toward the stairs, which were broad and marble, leading to offices on the second floor. There was less destruction here, and they moved easily up the stairs. To their relief, there didn't seem to be any more Japanese soldiers. The stairs grew narrower as they climbed from floor to floor, away from the public eye, finally ending in a utilitarian set of wooden steps that led to a hatch in the roof. They climbed out onto the roof, keeping low, not wanting to attract any attention in case enemy eyes were watching. Again, they were glad not to run into more enemy soldiers up here.

"Looks like we've got the place to ourselves," Deke said.

"Fine by me," Philly replied.

It turned out that the roof had a slight pitch to it, with acres of copper sheeting coated heavily in tar to keep the rain out. It wasn't the easiest surface to cross, and already the sun was making the black tar and metal surfaces unpleasantly hot. But that might be the least of their worries if the Japanese caught sight of them before they were in position. One burst from that Nambu might sweep them right off the roof.

Crouching, they ran around to the front of the roof that overlooked the square and the legislative building on the other side. Although the buildings were similar in height, the steeper roof of the bank building gave it an advantage, adding a few precious feet of elevation. This made all the difference because they could look down on the roof of the legislative building—giving Deke a clear shot at the machine gunner.

Deke got next to a chimney, which not only offered at least some cover but, more importantly, provided a solid surface to steady his rifle against. Philly set up on the other side of the chimney.

"I'll take care of business," Deke said. "You watch our backs. Maybe those Japs we saw earlier have some friends around."

"You got it."

Deke lined up his sights on the two machine gunners operating the Nambu. It was the longest shot that he had taken for a while, so he took his time steadying the sights, then raising his aim just a hair. If he missed, and they were spotted by the machine gunner, it was going to get unpleasant up here in a hurry, because there was precious little cover on the rooftop. First, he fired to take out the man feeding the ammo belt into the gun, the sound of the Nambu masking his shot. The man slumped down, but his comrade on the machine gun didn't notice. Deke worked the bolt and fired again.

The machine gun fell silent.

Next, he turned his attention to the square below, where he could see Patrol Easy trying to advance against the superior numbers of the Japanese force defending the legislative building. The Americans and Filipinos were clearly outnumbered.

"There's too many Japs," Philly said.

"Let's see if we can even the odds," Deke said, putting his eye back to the rifle scope.

CHAPTER TWENTY-THREE

Across the square in the legislative building, the fleeing prisoners led by MacGregor had reached the rooftop. To his surprise, the two-gun crew was slumped behind their wall of sandbags, clearly dead. Briefly, MacGregor thought about taking command of the machine gun and using it against the Japanese, but there simply wasn't time. Already the Japanese were in the stairway landing.

"Close the door!" he shouted as the last hostage made it through. The nurse turned and helped him slam the door shut. There was no lock on the outside, but he grabbed a length of broken board and jammed it under the doorknob. Already the soldiers on the other side were pounding on the door until it bounced in its frame. The door wouldn't hold for long.

"What should we do?"

He looked around. It was a good question. They were trapped up here. He began to doubt the wisdom of having fled to the roof, but they were out of time or options.

"Everyone scatter and hide as best as you can," he said. "Littleton and I will hold them off as long as we're able to."

The door shuddered again, then started to splinter. Littleton fired a shot through the door, then another. That slowed the enemy but did not stop them. A spray of bullets followed, wounding Littleton, who didn't go down but limped away, turning and firing as he ran.

Then the door gave way and the Japanese came pouring out.

* * *

DEKE WAS ABOUT to start picking off enemy soldiers in in the square below when he noticed a flurry of activity on the roof of the legislative building. He squinted through the scope to take a closer look. To his surprise, he saw the prisoners spilling out onto the roof of the legislative building. A couple of the men hung back, apparently trying to barricade the door.

"Philly, get a look at this," he said, pointing toward the rooftop.

Philly glassed them with binoculars. "I'll be damned. Those are the prisoners," he said. They had both recognized the tall fellow, MacGregor, father to the boy who had fallen in with Patrol Easy. "But where are they going? They're trapped up there. I see that they're trying to barricade the door, but that won't stop the Japanese."

As if to prove the point, the door leading to the rooftop suddenly banged open, scattering the two men who had been trying to hold it closed against the Japanese. Enemy soldiers boiled out of the door like angry hornets looking for someone to sting. The last soldier out wore an officer's uniform and carried a sword in addition to a rifle. Deke realized it was none other than Major Tanigawa.

For the prisoners trapped on the roof, the situation had just gone from bad to worse.

Within moments, he and Philly watched a drama play out on the rooftop, feeling helpless to do much about it.

Pursued by the Japanese, they could see that there was nowhere for the prisoners to go.

Deke glanced at the square below, where Patrol Easy was fighting for survival as the Japanese forces advanced. The next few minutes were going to be critical both on the roof and down in the square. With a sinking feeling, Deke realized that he had a choice to make. He and Philly could either save some of the prisoners, or they could help Patrol Easy. Which was it going to be?

* * *

As the door to the roof flew open, MacGregor turned to run, not sure where to run to. He dove behind a wide chimney before the Japanese spotted him. To his surprise, it was Inaba who went running past. On an impulse, MacGregor stuck out a long leg and tripped him.

Inaba went sprawling, his submachine gun flying out of his hands and clattering across the rooftop.

MacGregor marched toward him as the Japanese sergeant regained his feet. Inaba saw him coming and took a fighting stance, his weight on his back leg, body coiled, his arms raised in some kind of Japanese fighting position. Inaba made a noise that perhaps was intended to be a battle cry, more like a bellow than any kind of word. MacGregor thought it sounded like a noise that an upset steer would make.

"Kee-yiii!"

The big Texan was not impressed. This wasn't his first rodeo—you didn't grow up in Texas without getting in a fistfight or three. MacGregor expected an easy fight, but he soon found that he was sadly mistaken. Inaba turned out to know a trick or two.

Overconfident, MacGregor swung. The Japanese sergeant easily dodged the blow and instantly hammered the American in the ribs with a quick one-two punch combination. Like lightning, a fist connected squarely against MacGregor's face. He felt the wind knocked out of him and he sat down rather unexpectedly. Inaba was stronger than he looked, and a whole lot quicker.

Grinning, Inaba waited for MacGregor to get up again. The Japanese seemed to be enjoying this.

MacGregor shook his head to clear it. He got back on his feet and advanced on Inaba, more cautiously this time. He made the mistake of keeping his eyes on Inaba's hands. He didn't expect Inaba's foot to suddenly come flying at him. The kick sent Big Mike sprawling.

Once again, he got to his feet. Once again, Sergeant Inaba was waiting for him. MacGregor didn't plan on disappointing Inaba, but he decided to change his tactics.

He was at least a foot taller and fifty pounds heavier than Inaba, emaciated though he was. The ropy muscles that he had developed on the family ranch had never left him. Inaba had taken up his fighting stance again. This time, MacGregor kept his distance. With his long reach, he swatted Inaba's hands away, leaving the man's chin nicely exposed.

MacGregor swung his fist, putting all the frustration of the last few weeks into it. He struck Inaba a hammer blow squarely in the face, sending the man reeling.

"I've got to say, that has been a long time coming," MacGregor said.

MacGregor raised his fists to hit the man again, but it wasn't necessary. Staggering, Inaba had reached the edge of the roof. Trying to find his balance, he took one more step back—into thin air. His eyes went wide as he realized his mistake. And then Inaba fluttered his arms like a flightless bird and ever so slowly tipped over backward into nothingness.

He screamed on the way down.

But MacGregor's sense of victory was short-lived. The last Japanese soldier through the doorway was Major Tanigawa. He emerged onto the rooftop, carrying his double rifle, which he pointed at MacGregor.

From the Texan's perspective, the dual dark muzzles were big as twin cannons pointed right at him.

"Now hold on, Major," MacGregor said, raising his hands. "I'm a prisoner."

"No," said Tanigawa. "You are a dead man."

MacGregor closed his eyes, not wanting to see what was coming. It wasn't fear—he just didn't want Tanigawa's ugly mug to be the last thing he ever saw. Instead, in his mind's eye, he pictured his family—his beautiful wife, his daughter, young Roddy. They would be his last thought in this world.

The moment stretched on. He heard the crack of a rifle some distance away, but still Tanigawa didn't fire. MacGregor opened his eyes and glared at the Japanese officer. "Just get it over with, will you?"

* * *

DEKE HAD MADE up his mind. He reminded himself that the whole reason they were here in the first place was to rescue the prisoners. He turned his rifle toward the last stand on the rooftop, leaving Patrol Easy to fend for itself for now. Quickly, he picked off one of the enemy soldiers, then another. He desperately wanted to get Sergeant Inaba and Major Tanigawa in his crosshairs, but he had lost sight of them for the moment.

Finally, his luck changed. Across the square, through the scope, Deke saw MacGregor scuffling with Sergeant Inaba, who seemed to have lost his submachine gun in the fracas. Deke tensed at the sight of the Japanese sergeant confronting the much bigger American. Deke held his fire—it was a long shot and the angle wasn't good, so he was afraid of hitting MacGregor. Twice, Inaba knocked the bigger man down. But then the tables turned. MacGregor punched Inaba, and Deke watched in surprise as the sergeant staggered backward and then toppled from the roof.

"I'll be damned," Deke said. He let out a low whistle. "Did you just see that?"

"I saw it, all right," Philly replied. "That son of a bitch flew about as well as a brick."

Deke wanted to cheer. He was about to turn his attention back to Patrol Easy down in the square, but what he saw happening next let the air out of that balloon. Major Tanigawa had found MacGregor and was pointing his double rifle at the American. MacGregor was unarmed, and there would be no punching his way out of this situation.

"Can you get him?" Philly asked.

"I reckon," Deke replied.

The machine gunners on the roof had been easier. This was at a longer range, on a different part of the roof. He had to hurry —he was literally going to get only one shot at this.

He picked up a handful of dust and grit, then tossed it into the air to see which way the breeze was blowing. It wasn't much of a breeze, but it blew fitfully, promising to snatch his bullet off course during the second or so it needed to cross the distance. One second didn't sound that long until you measured it out loud, muttering *one blue mountain* or *one Mississippi*. Either of those phrases took about one second to say. Plenty of time for a stray eddy of wind or a pocket of humid air to send his bullet off course.

"Any day now," Philly said. "I don't want to be the one who has to tell young Roddy that his father is dead."

Neither did Deke, but some things couldn't be rushed. *Take your time killing him, Tanigawa,* Deke silently urged. *Take all the time you want.*

Deke knelt and pressed the rifle against the warm bricks, letting the rough surface dig into the wooden stock, holding it steady. He let out a breath, drew one in, and held it. When his father was teaching him to shoot, he liked to say, *Breathe out fear, breathe in courage.*

He settled the sights on Tanigawa.

The breeze touched Deke's face, then faded away.

Deke squeezed the trigger.

* * *

ON THE ROOFTOP of the legislative building, MacGregor was waiting to die, staring into the muzzles of the Japanese officer's double rifle, intended for the likes of tigers, lions, and water buffalo. MacGregor knew that he didn't have a prayer.

He saw that Tanigawa was looking in his direction, but that his eyes were unfocused. Puzzled, MacGregor noticed that a red stain had appeared in the middle of Tanigawa's chest, rapidly growing in size. MacGregor realized that the distant rifle crack that he'd heard earlier must not have been random.

The Japanese officer sank to his knees, then collapsed.

MacGregor turned and looked in the direction that the bullet had come from. As far as he knew, all the soldiers were fighting down in the square. Who in the world had shot Tanigawa?

Across the square, from another rooftop, he saw a soldier give him a big sweeping gesture, what they called a "hillbilly wave" back in Texas. Even at this distance, he could see that the soldier wasn't wearing a helmet, but a bush hat with one side pinned up. He must be either a Filipino or a stray Aussie. No matter—MacGregor owed that eagle-eyed bastard his life.

He grinned and waved back, thinking, *That was one hell of a shot.*

Then he picked up Tanigawa's rifle and fired at the closest Japanese soldier. The big round from the double rifle was as good as kicking the Jap in the chest, and down he went. Following MacGregor's example, a couple of the other prisoners had retrieved the rifles dropped by Inaba and the other Japanese and were now shooting back.

MacGregor aimed the rifle and fired again, then reached down and dug around in Tanigawa's pockets for more cartridges. They were big brass shells, practically the size of railroad spikes, or so it seemed. He grinned as he shoved two more shells into the rifle and snapped the breech shut.

Maybe a fight wasn't what the Japanese wanted from their hostages, but it was a fight they were going to get. And right now they were losing it.

* * *

DOWN IN THE SQUARE, while Deke and Philly were occupied by the fighting on the roof, the rest of Patrol Easy was managing to advance. It turned out that the Japanese had found one of their infamous knee mortars and were using it to walk rounds toward Patrol Easy.

"Juana, take care of that!" Lieutenant Steele shouted, frustrated that the mortar squad was beyond shotgun range. With Deke and Philly out on their mission, she was the best shot that he had left.

He recognized the high-pitched crack of her Arisaka rifle—once, twice—and that was the end of the mortar attack. After that, the enemy fire slackened, but there was still plenty of it coming at them.

It helped that the Japanese were rudderless, having lost their command structure. Unlike the Americans, the Japanese soldier was far more dependent on his officers telling him what to do. The Japanese didn't like soldiers to think for themselves. Maybe there were some benefits to that for the Japanese and their brutal tactics, but not in this situation.

The enemy began to fall back and scatter, some returning toward the legislative building and others simply melting into the rubble and ruins. The surrounding streets were filled with smoke and debris. The destruction was immense, several more dead bodies now scattered in the rubble.

Amid the chaos, Steele heard a familiar voice calling his name. It was Danilo, their fearless Filipino guide. He was on his knees, both hands gripping his midsection as if trying to hold something in. Blood so thick and dark that it was more like chocolate pudding oozed from between his fingers. The lieutenant started to reach for the man's hands to pull them away so that he could apply a bandage, but then he hesitated, afraid of what he might find. The lieutenant was far from squeamish, having seen just about everything you could see in terms of how a human being could be killed in this war, but even he had to admit that it was an ugly wound.

"Dammit, Danilo. Do not die on me. That's an order."

The tough guerrilla just shook his head. As usual, it was unclear just how much English he understood. But the severity of his wound was clear enough. However, there was no fear in his eyes, just resignation.

Juana was suddenly beside them. She propped her Arisaka rifle, its barrel smoking hot from the multiple rounds she had put through it, against a block of broken concrete and reached for her medical kit. "Go on," she said. "I will stay with him. There is nothing more you can do."

Knowing that she was right, but still reluctant to leave their loyal guide, he gave Danilo's shoulder a squeeze. A final look passed between them; then Danilo nodded and looked away, as if giving the lieutenant permission to go.

There weren't any medics to call because Patrol Easy was on its own. It wouldn't have mattered. Danilo's ragged breathing indicated that he was now struggling to stay alive.

Steele filled with grief and anger. Danilo had been through a lot with Patrol Easy—they might not have survived without him. The lieutenant promised himself that he would make sure that whatever happened to Danilo wouldn't be in vain.

If any of them survived. Bullets still whined overhead, bouncing off the rocks and debris around him. It was a wonder that the rest of them hadn't already ended up like Danilo. *I really ought to keep my head down,* Steele thought. But he'd be damned if he did that, not when his men needed him.

The lieutenant got to his feet.

He looked around, seeing that what was left of his patrol had lost momentum. There was Rodeo, on his belly, firing shot after shot at the Japanese. Yoshio was doing the same, hurling insults in Japanese at the enemy between squeezing off rounds. Captain Oatmire was firing from behind a chunk of stone. The guerrillas had seemingly melted into the debris, taking cover wherever they could.

No, they couldn't stop. If they halted their advance now, the Japanese might be able to regroup. He glanced at his watch. To make matters worse, the bombardment was set to recommence soon. The last thing he wanted to do was leave his patrol out here in the open, exposed, once the Long Toms finally resumed their deadly work.

"Let's go!" Lieutenant Steele shouted, leading his patrol forward. Soon they were a hundred feet from the front door, then fifty, then climbing the wide stone steps leading toward the entrance.

A Japanese sprang from the shadows near the door of the

legislative building, running at the lieutenant with a fixed bayonet. Steele fired the shotgun, and that was the end of that particular problem.

Moments later they were inside the building itself. Any able-bodied soldiers seemed to have fled out the back like the rats the Americans thought they were. The lobby had been turned into a makeshift hospital, with Japanese dead lined up on one side and the still-living on the other.

"Japs!" Rodeo shouted, swinging his rifle at them.

"Don't worry about them. They aren't going to bother anybody," Honcho said, giving him a shove toward the door.

Unarmed and helpless, the wounded watched them with furtive eyes, but Honcho and the others kept going, not even Yoshio giving them a second glance. They moved deeper into the building's interior. The only thing he cared about was getting the prisoners out before the US Army rained the wrath of God down on everyone's heads in the form of heavy artillery.

He heard a deep, booming voice ahead. "Don't shoot!"

Seconds later, a tall figure appeared, leading the rest of the prisoners. A couple of the prisoners were wounded and had to be helped by the others.

"Is this everybody?" Steele asked.

"All present and accounted for," the tall prisoner said. "All twelve of us, in various states of repair."

"Then let's get the hell out of here."

They turned and headed out of the building, passing the silent wounded again.

"What about those wounded Japanese?" Rodeo asked anxiously.

"To hell with 'em," Honcho replied, rushing past the men lying on blankets on the marble floor. "They'll all be dead in about ten minutes, and so will we if we don't get out of here."

Juana was waiting for them on the steps. The lieutenant looked at her questioningly, but she shook her head.

Danilo was gone. Though it was no surprise, the finality of it hit the lieutenant hard. He pushed that thought down, not having time for it, and led the patrol back the way that they had come.

Out in the square, there was one more important piece of business waiting.

"Papa!" cried Roddy, who had crawled under a fallen column, keeping out of harm's way just like Lieutenant Steele had told him to do.

"Son!"

The two embraced, a couple of tears leaving tracks in MacGregor's dusty face.

Steele told himself that the reunion somewhat made up for Danilo. Life went on. He couldn't help wondering who would grieve for their dead guide. Like so much about Danilo, the existence of any family that he'd had remained a mystery.

He glanced at his watch. Almost noon. Turning to the prisoners, he said, "We need to get out of here, and fast."

The urgency in the lieutenant's voice said it all. They did as they were told, or as best as they could. Rodeo and Yoshio, along with Captain Oatmire, jumped in to help the injured prisoners. At the edge of the square, they were rejoined by Deke and Philly, who hadn't wasted any time getting off the roof of the bank building.

"You guys are a sight for sore eyes," Philly said. "I was thinking—"

Whatever thought he'd wanted to share was interrupted by the high-pitched wail of incoming artillery. Right on schedule, the artillery officer was opening fire.

"Run!" Steele shouted.

The first shells hit, making the ground shake. The front

corner of the legislative building shattered in a tremendous explosion that sent debris skyward.

Fortunately, the battered band of soldiers and prisoners had made it across the square.

"This way!" shouted Juana, leading them down an alley. They cut through one street after another, shells landing ever closer, and didn't stop until they had reached the nearest gate of the walled city.

Behind them, what was left of the old city of Intramuros was being reduced to rubble, along with any remaining Japanese holdouts.

EPILOGUE

THE STUBBORN JAPANESE resistance was no match for the determined artillery barrage. Wherever the enemy took refuge in the city, the building was simply leveled. While the approach was brutal to the city itself, it saved American lives that might have been lost in street-to-street fighting. The sturdy legislative building remained standing, but with the corners knocked off and the roof sagging, it resembled a collapsed soufflé. Any remaining Japanese within had either fled—or died when chunks of the building fell on their heads.

Admiral Iwabuchi had been the driving force behind the horrific battle that had destroyed the city. With the Americans closing in, Iwabuchi decided to commit suicide in the manner of a samurai warrior. Kneeling on the floor of the dirty dugout that served as his headquarters, Iwabuchi unbuttoned his naval officer's tunic and used a *tantō* knife to slit open his own belly.

As Iwabuchi's blood and offal ran out into the dirt, one of his staff officers then swung a sword with all his might, grunting with the effort of cutting off Iwabuchi's head. It was not cleanly done, but then again, beheading was not something that he'd had the opportunity to practice. Shaking, with tears in his eyes, the younger officer then shot himself.

It wasn't long before their bodies were found and identified. Ritual suicide was a gruesome and brutal act that was hard for the typical American soldier to fathom, but they had seen it done before. One of the intelligence officers used the toe of his boot to roll the head over and said, "That's Iwabuchi, all right. It's too bad the son of a bitch didn't kill himself from the get-go and spare the whole damn city."

With the city firmly in US control, word came down that Patrol Easy would be shipping out soon to rejoin the rest of the 77th Infantry Division. But first there were a few goodbyes to make, starting with young Roddy and his father. Fortunately for them, their home had been spared from destruction, and the MacGregor family had been kept safe inside their walled compound.

"I can't thank you enough for taking care of Roddy—and helping us get away from those damn Japanese," MacGregor said as Patrol Easy gathered around. He looked as if he had finally gotten a decent meal and was no worse for wear, except for a bandage on his left ear where a Japanese bayonet had caught him during the scuffle on the rooftop of the legislative building.

"We couldn't have done it without Roddy," Lieutenant Steele said. "You have a brave son there."

"Indeed I do," MacGregor said, reaching down to ruffle the boy's hair, much as Honcho had done from time to time when the boy was helping to guide them through the city ruins. Roddy jerked his head away as if annoyed—acting like he was too old for that nonsense—but he was smiling as he did it. "Now we have a lot of rebuilding to do. This city is just about destroyed."

"At least you won't be doing it alone," Honcho said. Already, in the distance, crews of army engineers were using bulldozers to clear the streets. General MacArthur had made sending help to

Manila a priority, although any real construction would have to wait until the end of the war. Other crews made up mostly of Filipinos worked to bury the dead—of which there were far too many civilian casualties.

"We're glad to have all the help that we can get," MacGregor agreed. "As for you fellas, go give the Japs hell. If you get to Tokyo, give Hirohito a punch in the nose from me."

Of course they were not the only prisoners glad to get home and see families and friends from whom they had been separated. No one rested for long because survival in the city ruins required nothing but hard work. The two Red Cross nurses, including the redoubtable Catherine Rooney, had immediately gone to work helping wounded soldiers and civilians. Rooney could be heard muttering under her breath about "conditions," but that didn't stop her from doing everything from bandaging a wound to holding the hand of the dying. Deke decided that the nurses were two of the biggest-hearted, toughest people he had met in Manila.

* * *

ANOTHER GOODBYE CAME when they buried Danilo. There was no one to claim his body, considering that his family was far away on Leyte.

"Dammit, I figured that nobody could kill that tough bastard," Deke said.

"When your number's up, it's up," Philly said. It was a philosophy shared by many soldiers, and in some strange way it made the loss easier to bear.

Considering that Danilo had died during the most critical moments of that fight in the square, Deke had blamed himself because his crosshairs had been focused elsewhere. But when he said something aloud about that, Lieutenant Steele had been quick to dissuade him of that notion. "You made the best of two bad choices," Honcho said. "If you hadn't acted, every last one of those prisoners might have died. Don't forget, those prisoners were the reason for us being there in the first place."

Deke shook his head. "But still—"

"Listen, Deke. The enemy killed Danilo. It had nothing to do with you."

Looking down at the bundled blanket—a bundle that looked much too small to contain a force of nature like Danilo—Deke tried to decide how he felt. He would not have called Danilo a friend, because he had scarcely known him, but they had fought side by side. Danilo also had taught him a great deal of jungle craft in an environment so very different from the mountains back home. Maybe Danilo hadn't exactly been a friend, but he'd certainly been a kindred spirit.

"I do know one thing," Deke said. "Danilo would not want to be buried in the city."

At Deke's insistence, they managed to commandeer a jeep to take them beyond the city, to where the green hills began to march down to the slow-moving Pasig River. The soil here was soft, and they soon had a grave dug under a grove of banyan trees. Patrol Easy kept a wary eye out because it was no secret that some Japanese fighters had made their way to the outskirts of the city and were now hiding in the agricultural lands and forests.

Also, they were not alone. None other than Father Francisco had found them in the ruins of the city just the day before and had agreed to preside over the burial of one of his old guerrilla fighters.

"Requiem æternam dona eis Domine," he said in Latin.

The first shovel of rich earth pattered down on Danilo's body, making him forever a part of his beloved country for which he had fought and died.

* * *

BURYING DANILO HAD BEEN TOUGH, but for Deke the hardest goodbye was yet to come.

Finally, the orders arrived for them to get down to the harbor, where they would be boarding a troop transport. He had been dreading this moment. It wasn't the thought of what was next, but what he was leaving behind.

Juana would be staying in Manila, helping the occupation take out the few remaining Japanese defenders who had fled to the hills. At some point, she would put her rifle aside and begin the important work of rebuilding her country.

She accompanied them down to the port, where a ship was waiting to carry troops to the next islands, that much closer to Japan. The port was a flurry of activity, soldiers in olive green uniforms bustling about with the shouts of NCOs ringing in their ears. The ship stood tall and formidable, its drab metal exterior failing to look cheerful even in the bright sun. In the harbor beyond, the water sparkled a deep blue, its waves lapping against the ship's sides. Considering that up until a few hours before the harbor front and surrounding city had been a scene of intense fighting, the peaceful setting felt surreal.

Father Francisco offered to marry them on the spot, but after considering it briefly, they shook their heads in unison. They both knew that fate was carrying them far apart, rather than together.

Juana stood stiffly as if holding in her emotions, still carrying her Arisaka rifle slung over one shoulder. Deke had the Springfield slung over his own shoulder. *Birds of a feather,* he thought. For a long moment they simply stood facing one another. Then something passed between them, and they stepped closer and embraced. They would have melted into each other if they could have. Then the moment passed and they stepped apart. It was only a short step, yet it felt as if the entire world had slid between them in that instant.

"Take care, *mi soldado*," Juana said, reaching out to trace her finger down the unscarred side of Deke's face.

He put a stray tendril of hair over her ear. "You do the same, *mi guerrera*."

Then Deke turned and started up the temporary quay toward the waiting ship. He didn't look back, because that was bad luck.

Once they were aboard, Deke stood at the ship's rail and finally looked back toward the spot where he had left Juana, but she was gone. He felt a sudden emptiness, as if a piece of him had been removed. It was an unexpected feeling, and he took a moment to try to understand it.

After all, Deke had always reckoned that he was destined to live a lonely life, that he didn't need anyone in it. He recalled the softness of Juana beside him, her warm body, even the smell of her skin and hair. Just maybe, he realized, he'd been wrong about never needing anyone.

"I guess that girl finally got through your shell," said Philly, who was standing next to him. "Maybe Deacon Cole isn't as tough as he lets on."

"Just keep it up and you'll find out," Deke said, some of the old steel back in his voice. But after a moment he wondered, "Do you think I'll ever see her again?"

"We're still in the middle of a war, Corn Pone. None of us know if we'll live to see the next sunrise. Right now we've got to cross an ocean that's crawling with Japanese submarines and a sky that could fill up with Zeros any minute. I wouldn't go buying any green bananas."

Deke nodded. He supposed that Philly was right and he was better off not counting on seeing Juana again. Hell, they hadn't even agreed to write to each other, although it seemed unlikely that their letters would find one another in the chaos of war. If nothing else, he had his memories.

* * *

HAVING BOARDED the ship that was crossing Manila Bay bound for the vast South China Sea, Patrol Easy was leaving another chapter of the war behind. The fight had left them battered and bruised, having lost three men over the months of bitter battles, including Danilo. It was all a bitter pill to swallow. And yet it was satisfying to know that the Philippines was finally being restored to American hands.

"Hey, Honcho, where are we headed?" Philly asked. He had spotted the lieutenant on deck, coming away from a powwow with a handful of other officers. They all looked dead tired, maybe Lieutenant Steele most of all, considering that he was clearly the oldest of the bunch.

"We're going to the Ryukyu Islands to handle some trouble there," the lieutenant replied. "It's a place called Ie Shima. Among other things, rumor has it that the Japanese Navy has a base there with suicide speedboats that they are sending out against our navy."

"I guess when they need a job done right, they know who to call. No rest for the weary."

The lieutenant clapped him on the shoulder. "Gee, Philly, you're finally catching on."

There were a few bright spots now that they were leaving Manila behind. Aboard the ship, they were reunited with Private Egan and his war dog, Thor. Deke realized that Patrol Easy had suffered even more losses, if you included Egan's first war dog, Whoa Nelly, killed in the fighting. While the rest of Patrol Easy had been engaged in Manila, Egan and Thor had been doing guard duty at the port, alert against Japanese saboteurs as American vessels began to fill the waterfront.

Deke reached down and scratched Thor's ears. "Nice to see you again, boy," he said.

Egan had been watching with some concern, ready to pull back on Thor's leash. "Thor doesn't let just anybody do that, you know."

"I reckon he's a good judge of character," Deke said, who continued scratching Thor's ears. He always had liked dogs and had mixed emotions about them getting dragged into the war.

"There's something to be said about that," Egan agreed. "He knows he can trust you."

Deke gave Thor a final pat and then looked out to sea, where diamonds of sunlight tipped the waves. Overhead, a formation of fighters buzzed low, serving as their eyes and ears as the small flotilla steamed forward. There was nothing out there but water, but he knew that on the other side of that vast ocean lay another island, and more islands beyond that, stretching all the way to Japan.

He wondered what Juana was doing at that moment, whether she was also thinking of him, or if she had already forgotten about him. Deke smiled to himself and shook his head. Maybe Philly was right—when it came to Juana, he'd gotten it bad. It would take a while for that missing piece of him to grow back.

He glanced over at Thor, who seemed to have the right idea. The dog was stretched out in the sunshine, taking a nap. Lieutenant Steele had added that they had more than a thousand miles of ocean to cross before they reached Ie Shima, so they were settling in for a long voyage. Men had taken up whatever space they could find on deck, some of them reading like Yoshio, his nose already buried in a Western, or they smoked cigarettes, or wrote letters home.

Philly had gotten a card game together, and he tried to wave Deke over, but Deke just shook his head, not interested.

Instead, Deke lay down next to Thor, feeling the sun warm him and the tropical breeze brush his hair. He was normally on high alert, but here on the ocean he had no choice but to put his trust in the ship's crew. Realizing that, it was like a weight had lifted, and he felt more relaxed than he had in weeks.

He closed his eyes and felt his mind drift. That was all right; there would be more fighting, and when it came, he would be ready.

* * *

CAPTAIN JIM OATMIRE had returned to headquarters. He had not thought that he would ever look forward to mess hall cooking or his bunk, but they were far superior to C rations and sleeping on the ground. He didn't miss any part of that. However, he did find himself missing the soldiers and guerrillas of Patrol Easy. They had an easy camaraderie that did not exist among the headquarters staff, where there were many egos to navigate and toes to step on. Although he was an officer, the soldiers had accepted him once he had proved his worth.

His original assignment to negotiate the release of hostages from the Japanese had taken some twists and turns, not going at all the way he had expected, but ultimately the hostages had survived. He knew well enough that Patrol Easy had saved the hostages, though, not him.

He didn't feel that he deserved it, but back at HQ the outcome had earned him an attaboy—and something more. None other than General MacArthur's chief of staff had some news for him. He had summoned Oatmire to a meeting.

"You've done such a good job, son, that the Old Man is sending you to Okinawa for the big show."

"What the hell am I supposed to do there?" He waited a beat and added "sir," realizing that Patrol Easy had rubbed off on him in more ways than one.

"I guess you could say you're going to be a troubleshooter. Get some sleep and some chow. You'll head out tomorrow."

"Yes, sir. That's great," Oatmire said, realizing with a sinking feeling that his hopes of a few days of rest had just evaporated like the morning mist in the rays of the rising sun. "That's really great."

* * *

THE RIPPLES LEFT by the fighting in the Philippines kept flowing months and even years after the war. On July 4, 1946, the Philippines was recognized by the United States as an independent democratic nation. For the first time in centuries, the people of the Philippines could determine their own destiny. More than seventeen thousand Americans would stay behind as permanent residents, men and women who gave their lives fighting Imperial Japan, forever sleeping in the Manila American Cemetery and Memorial.

There was also unfinished business from the war. Early one morning in 1946, General Tomoyuki Yamashita put on his dress uniform that had been stripped of any rank or insignia. Slowly and with dignity, he climbed thirteen steps to a platform where a rope with a hangman's noose waited. It had taken him less than a minute to climb the stairs, but his journey to this fateful moment had taken months, if not years.

After the defeat in Manila, there had been no good end for the Japanese forces that remained in the Philippines. As the overall Japanese commanding general, Yamashita had remained behind with his troops, fighting as best they could despite running out of food, medical supplies, and ammunition. They had been abandoned by Japan. In the end, his forces became little more than a nuisance rather than a military presence. Finally, Yamashita had seen no choice but to surrender.

He lingered during the next few months as one of the highest-ranking Japanese officers held prisoner. After the war, he was put on trial for war crimes. There had to be some justice for so many civilian deaths. Some might even have called it revenge. The military trial had been a matter of going through the motions. It was a foregone conclusion that Yamashita would be found guilty of the killing spree that his troops had undertaken, although the actions of his desperate men appeared to be counter to the orders he had given.

During the trial, the general had tried to explain himself: "My command was as big as MacArthur's or Lord Louis Mountbatten's. How could I tell if some of my soldiers misbehaved themselves? It was impossible for any man in my position to control every action of his subordinate commanders, let alone the deeds of individual soldiers. The charges are completely new to me. If they had happened, and I had known about them, I would have punished the wrongdoers severely. But in war someone has to lose. What I am really being charged with is losing the war. It could have happened to General MacArthur, you know."

But that was not how the war had turned out. Ultimately, Yamashita's defense seemed to overlook the fact that a commander is ultimately responsible for the actions of his troops, even the lowliest private.

Swiftly, he was found guilty and sentenced to death for the war crimes committed by his troops.

Not being in a forgiving mood, President Harry Truman denied a request for a pardon.

And so Yamashita found himself climbing those steps, finally taking a drop into eternity. Justice had been done.

NOTE TO READERS

Thank you so much for reading and keeping some of our amazing American World War II history alive. I did want to clarify a few places and events in the story, because I have taken some artistic license here with the timeline that involved the 77th Infantry Division, the unit on which many of the adventures of Patrol Easy and Deacon Cole are based. Several of the events are inspired by the unit history *Ours to Hold It High: The History of the 77th Infantry Division in World War II*, by Max Myers. For example, the attack on the convoy crossing the two bridges in Chapter 1 is loosely based on an incident recounted in that unit history. Another helpful book that brought the hostage situation to life for me was the memoir *Manila Memories: Four Boys Remember their Lives Before, During, and After the Japanese Occupation*.

I've also used some of reporter Ernie Pyle's words in Chapter 2, where he describes soldiers' nostalgia for home. In Chapter 11, the article "On the Front Lines in the Pacific" is my attempt to write about Patrol Easy in Pyle's voice to give a flavor for his reporting (although he did not actually write those words).

Please consider it a small tribute to Pyle and his writing style from another old newspaper reporter. Pyle will appear in at least one more story in what I hope is a way to honor how he ultimately gave his life to bring the war home to so many. I often found myself dipping into the collection *Ernie's War: The Best of Ernie Pyle's World War II Dispatches*.

In the first part of the story, the soldiers are involved in wiping out the last of the Japanese on the island of Leyte, where US forces initially landed. According to division records, the unit lost 543 killed and 1,469 wounded during their participation in the fight for Leyte between December 7, 1944, and February 5, 1945. Japanese losses were catastrophic, with an estimated 19,456 killed during actions with the 77th Infantry Division. (It's worth noting that the overall population of Japan in 1941 was around 72 million, roughly half the population of the United States.)

Many of the defenders on Leyte were hidden inside deep bunkers like the one depicted or had taken refuge in the hills. (On a side note, the actual name for napalm was classified, although it made an appearance in the Pacific long before Vietnam.) It is notable that just 124 Japanese prisoners were taken—still enough to have kept Nisei interpreters like Yoshio busy. The Japanese mostly became prisoners only because they had been wounded or knocked senseless with bombs or rifle butts. There wasn't a lot of surrendering going on.

From Leyte, the soldiers embarked for Ie Shima and Okinawa, preparing for the big invasion of what was considered one of the Japanese home islands. The division itself apparently was not involved in the fight for Luzon, having already left for Okinawa, but Patrol Easy has been assigned to Manila for the sake of the story. Their skills would have been welcome at what has been called the "Stalingrad of the Pacific" because of its similarity to the street fighting and sniper battles in that Soviet city.

The villains of this story, Major Tanigawa and Sergeant Inaba, are a composite of several Japanese officers who behaved with unusual cruelty that went far beyond any sort of military necessity. Some of these officers took their own lives in the last days of the battle, and others were tried and hanged after the war. As mentioned in the epilogue, the overall Japanese commanding general, Tomoyuki Yamashita, and his chief of staff, Akira Mutō, were executed for the crimes committed in Manila.

In addition to the lives that were lost, it was heartbreaking to read about the destruction of what must have been a beautiful city filled with old Spanish architecture. General MacArthur had urged the Japanese to make Manila an "open city," as he had done in 1941, and withdraw to avoid this outcome, along with civilian deaths, but that was not to be. As often happened, helpless civilians got caught in the middle of the battle.

I've taken some fictional liberties with the geography of the final battle. The Japanese did use the imposing legislative building for their last stand, and it was mostly destroyed by the end of the battle, but has since been rebuilt and is now used as a beautiful museum of the arts. However, the legislative building actually stands just outside the old stone walls. I condensed locations to simplify the story but keep the flavor of that last, desperate battle. Intramuros has been rebuilt into a charming commercial district, its old stone walls and gates mostly intact.

Deke and Patrol Easy will soon be heading for Okinawa and rejoining the rest of the division as the Pacific war continues. I hope that you can join them.

I want to offer a heartfelt thanks to all those who helped with previewing or editing the book, especially Charles, Paul, Castle Walls Editing, and Intracoastal Media. Thanks to Rob for the opportunity to visit his collection of militaria. Tisa introduced me to her father's wonderful WWII sketches. Once again, the talented Scott Bennett brought the characters to life with his audiobook narration. The home team of Aidan, Mary, and Mike listened to my musings with patience. Your enthusiasm and support are deeply appreciated.

Finally, I wish to express humble gratitude to all those who have shared their family stories (sometimes even photographs or memoirs) of relatives who served in World War II. They are proud of their connection to the "Greatest Generation" and rightfully so. Remember that you can always reach out through my website or Facebook to share more of those stories because I appreciate each one.

—DH

ABOUT THE AUTHOR

David Healey lives in Maryland, where he worked as a journalist for more than twenty years. He is an author member of the International Thriller Writers.

www.davidhealeyauthor.com

Check in with him on Facebook at
https://www.facebook.com/david.healey.books

www.ingramcontent.com/pod-product-compliance
Lightning Source LLC
Chambersburg PA
CBHW022030240626
47154CB00007B/2345
* 9 7 9 8 9 8 7 2 8 0 8 4 3 *